THE Other Room

Door Peninsula Passions Book Two

KATHERINE HASTINGS

Flyte Publishing

THE OTHER ROOM

Copyright © 2019 by Katherine Hastings

This book is a work of fiction. Names, characters, businesses, organizations, places, events and incidents either are the product of the author's imagination or are used fictitiously. Any resemblance to actual persons, living or dead, events, or locales is entirely coincidental.

For information contact :

http://www.katherinehastings.com

Ebook ISBN: 978-1-949913-14-9

Paperback ISBN: 978-1-949913-26-2

Second Edition: March 2021

Editing: Tami Stark
Proofreading: Vicki McGough
Published by Flyte Publishing

THE OTHER ROOM
Door Peninsula Passions
Book Two

THE OTHER ROOM is the second romantic comedy in the Door Peninsula Passions series. While each book can be read as a standalone and features its own love story with a HEA, they feature reoccurring characters on a continued timeline. If you don't want any spoilers about a previous couple, then start at the beginning and enjoy them in order.

CHAPTER ONE

MATT

A loud splash broke the silence surrounding me. Holding my pole tighter, I leaned back and held steady while the whirring of my reel announced the fish was making another run for freedom. Smiling, I waited him out, careful not to put too much tension on the line. *Patience.* The top virtue of any successful fisherman, and I possessed an ample amount of it. Years of fishing at these docks in Baileys Harbor had taught me that. And today would be no different. I would wait this big Northern out.

"Hey, Matt. Walleye?"

I glanced over my shoulder to see Jake Alton, my best friend since diapers, waltzing down the dock, fishing rod in one hand and a tackle box in the other. His black lab, Hank, trailed just behind him.

"Northern. Tough son of a bitch, too. I've been at

this for almost half an hour."

"Gotta love the ones that battle hard." He set his box beside me and leaned against the post jutting up from the wooden dock.

"You know I love a good challenge." I grinned but stiffened when I felt the fish surge left. "Quit distracting me. I'm not going to lose it this far in."

"Hand me the pole and I'll end this battle in under sixty seconds," he taunted. Even though I didn't take my eye off the line zigging and zagging below me, I could picture his smug smile.

"Yeah, right. Just shut up and watch the pro get it done."

"By all means."

Tossing him a quick smile, I started carefully reeling in the fish. Inch by inch it drew closer, and I felt his fight subsiding. As I gave the line another crank, the weight in my hand doubled and I braced for another explosion. The defiant fish leapt out of the water, twisting in the air, and when it landed with a splash, my rod snapped back, and the sudden loss of tension nearly sent me tumbling back onto my ass.

Jake's roar of laughter combined with the last echoes of the waves signaled my defeat. The waves created by the wake of a fish sprinting to freedom.

"Shit!" I grumbled, clenching my fist tight around my rod.

"A real pro!" His deep laugh only added insult to injury.

"You distracted me. Made me rush."

His snort exploded into the still air. "Is that your excuse? *I* made you lose it?"

With a deep sigh, I started laughing with him. "Well, I have to blame it on something. And you're here, so yeah. You made me lose it."

"You're an ass." He smiled and reached down into his tackle box, pulling out a lure. Hank flopped down at his feet, the loyal dog knowing the sight of Jake setting up his rod meant they would be here for a while.

I ran a hand through my hair. "Well that was a half hour of my life I'm never getting back."

"Ah, but a half hour spent fishing is never wasted."

A melancholy smile tugged at my lips. "True. I could be working."

"You really should get into commercial fishing. You're good at it and then you can be like me and fish for a living."

Jake's commercial fishing business took out charter clients and he'd been trying to get me to join him for years. Shaking my head, I set my rod down.

"Nah. You know how I feel about that. If I fish for a living, then I won't want to fish for fun. I'd hate to suck the joy out of my favorite thing in life."

Shrugging, he cast into the water. "Yeah. It's a risk.

I still manage to make it fun on my off hours, though."

I shook my head. "Maybe next year."

"How is the maintenance job for the town going? You still like it?" he asked as he started reeling in his line.

"Yup. I think I might have found my calling. I get to work with my hands. Every day is something different and challenging, and the flexibility is pretty sweet."

"So, you finally found a job you want to stick with? You're done wearing twenty hats every summer?"

Living in a summer tourist destination like Door County, that all but shuts down every winter, meant finding a year-round job I loved proved even more difficult than reeling in that Northern. Each year I tried something new. Serving, painting houses, construction, kayak guiding... just hoping that maybe my current choice would be the one that stuck. So far, doing maintenance for the town was the closest I'd come to finding something fulfilling in my life. So much for those four years I'd busted my ass in college getting an advertising degree. Turns out working in an office and on computers was my version of hell on earth, and I'd hauled ass back to Door County to find a job that let me spend my time outdoors. "The job is good. I like it, but it turns out I may not be living in Baileys Harbor next week, so I'm not really sure what I'm going to do if that happens."

"What?" He stopped reeling and all his attention focused on me. "What the hell do you mean you're not going to be living here? We're Harbor boys. Always have been, always will be."

Blowing out a puff of air, I sat down and leaned back against the post of the dock where he and I had been fishing since we were three. "Yeah. Shitty news. The house I've been renting for six years just sold, and instead of renting it to locals, they're putting it up for seasonal rentals on VRBO. This guy is officially homeless this weekend."

"Why didn't you tell me?"

A heavy sigh escaped my mouth before I could shove it back inside. "You and Cassie were in your own little world after she got back from New York last week. I didn't want to come dumping in on your happy little reunion with my crap."

"Holy shit, man. That sucks."

"Yeah. Seriously sucks. I love that house. If I'd have known they were selling, I probably would have tried to buy it. He sold it to his niece or something though. Never even gave me a shot."

He lifted a dark eyebrow. "You have the money to buy a house in Door County? The prices of real estate here have skyrocketed if you haven't noticed. Unless you have some secret stash of dough I don't know about, there's no way you'd have been able to buy that place." He chuckled, knowing full well I lived my life in the moment and things like savings accounts and retirement planning were foreign concepts to me.

"True." I grinned. "You and Cassie want to buy me a house?"

Laughing, he shook his head. "I love you, man, but hell no."

"Come on," I teased. "You guys are worth *billions*. Don't you think you could spare a couple hundred thou for an old friend? That's like ten dollars in your world."

Jake had fallen in love with Cassie before he discovered the size of her bank account. Now my best friend and his heiress had figured out how to blend their vastly different lives together, and they were living the dream up here in Baileys Harbor with Cassie flying back to New York on occasion to run her empire.

"Do you really need money?" he asked, glancing down at me. "Cassie adores you, and I'm sure she'll lend it to you if you need it."

"Nah. I'm just kidding. It's my own damn fault for not prioritizing buying a house when we could still afford to buy one up here. And now finding rentals is near impossible with the vacation rental boom. But I'll figure it out."

My friend's eyes narrowed. "You sure? Cassie still has that little cabin next door that no one stays in. You can always crash there if you need a place for a while."

Scoffing, I pulled a face. "Dude. I would rather sleep in my truck than spend a night in that deathtrap. How is it even still standing? One strong wind and you'd be digging my corpse out of a pile of rubble."

Jake laughed and shrugged. "When Cassie's grandpa kicked her out of the penthouse and shipped her up here to Door County, she survived a whole summer in it before I moved her into my place. Are you saying you're not as tough as a city girl?"

"I am saying exactly that. She has my respect since she endured living in that dilapidated shack. Massive respect."

"Well, it's yours if you need a crash pad."

"Thanks, man. But I'll figure something out. I gave up on finding a place in Baileys Harbor, though. Being August in Door County, I'm having a hell of a time finding a place to live. I'm sure I would be having better luck if it were fall and all the summer workers were gone, but I don't have that kind of time. My search is now extending all over Door County. Something has to pop up sooner or later. Hopefully sooner, since I only have a few days left."

"I can't believe you won't be living down the road anymore."

"Yeah, but what are you gonna do?"

"Well if you need something, just say the word. Cassie and I are happy to help."

I tried not to let the frustration creep into my voice. "Yeah, two-week's notice to find a new place to live isn't exactly ideal."

"That's bullshit, man. Can you fight it?"

I shook my head. "Nope. We never had a lease contract and I pay cash. Didn't really think that one through."

"That sucks."

"Yeah. But I'll figure it out. I always do."

"You're like a cockroach. You survive everything. Even my wrath." He arched a brow and lifted a balled-up fist.

Rubbing my jaw, I nodded. If I'd been this close to Jake last year I would have been bleeding on the ground. In fact, I had ended up a bloody pulp after he saw me one night at the Blue Ox. Not that I didn't deserve it. I'd had a crush on his ex-fiancé since high school, and like a dumb ass, I'd gotten drunk and didn't push her away when she'd kissed me. Talk about feeling like a cockroach. The lowest of the low. Luckily, I'd come to my senses before our clothes went flying, but I'd still broken his trust and obliterated a lifetime's worth of Bro Code. But I'd left that version of me behind, and I'd never slip up and hurt a friend while under the influence again. And not just because I wanted to avoid another well-deserved beating, but because I'd come only a sliver away from ruining the most important friendship of my whole life.

I moved my jaw back and forth like a seesaw. "It still hurts when I chew, you know."

"Good. That'll remind you to keep your mitts off my Cassie." He smirked, and even though his eyes twinkled, I heard the veiled threat laced between the playful words.

"Never, man. I'd sooner chop off my own arms. One time. I fucked up *one time* and that was enough for me. Bros before—"

"Don't call Cassie a ho."

I lifted my eyebrows. "Bros before classy ladies?"

Laughing, Jake tossed out another cast. "Bros before classy ladies. Although, I'm still picking Cassie over you if push comes to shove."

"Can't blame you for that." Laughing, I pushed myself back up to my feet and tucked my fishing pole underneath my arm. "I gotta get home and finish packing. And keep up the hunt for a new place."

"Catch you later, man." Jake stuck out his hand, and I gave it a slap. Then I paused and gave Hank a scratch before heading back down the docks. While I climbed into my truck, I glanced back down the dock to see Jake give me a last wave goodbye. It had been a year since Jake and I had mended fences after my drunken screw up, and the feeling of knowing I had a best friend, a brother, who had my back was something

I'd never take for granted again.

With a quick wave, I put my old truck in gear and pulled away from the docks. The drive to my house took only a few minutes, and soon I pulled up into this truck's six-year parking spot with a heavy sigh. After next week I had no idea where I'd be parking and laying my head to rest at night. With an internal grumble at my self-inflicted situation, I climbed out and headed into the little grey house I needed to vacate by the weekend.

I walked in through the garage, dropping my boots in the kitchen. A few cardboard boxes with my minimal belongings were stacked by the stove I'd only used for cooking pizzas. Stepping over them, I looked around to see what else I needed to pack up. The house had come furnished, so at least I wouldn't have to drag all this furniture with me to wherever I landed. Just my clothes, a few boxes of dishes, and all my fishing gear needed to vacate this bachelor pad with me.

As I settled back on the floral couch I'd always hated but saw no need to replace, my cell phone dinged. Picking it up, I looked at the screen. My friend Aaron. Another buddy I'd grown up with in Baileys Harbor.

Aaron: *Hey man. Drinks tonight?*

Hell yeah, I wanted drinks tonight. Something,

anything, to take my mind off the fact I had no place to go. But I needed to buckle down and find a place to live, so I groaned and answered back.

Me: *I wish. Gotta find a new place to live. Can't hang tonight.*

Aaron: *That sucks. Tony told me you had to move out. Maybe you should just come drown your sorrows for a few hours. We're going to downtown Sister Bay and then JJ's for margaritas. Come on. Party time.*

Margaritas at JJ's? I didn't get to Sister Bay often, and a margarita did sound like something I could use. Scratching the scruff on my chin I realized needed a date with the razor as I contemplated my options. Sit home alone scouring the internet for affordable year-round Door County rentals that were rarer than a unicorn, or head out for some drinks with my friend and work on finding a place to call home later?

Me: *What time you picking me up?*

Aaron: *Hells yeah! Be there at 7.*

Me: *See you then.*

What the hell. If I knew anything about living in Door County, I had a better chance of finding a place to live through word of mouth than I did on the internet. I'd make sure to ask around tonight, and maybe, just maybe, I could find a new place to call home. I hadn't spent much time looking outside of Baileys Harbor, not wanting to leave the town I'd lived in my whole life, but Sister Bay was booming and there was a better chance of finding a place to live there.

Pushing myself off the couch, I headed into the bathroom to shave my face and jump in the shower. If I wanted to convince someone to rent me a house, smelling like fish wasn't a big selling point.

CHAPTER TWO

JO

A beep from the drink printer behind me sounded like fingernails on the chalkboard. Over and over throughout this insanely busy night it went off each time a server put in a drink order. It was now the soundtrack to my nightmares... nightmares that consisted of me drowning in paper while I tried to make a never-ending stream of drinks.

Beep. It went off again, and I groaned, turning around to see the printer spitting out more tiny white sheets that looked more like losing lottery tickets. Gah! More drink orders on top of the other drink orders I still scrambled to keep up with making. I eyed it as it hissed and spit, wishing I could smash it with a sledgehammer.

"Hey, Jo!" Hanson called from the corner. "Add another regular marg on that!"

"On it!" I called back, then ripped the paper off the

printer, eyes bulging at the long list of drinks I needed to make on top of the full bar of customers all vying for my attention. I'd known it would be a big change switching jobs from bartending at the laid-back Blue Ox in Baileys Harbor and jumping into the fray at JJ's La Puerta, one of the busiest restaurants in Door County, but I had seriously underestimated the number of margaritas that passed over this bar each night. Paired with an extensive bar menu, the pace of this new job resulted in a serious shock to the system. Lucky for me I'd started in May before tourist season hit full swing in July and I'd had a couple months to learn the ropes before getting pummeled every weekend.

At the Blue Ox, I'd primarily cracked beers and dropped off baskets of cheese curds. Sure, it got busy there, but nothing like it did at JJ's. This was like the Blue Ox on steroids. Like going from high school sports straight into the big leagues. Even though I'd loved my gig at the Ox, when I'd made the move to Sister Bay it made more sense to work here... only a sixty-second walk down the road from my new cabin. The money was great, the owners awesome to work for, and the customers were all pretty fun. But on Friday nights, when you couldn't even walk through the sea of people crammed into this little waterfront restaurant, I seriously questioned my sanity in thinking I could survive the summer season working in Sister Bay.

"Jo! Can we get more margs! One strawberry, one regular," Andy, one of my regulars, called.

"Yep. Just a minute." With a deep breath, I tried to quell the anxiety churning in my gut from the feeling I would never catch up. I was "in the weeds" as we called it, and as my breath caught in my throat, I couldn't even begin to see the way out. But panic wasn't something I had time for, so I focused on the drink order in my hand and went to work shoveling ice into the blender to make a pitcher of margaritas.

After another hour of juggling the Mt. Everest of orders, I dropped off a drink at the end of the bar and bolted back to the printer to start the process again. Skidding to a stop, I smiled when I saw no little white pieces of paper pouring out of it. I waited for the beep, for the printer to start spitting out orders again, but after a few moments I exhaled a long breath filled with relief.

Hanson stepped to my side, puffing hard. Our gazes slid across the restaurant, passing over the few patrons left at the bar, and over to the dining room tables. Only a few scattered customers remained.

"Holy shit. Are we caught up?" he asked, smoothing the ruffled mess of blonde hair that looked like he'd been victimized by a Midwestern twister. I hadn't had time to check mine in hours, and I wondered now if it resembled his messy mop from the speeds we'd hit serving drinks tonight.

"Don't jinx it!" I slapped him on the shoulder.

"Sorry. I should know better."

"Yeah, you should." The printer beeped and our groans mingled into one. "Damn it, Hanson! You've been bartending here for over twenty years and you *still* manage to break the cardinal rule of saying we're caught up and jinxing us."

"My bad. I've got it." Sucking the air through his teeth, he grimaced then reached across me and plucked the piece of paper from the printer. "Only a couple of Bernies. Phew."

A Bernie was the house shot at JJ's. It consisted of a shot of tequila topped with an orange sprinkled with cinnamon and sugar. A shockingly delicious combination, and we served as many Bernies a night as we did margaritas.

After taking a moment to catch my breath, I went to work washing the glasses we'd abandoned during the dinner rush. Hanson dropped off the Bernies and joined me in stacking the clean ones on the drying rack and loading the dishwasher again.

"That was freaking nuts," I said while I grabbed a rag and wiped the drink rings off the bar.

"Yep. Gotta love summer in Sister Bay. You regretting leaving the Blue Ox yet?" He taunted me with a grin.

Chuckling, I pointed to the tip jar. "There's enough money in there for me to pay my property taxes and insurance for the month, so no... no regrets here. Sore feet, shattered confidence, and anxiety like I've never experienced in my life? Yes. Regrets? No."

"That's what I like to hear." He patted my back and smiled. "You're a great addition to the team. I'm glad you joined us. You're fast. You're little so you don't take up much space and I'm not always running into you, and the customers love you."

"I'm glad I get the coveted Hanson stamp of approval."

"Hanson. It's still going to take me awhile to get used to that, but it's starting to stick."

His name was Joe Hanson, but we'd decided it was too confusing having Jo and Joe behind the bar, so we'd rolled a round of bar dice to decide who got to keep the name and who'd have to start using a nickname. I'd won three rounds in a row, and we'd settled on calling him by his last name.

"I like it, Hanson."

He gave me a wink. "It's growing on me."

Grabbing a few empty glasses off the bar, I walked back over to the dishwasher. "I thought we were busy when I started here in May. That was a cake walk compared to what's it been like since July."

"Don't worry, you get used to it. I stopped going

home, curling up into a ball and sobbing after summer weekend nights years ago."

I burst into laughter and bumped him with an elbow. "Damn. That was my plan for the rest of the evening."

"We're over the rush now, so why don't you help me clean up and then you can be done for the night. I'll be able to handle the night crew on my own."

"Yeah? You sure?"

"Yep. We've got another couple of months of this, and I don't want to burn you out and lose you before the season's over, so consider this a 'please don't leave me' bribe."

"Bribe accepted!" I extended my hand, and he took it, giving me a nod while we shook on it. The movement caused his glasses to slip down his nose, so he pushed them back up before getting back to work.

It took me a half hour just to clean up the mess left behind from the dinner rush, stopping only to refill the drinks of the night crowd while they shook the bar dice cup, cheering over their wins and groaning over their losses.

"Shit. I put the wrong brand of tequila in this one." Hanson walked over holding the margarita glass rimmed with a healthy portion of salt. "Here. It's yours. Punch out, take a load off and enjoy a cocktail."

With a sigh and smile, I took the margarita into

my sore hands. "No need to tell me twice."

After punching out, I climbed into a seat at the bar leaving one space between myself and the mannequin who had lived there for decades and startled most of the new customers. The blonde-haired "woman" we called Wanda received a shocking amount of "sorry" and "is this seat taken" every evening, and I didn't think it would ever get old watching people's faces when they realized plastic women don't answer.

At the Blue Ox a mannequin sat by the window named Captain Bailey. At JJ's it was Wanda. As a local who grew up in Door County, I never really gave much thought to the trend of mannequins taking up space at our bars. Yet here I was again, working at bar with a mannequin and listening to customers apologize to an inanimate object after they bumped into it.

Never got old.

"You want anything to eat?" Hanson asked as I settled in.

"Nah. I snacked on tortilla chips all night. I'm full."

"Great job tonight. Here, count the tips."

"With pleasure." Grinning, I took the overflowing pitcher of money from him and dumped it out on the counter. Bartending here was hard work... exhausting, sanity-stripping work. But this blissful moment every night made it worth it and stopped me from running back to the slower pace of the Blue Ox.

Between sips of my margarita, I smoothed out the crumpled bills and stacked them in piles of singles, fives, tens, and twenties. While I separated them into equal piles of two that Hanson and I would split, I heard new voices flood into the bar. I looked up to see a few guys filing in through the door, and I groaned when I recognized the one face I'd have happily never seen again.

Matt Michaelson.

"Jo?" Matt said, and I curled my lip at him in return.

His face dropped at my response. Even with his muscular build, strong cut jaw, and piercing eyes, he still managed to look contrite. Good. Let him swirl in the vortex of his own sins.

Matt, Aaron, and Tony headed toward me. I'd grown up with all three of them, and had always considered them friends, only one no longer got to wear that title. The one who used to wear the title of best friend, and the one I now considered beneath my notice.

Matt. Matt the betrayer.

"Jo!" Aaron grinned, his lips parting between his bushy red beard. "What up, girl? I forgot you worked here now."

Before I could answer, he wrapped his arms around me and pulled me off my stool, squeezing me so tight I struggled to inhale.

"Hey, Aaron." I managed to grunt out. "Hey, Tony."

"Hey, Jo!" Tony patted me on the back. "Long time, no see!"

Aaron set me down, and I slid a glare to Matt. Through gritted teeth, I growled out, "Matt."

Lifting his chocolate eyes to meet mine, he pulled his lips into an awkward smile. "Hey, Jo. How you been? You ready for a little Family Guy marathon soon?" His awkward grin lifted into a genuine smile. "Oh! Or I got this new video game. You'll probably kick my ass like you always did, but it's really fun. First-person shooter. And we get an RPG launcher straight off the bat. Your fave!"

I didn't answer, just lifting a brow and staring at him until he gave up first and glanced away. As the irritation of past memories laced with his bad behavior bubbled up within me, I thought about how good it might feel to slap him. Hell, he was lucky I didn't kick him in the crotch, , or maybe even smack him upside his head with the drink pitcher just within my reach.

Guilt rose up and almost softened my expression. Almost softened my heart. But only almost. With a flare of my nostrils, I shoved that shit back down and told it to stay put. I quickly reminded myself that even though he looked like a scolded puppy who just needed a hug, he was anything but. He was the selfish liar, the betrayer who'd hooked up with Jake's fiancé and shaken our little friend group right to the core.

Okay, so we'd only *thought* he'd slept with her for the better part of the summer, but it had turned out he'd only kissed her. But still. Sex. Kiss. Didn't matter. That kind of betrayal was the gun that wouldn't stop smoking. Trying to steal your best friend's girl in any way, shape, or form? Despicable. And not a quality I ever wanted in someone I called friend. So despite the pain and regret, I'd cut the man loose.

Friendship over.

Done and dusted.

I sat back down, and Tony settled into the stool beside me.

"We miss you at the Ox," he said.

"Yeah, it's been a big change moving to Sister Bay."

It was only fifteen minutes away from where I used to live and work, but the faster pace of Sister Bay was a big change from Baileys Harbor, the place locals referred to as "the quiet side" of our little peninsula in Wisconsin.

"Are you done for the night?" Aaron asked, grabbing the stool on Tony's other side.

"Yep. I survived another crazy Friday night. I thought I was prepared for working a summer in Sister Bay... I was drastically wrong." Laughing, I took a well-deserved sip of my margarita.

The sweet and sour flavors combined with the salt

from the rim and I closed my eyes, letting the tequila work its way into my aching body.

Matt shifted beside me, and I saw him glance at the last open stool on this side of the bar. The stool that would seat him next to me. One cautious move at a time, he slid into his seat, pausing to look at me before settling all his weight down.

"You gonna throw elbows if I sit here? I've been on the receiving end of those bad boys a couple times. You've got some bony ass elbows and they hurt like hell."

I tossed him my best side-eye, daring him to continue his half-assed groveling.

"Hey guys!" Hanson came around the corner and tossed drink coasters in front of them. "What are we having?"

"Pitcher of margaritas and a round of Bernies, please," Aaron answered. "You want a Bernie, Jo?"

Scrunching my nose, I shook my head. "No, thanks. I poured enough of those tonight, so I never want to see one again."

"Coming right up." Hanson smiled and spun around, heading for the tequila bottles.

"Not guzzling beer tonight?" I asked, turning my body to block Matt out of the conversation.

"We stopped for beer along the way, but you can't come to JJ's and not do margaritas and Bernies,"

Aaron answered.

"Valid." I lifted mine and took another sip.

"So, what's it like over here in Sister Bay? We rarely make it over here. But Tony agreed to drive tonight so Matt and I can booze it up."

"You're driving next weekend," Tony answered, pointing a finger in Aaron's face.

"Deal."

"Sweet." Tony grinned, his white teeth gleaming as much as his perfectly shaved bald head.

"It's good. My cabin is pretty awesome, and right on the water, which is amazing. And it's right over there." I jutted a finger out the window pointing in the direction of the cabin I'd inherited just a short jog away.

"I can't believe you scored waterfront property in Sister Bay. That's freaking awesome." Aaron shook his head.

"Yeah. It's pretty crazy."

When my great uncle passed away this winter, my mom, his only heir, had inherited the property. Since my parents had a house they loved out in the country, they'd offered it to my sister, Jenna, and I. She'd taken one look at the small "rustic" cabin and turned her nose up at the offer to split it, choosing to stay in the fancy new house she'd just built. I'd been overjoyed at the thought of getting out of my apartment and getting my own place on the water... even if it did need a little TLC.

Okay, a lot of TLC.

Hanson arrived carrying a pitcher of margaritas, setting three glasses down then returning with three Bernies.

"I'm driving," Tony said, pushing the shot away.

"Oh shit, that's right." Aaron grimaced, then his lips pulled into a smile. "Jo can do it."

"Oh God, I do *not* want a Bernie." I laughed, but Hanson pushed it my way.

"You earned several Bernies tonight, Jo. It will help numb the pain you're going to feel later tonight."

"Oh, that pain is already alive and well." I chuckled and picked up the cinnamon and sugar-coated orange that was lying on top of the glass. "Why the hell not?"

"Cheers!" Aaron lifted his orange and tapped it against mine, the traditional way to take a Bernie. He leaned over me and bumped his orange against Matt's, and all eyes fell on me while Matt held his orange slice waiting for me to give him the obligatory cheers. Rolling my eyes, I bumped his hard, nearly dislodging the piece of fruit from his grip.

"Cheers," I said, then licked the cinnamon mix off my orange and we all downed our shots then chomped into the fruit.

"God that's good!" Aaron announced as he chewed

on the remains of his orange.

The warm liquid burned a trail down the back of my throat, but in only a few moments I felt it start to work its magic. The tension from my busy night slid off my shoulders and I relaxed into my seat.

"Can we get the bar dice cup?" Tony asked. "I may not be drinking much tonight, but I can still kick their asses in bar dice."

"You got it," Hanson answered, leaning down and returning with the black plastic cup filled with five dice. It was a traditional Wisconsin drinking game I'd mastered during all my years of bartending. The loser of each game bought the winners a round of shots, and it was often the catalyst to a night spent out drinking far more than you'd intended.

"So, you've been good?" Matt asked, still trying his best to strike up a conversation after I'd been ignoring each attempt for the better part of a year.

"Yep. Fine." I picked up the bar dice cup, giving it a shake and slamming it down with enough force to shake the whole bar.

"Jesus, Jo. Whose face were you picturing pummeling with that roll?" Hanson asked.

My glare slid over to Matt, who seemed to be obsessed with shredding his cocktail napkin.

"Forty-six in one." I pushed the dice cup over to Tony.

"Damn. That's hard to beat." He blew out a puff of air and shook the cup, slamming it down with far less rage than me.

"Twenty-four. Shit."

I didn't try to hide my victorious smile while he slid the cup over to Aaron.

Aaron rolled a thirty-two, leaving me sitting in the winning seat. With a grumble, he slid the cup and dice back down the bar, and I pushed it in front of Matt.

"Thanks," he said, but I just pursed my lips and turned away.

When he finished his roll with a forty-four, I grinned and leaned back in my chair.

"Jo's out," Aaron said, shaking his head. "Of course, Jo's out. She always wins."

"And don't you forget it." I waggled my brows.

While the three of them continued shaking the dice to narrow down the loser, I sipped on my margarita, helping myself to a refill from the pitcher sitting in front of us. The last round ended in a tie between Matt and Aaron, and I cheered on Aaron while he tossed his last roll.

"Yes! You lose!" Aaron jutted a victorious finger at Matt.

"Yep. Matt's a loser. Surprise, surprise." I smiled, and the unveiled insult caused Matt to widen his eyes and blink back at me.

"Damn," he blew out a breath. "Looks like I'm still in the doghouse. Long memory, huh? Do I at least get a fancy collar or a new dog bed? Blue is still my favorite color if you want my collar and bed to match."

He grinned, leaning over and bumping me with his shoulder. Another attempt to disarm me with his charm and sense of humor. And when nostalgia whispered to give the guy a break, I willed it to stand down. Another attempt failed.

Ignoring him, I slid my finger around the rim of my glass and licked a little salt off my finger.

"Jo, seriously. Everyone else has forgiven Matt for the Nikki situation. Now it's your turn," Aaron said, having taken notice of my icy attitude to my former best friend.

"Good for all of you. I'm not the forgiving type." Crossing my arms, I turned in my seat, leveling Matt with a glare. How dare he think he can just waltz right in here and try to charm me into giving up my carefully crafted ire? Letting him off the hook made me look weak and sappy when I was neither of those things. Matt could go pick one of the docks and take a flying leap into the lake.

"Jo, I'm sorry. Seriously. It was a fucked-up thing to do, but Jake forgave me. Why can't you do the same?"

Why couldn't I do the same? It wasn't like he'd kissed *my* fiancé. And it was just a kiss. One kiss. I *should* put this behind me like everyone else, but the betrayal to Jake cut too deep. The three of us had been best friends our entire lives, the Three Amigos as our parents used to call us. We'd played in the sandbox together as kids, learned how to drive together, had our first drinks together, and had maintained that close friendship into adulthood. That was until Matt went and shoved his tongue in Nikki's mouth last year, breaking up the Three Amigos and destroying a lifetime of loyalty. Even though Matt had won back Jake's forgiveness, and Jake was now happy with his new fiancé, Cassie, I didn't think he would ever win back mine.

Was I mad at Matt? Yeah. But I was even more mad at myself. Because when push came to shove, I'd spent years thinking my best friend was someone he wasn't. I guess I'd put Matt up on a pedestal and when he'd tumbled off it and hit the ground, he'd lost my respect. And that stung. It burned so deep and hard it had become a constant companion – a dull ache in my heart that wouldn't ease.

It was a best friend's duty to hate the traitor who wronged them until the end of time. That was best friend code 101. Hell, I still hated Lucy Atlee for that time she stole Matt's favorite lunch box and tossed it in the lake after he didn't give her a valentine that year. He'd been beside himself watching his favorite

Transformer sink out of sight. Knowing he could never hit a girl, I'd taken one for the team and punched her in the nose and got grounded for a week. It was a long week with no TV or video games, but it was worth it to defend him.

Despite that incident happening over twenty years ago, I still snarled when I thought of how upset she'd made my friend. My grudges over people who hurt my best friends were for life. This time though, it all felt awkward at best and intolerable at worst. One best friend of mine had wronged the other, leaving me smack dab in the middle. But my mom raised me with morals. *Values*. So it wasn't even a question where my loyalty slid when Matt crossed the line.

Matt had been the betrayer. The harmer to my friend. The bomb that blew up our entire lifetime as a trio of best friends.

It was me who'd taken care of Jake during the aftermath of losing his fiancé and his honorary brother in one fell swoop. Me who'd helped him crawl out of the hole Matt's selfish actions had tossed him in. After seeing the wreckage Matt left in his wake, I didn't think I could ever forgive him... or want to for that matter. To me, loyalty and honesty were the core of friendship, and if he could betray Jake, then I knew I would never truly trust him again. Matt's true colors had shown through in all their vibrant glory, and they weren't the kind of colors I wanted in my life.

"Because you're an asshole. And I'm not friends with assholes, Matt."

"Jo, come on. You have to forgive me. I miss you." He reached for my hand, but my icy glare slid over the movement and caused him to pull it back.

I inhaled, trying to suppress an explosion. "I don't have to do shit, Matt. You made your bed, now you can lie in it."

With a heavy sigh, he flagged Hanson over. "I lost. Another round of Bernies."

Hanson nodded and disappeared around the corner to make our shots.

"Why do you have paint on your hands?" Aaron asked, pointing to the brown specks of paint I'd missed when I washed them before work.

Staring down at the tiny flecks, I wrinkled my nose. "I'm staining some trim in the spare bedroom of my cabin. The whole thing is in pretty rough shape, but I thought a little stain would at least brighten it up until I can afford to pay someone for repairs."

"A spare bedroom?" Matt asked, and I turned to glower at him.

"Did I stutter?"

"Is, uh, is anyone staying in that spare bedroom?" he asked.

Furrowing my brow, I shook my head. "Nope. No

roommates for this girl. Too much stress."

"Hmm." He pursed his lips, and I could almost see the wheels turning inside his mind.

I stared, throwing a mental stick into those gears, but if anything, his expression just brightened.

"There you go, Matt!" Tony slapped the bar. "You can live with Jo!"

"What?" I choked on the sip of margarita I'd just taken.

"Matt lost his place to VRBO, and as of this weekend he's homeless," Aaron said. "I offered to let him sleep on my couch, but he said no."

"I've seen the chicks you bring home to that couch." Matt shuddered, and the visual caused me to do the same.

"My girlfriend isn't keen on having another dude in the house, something about toilet seats and dirty underwear, so I'm out," Tony said. "So yeah, you can move in with Jo! It's perfect!"

"Hell. No." Shaking my head, I crossed my arms.

Matt waggled his eyebrows and bumped me with an elbow. "Oh, come on, Jo! Remember that summer we crashed together my sophomore year of college for like a month? We had a blast! Campfires and s'mores at night. Video game marathons. Beer pong. Sunday morning bacon and eggs. With extra, extra, *extra* bacon, remember?"

"We're not twenty anymore. I don't want a roommate. Especially not you." I challenged him with a glare, but deep down those memories did warm me up a little inside. It had been the best summer of my life if I was being honest, and the two of us had been as close as we'd ever been.

But that was then. *Before* he turned out to be a sleazy cheater.

"Oh, come on, Jo." Tony leaned his shoulder into me. "He was your *best friend*. Are you really going to make him homeless when you have a bedroom he could live in?"

"Yep."

"Jo," Aaron soothed. "It's time to get over this. You need to forgive him. We all forgave him. It's your turn."

"Nope."

Forgiveness was not my thing. It felt too much like weakness.

"You'd really turn your back on a friend in need?" Tony shook his head.

"No. I would never turn my back on a friend in need. But Matt isn't my friend anymore, so it's irrelevant."

"Guys, it's fine. I don't expect Jo to let me move in with her. I'll figure something out."

The defeat in his voice plucked away at the tiny threads of empathy residing somewhere deep inside me. But I waged a war to stop their resonating before they grew too loud to ignore. Matt was a betrayer. Matt didn't deserve my forgiveness or my mercy. Nope. I wouldn't lose one second of sleep over where Matt would lay his two-faced head.

Then why do I feel so guilty saying no?

Shaking off the nagging guilt brewing inside me, I lifted my chin and tried to change the subject. "Who's up for another round of bar dice."

"I'm in." Aaron grabbed the cup.

"I lost. I go first." Matt reached across me to confiscate it. When his hand brushed across mine, I yanked it back, startled by the sensation from the touch that used to be so familiar. So natural. His wide eyes locked onto mine for a moment before darting away.

"Sorry."

"It's fine."

"And I'm sorry those guys are trying to force you to take me in. I don't blame you for saying no. It's fine," he said, chuckling to hide the desperation lingering just below the surface.

I didn't answer. A flurry of memories and ghosts from the past swirled inside me, demanding to be acknowledged. Instead of surrendering, I tapped my toe on the barstool.

"Although, if you happen to change your mind," he said, then raised his hands in submission, "though I don't expect you to, I am super handy and can help you fix up the cabin. Bob Vila ain't got nothing on me."

The cabin did need a lot of work. A new roof, new flooring, work on the plumbing, new appliances... the to-do list was longer than my arm. Having grown up as a tomboy, I was pretty handy with tools, but complex projects were a little out of my skill set. But Matt possessed that skill set in spades.

Ever since we were kids, he could fix any problem that came up and build anything he dreamed of creating. Since my father wasn't around while we were growing up, he'd even helped out around my house when my mom needed work done. He'd repaired broken faucets, retiled our bathroom, installed new flooring, and offered to help her with any handyman projects that popped up. He'd always refused to be paid even when she insisted, knowing our money was tight. But to quell her guilt over all the free work, he'd always accept a batch of his favorite cookies.

For a moment I contemplated his offer, thinking having Matt and his extensive skill set with construction and building would be a smart move. Hiring out all the work was going to be a lot of money, and it was all work that Matt could do with ease. Considering his offer for a heartbeat, I shook my head.

"I can't. Sorry." My heart stumbled. "After what you... you know... I just can't."

"I get it. It was unforgiveable. Hell, I'll never forgive

myself for falling for Nikki's temptations and betraying Jake." He looked up, those dark eyes meeting mine. "But, I did. And there's nothing I can do to take it back. But I really am sorry, Jo. I miss you. So much."

I missed him, too. More than I would ever admit to anyone, and it would seem even myself, because sitting next to him after spending a year apart was like torture. I missed how hard he could make me laugh, how comforting his hugs were after a bad day, and how easy it was to be with him. He got me. He always had, and I missed the best friend who'd been at my side since the day I could walk.

But he is a liar. A cheat and a liar. And that violates the friend code. More importantly, it violates the Jo code.

That realization stung the worst. The man I would have trusted with my life had morphed into the lowest of the low, and finding out the person I thought I'd known better than anyone in the world was an untrustworthy piece of crap had shaken my world to the core.

Fighting to keep the words *I miss you, too* lodged inside my mouth where they belonged, I took a sip of my margarita to keep it busy.

"Hopefully someday you'll forgive me. But until then, I'm not going to stop trying. And you know how persistent I am, so eventually I'll wear you down. I'll be peeling your cold, unforgiving layers off one at a time. Like you're a stinky, grudge-holding, irrationally angry onion."

With a cocky smile that almost inspired one in me, he shook his bar dice and spilled them out onto the bar.

"Fifty-six in one. Beat that, Jo." He smiled and pushed the cup my way.

The softness of his smile, and the warmth he radiated with it, assaulted the icy wall I'd built around myself whenever he came near. Fighting to resist the heat threatening to turn it into a puddle at my feet, I glared at him and took the dice cup.

"You're on."

CHAPTER THREE

JO

"Ugh," I groaned into my pillow. Six hours of running at break-neck speed behind the bar last night, and the four winning rounds of bar dice I'd played that ended with Bernie shots, had taken a toll on my body. Every muscle screamed for relief and jockeyed for position in the pain department, competing for first place with the throbbing in my head no doubt caused by too much tequila.

With a desperate need for a giant glass of water forcing me to move my aching bones, I pushed off the covers and sat up in bed. Petunia, my new cat, sat at the end of the bed, her green eyes penetrating me while she stared, her silent demands for breakfast well understood.

"Morning, Petunia," I said as I stretched. "Don't ever drink tequila. Tequila is bad. Very bad."

She sat unmoving, and I followed her demanding gaze as it slid to the partially empty food bowl in the corner.

"It's not even empty yet. There are starving cats in the world who would kill for the leftovers you seem too good to finish."

She just blinked her response.

"Fine. I'll fill it, but this is the last time. From now on you finish it before I fill it again. We aren't wasteful in this household, Petunia."

Rubbing my head, I leaned over to my bedside table, picking up my phone to check the time. Nine in the morning. Not bad. As a bartender, sleeping until noon wasn't unheard of, and since I was nocturnal by nature, it was a good career fit for me. However, with the number of things I needed to get done around the cabin today before heading back to work, I'd take those extra hours of awake time. Two new messages sat unopened on my phone, so I clicked the unknown number and gasped when I saw the string of words that addled my brain and flipped my heart over.

Morning, Roomster! I'm packing up my truck right now and heading over before you can change your mind. Last chance to say no. I know tequila greased the wheels into getting you to agree to this, so just text me if you don't want me to move in. I'll understand.

Roomster? Move in? What the what? Whose number was... I gasped, clasping a hand over my mouth. I may not know the number, but I knew who'd sent the message. *Matt.* I'd deleted Matt's number last year when I'd vowed to never speak to him again, but there was only one person who would be texting me about moving in. Memories of last night assaulted my body like incoming enemy fire. The pleading eyes. The insistence from Tony and Aaron that I let him move in. The last round of bar dice when I'd gambled away the spot in my empty room and... lost.

Shit! I *hadn't* won every round last night. There had been a fifth one... the round where I'd agreed to let Matt move in if I didn't win. Then I remembered him tossing his arm around my shoulder and calling me "Roomster" after I'd rolled a losing round of nothing but aces.

Like the universe was conspiring against me.

No. No, no, no, no, *NO!*

What time had he sent this message? Maybe I still had time to respond and tell him no. Hell no, in fact. But I scrolled down and saw the message had been sent at eight in the morning, and there was another message he sent a half hour ago.

Okay! Since you haven't messaged to tell me no, I'm officially on my way, Roomster! Thank you, Jo! You're a lifesaver! You won't regret it! Beer pong and bacon buddies reunited!

Scrambling to text him back before he pulled into my driveway, hoping to send him back to anywhere that wasn't here, I started typing a message back. But then I heard tires grinding on the gravel just outside my cabin, and I groaned. I was too late.

Glancing down in horror at my underwear and tank top, I leapt out of bed and hopped into a pair of shorts, tripping over my feet while I tried to yank them on.

"Hey, Roomster! I'm here!" Matt called, and I heard his footsteps coming up the stairs to my porch.

"Just a second!" I realized my shorts were on backward, so I ripped them off and hurried to get them back on. In my rush, I put both legs in the same hole, and when I went to pull them up, they stopped just short of my thighs. As I stood with my legs mushed together, stretching the one leg hole of my shorts to near ripping, I looked up to see him arrive at the screen door that was kitty-corner from my bedroom. Our eyes met, and he took one look at my black boy short underwear and then looked up at my horror-stricken face and spun around.

"Sorry, I didn't realize you weren't dressed, and the door was open."

"The door isn't open," I spat, pushing the shorts down and getting my legs into the appropriate holes.

"Well, it's a screen door, and totally see-through, so it's pretty much the same thing as open. I'm really sorry... I just—"

I could hear the laughter laced with the words, and his amusement caused my temper to flare. "Just forget you ever saw anything." The elastic waistband snapped into place.

"Are you decent?"

"Yes. I'm decent."

"I'm turning around now." Covering his face, he slowly spun on his heel, peeking out between spread fingers. When he saw me wearing the shorts correctly this time, he pulled his hand from his face, a sexy smirk still tugging his lips upward. "Can I come in?"

With a heavy sigh, I nodded. As he stepped through the door, his gaze slipped to my breasts for a beat before wide eyes lifted to meet mine. My eyes bulged when I realized I may be wearing a tank top, but I wasn't wearing a bra. Heat scalded my cheeks as I crossed my arms and covered the breasts this thin tank top did little to hide.

"I'll pretend I didn't just see that, too," he said, forcing his eyes to stay with mine.

"Give me a second." I spun on my heel and disappeared into my bedroom, slamming the door behind me. My plush white robe hung on the back of the door, so I tossed it on, tying the waist sash tight.

With a deep breath, I opened the door and stepped back out.

"Are you *actually* decent this time?"

"Yes," I said, still struggling to force the heat from my cheeks.

"Did you... did you forget I was coming? Forget about last night?" The mirth that usually resided in his eyes flickered out, and a heavy layer of disappointment tugged them down to the ground. Back in the day if someone had put that defeat in his eyes, I'd have given them a date with my fist, but this time I'd put it there. But this Matt wasn't the same one I'd have laid down in front of a train to save. Last year, that version of Matt had died a slow death.

"Listen, I had a lot of tequila last night and I was exhausted after my shift. I just... this isn't a good idea." I crossed my arms over my breasts for good measure.

"Oh." He rubbed a hand across the back of his neck, his eyes fixated on my wood floor. "Yeah. No, you're right. It was a stupid idea. I'm sorry I dropped in on you. I'll catch you later, Jo."

As he started to turn toward the door, shoulders slumped like the weight of the world pushed them down, that nagging guilt wrapped itself around my heart and squeezed. Hard.

Shit.

"Okay. Wait," I said, wishing the words would stop

falling out of my mouth. Him. Here. With me. That *was* a terrible idea. Not only did I not want a roommate, but having the man who I no longer trusted sharing this tiny space was a recipe for disaster. But when he turned back, the light returning to his eyes, I heaved a sigh. "Fine. You can stay. But..." I raised my hand. "Just until you find somewhere else more permanent."

"Really?" His mocha eyes flickered even brighter. "Seriously? I can stay?"

"For a little while," I reminded him. "Just until you can go somewhere else. I may hate your guts, but even I'm not a big enough asshole to make you sleep in your truck when I have an empty bedroom."

Clutching his hands to his heart, he stepped toward me. "You are not going to regret this, Jo. I swear to you that I'm going to be the best roommate *ever!*"

"Yeah, well you're already off to a bad start. But you're paying rent. I may have inherited this place mortgage free, but property taxes for waterfront property in Door County are a bitch."

"Done. I'll pay them."

"And you can help me fix up this place. It needs a *lot* of work."

His eyes sparkled with excitement. "Martha Stewart will be begging to live here when I'm done with it."

Pursing my lips, I sucked on my cheek while I

started compiling a list of ground rules in my mind.

Awkward silence settled between us. No longer were we the two old friends who never ran out of things to talk about, but instead it felt like we were two strangers struggling to find even an inch of common ground to stand on. The seconds ticked by as we shifted our gazes to anywhere but each other.

"So." Sliding his hands into his pockets, he rocked back on his heels.

I sucked the air through my teeth. "So."

More awkward silence. More shifting gazes. More of that sense of regret growing like a weed in my gut.

"Is this my room then?" He pointed a thumb toward the door opposite my bedroom.

"Yep." I nodded, then followed him in.

"This really is a tiny cabin. Just the two bedrooms, living room with the kitchenette, and the bathroom?"

"Yep," I answered, sticking with my one-word responses, more words ceasing to form as I let Matt's presence settle over me. Why did I have to do all those Bernies last night? If I'd have just grabbed my tips and gone home, I never would have seen those soulful eyes begging me for a place to stay. That tequila wouldn't have clouded my judgement and made me wager something as significant as a room in my house. Ugh. No more Bernies for this girl.

He slid his hand along the wooden logs that

comprised the walls of this old cabin. "Are you staying here all winter?"

"Yep."

"These are going to need a little insulation repair, so you don't freeze to death. See the cracks here?"

I followed his finger along the gaps between the logs I hadn't even noticed before.

"I can chink or caulk the walls and really help hold the heat in this winter. You'll save a lot on heating costs and it won't get so drafty."

"Wow. Thanks," I said, still trying to process the fact that Matt, who I'd sworn never to speak to again, was marching around my cabin. Or as of a few minutes ago, *our* cabin.

"The windows could use some updating, but I can handle that." He stepped around me and headed back out into the small living room. "I can refinish the floors and really bring out the natural beauty of the wood, and a pellet stove could fit right here." He pointed to the vacant spot on the exterior wall. "It will heat this whole place without any issue and save you a ton of money in the winter."

Speechless over his remodeling ideas, I followed him to the other side of the room to the bathroom. When he pushed open the door and looked inside, his face dropped.

"Whoa. This is... wow. This is a gut job." Laughing,

he poked at the shower stall that was little more than a thin plastic shell, then looked at the rusted old sink and the toilet that sat at an angle. "I'm surprised there isn't like a wooden barrel with a chain for the shower and a hole in the ground for a toilet. In fact, that may be an upgrade."

His laughter bounced off the walls of my bathroom, and I tried not to let it wear me down any more than that smile of his did when he aimed it at me. Charming. Infectious. Warm. All the things I adored about the Matt I used to know. The one who looked and sounded a hell of a lot like the one who was beaming at me right now.

He's a liar. A cheater. A traitor.

Nope. Jake may have found it in his big, softie of a heart to forgive Matt for his transgression, but I wasn't going to let it slide. The cut ran too deep. The damage too extreme. Stiffening against his charm, I lifted my chin. "Whatever you think is best, but keep in mind I can't afford a whole lot of extravagant upgrades. Just the basics."

"You don't need to pay me a penny for labor, and since I'm footing the property taxes, you'll have extra money to put into upgrades. See? Having me move in is the best thing that can happen to you!" His wide grin stretched across his unarguably handsome face, and I had to fight extra hard not to grin back at him. That same magnetic smile had sent me swooning when I was a young girl with a crush the size of Texas.

"Now, what about the roof?" He marched past me like a man on a mission and pushed his way out the rickety old screen door. "That needs some work, too," he noted as it wobbled on its old hinges.

I followed him out onto the small porch that wrapped around the back of the cabin and overlooked the bay.

"Jo. I still can't believe you scored property on the Sister Bay waterfront. This is amazing." He stopped, leaning his weight onto the railing while he stretched his gaze out to the water lapping at the rocky beach beneath us.

"Yeah. It's pretty incredible waking up to this every morning and going to sleep listening to the waves just outside my window every night."

"I bet I can put on my waders and fish right out the back door." Turning toward me, his smile grew. "Incredible."

"Yeah, it is." I stepped to his side, pressing my elbows into the wood while I took a breath and let the view and the sound of the waves calm me from the staggering shock that still lingered inside me over his arrival. When I pressed my weight into it, the railing creaked, the old wood buckling and giving way. I shrieked as I went with it, scrambling to stop myself from going over the edge and tumbling ten feet to the rocks below. Matt snagged me around the waist, pulling me into his arms and away from the ledge.

"Holy shit! Are you okay, Jo?" he asked, swiping a hand through my hair.

The gentle touch and the concern brewing in his eyes shook me to the core. The way his arm held me tight against his chest sent feelings through my body that were anything but anger.

Safe.

He made me feel safe, just like he had when we were kids. And teenagers. And even adults. Like the way he would toss handsy guys out of the bar when they went too far with me. It was that safety in his presence I'd lost when he'd betrayed Jake. That trust. He'd stolen that from me, and I missed it. I missed the feeling of having complete faith in him, complete faith that he was the kind of stand-up guy you could rely on no matter what.

Yet here I was, plucked from the clutches of danger and suspended in his embrace. Memories assaulted me in waves. It felt like the same embrace of the Matt who'd caught me before I fell off the back of the four-wheeler when we were fifteen. The same arms that had carried me back from the rock quarry when I'd sprained my ankle chasing him around in a game of tag on my eleventh birthday. The same hands that had pressed into the exact same spot on my lower back when he'd spun me around the dance floor at prom after Jimmy Hayes had stood me up. It was Matt who had appeared at my house like a savior after he heard the news Jimmy had ditched me for Lacy. When I'd opened the door, he'd stood there grinning and holding a corsage he'd made from wildflowers he'd picked on his drive over to rescue me from high school humiliation.

While I pressed up against him and his arms tightened around me, for a moment I forgot the hurt and the anger still raging inside me. For a moment, time stood still, and I was with that Matt again.

"Yeah. I, um, I'm fine." I forced myself out of his grip, struggling to suppress the emotions the brief encounter unleashed inside me. "Wow. I almost fell."

"Add a new railing to my list of house projects." Blowing out a breath, he scrubbed a hand down his face. "You seriously almost went over."

Peering over the now exposed edge of my porch down to the remnants of the railing scattered about the rocks below, I shook my head. "That was close."

"You sure you're okay?"

His hand settled on my shoulder, heat still searing through my robe and I nodded. "Yeah. Thanks for the save."

"See? You're lucky I'm moving in. If I hadn't been

here when that happened, we'd be scraping you out of the stones!"

Turning back to catch his grin caused me to cringe. Staying mad at Matt was hard enough when I could avoid him, which was exactly what I'd done the past year. Staying mad at Matt when he could assault me with his charm every hour of the day was going to prove more difficult than keeping up with all those drink orders last night.

Petunia's hoarse meow shook me back to my senses, and we both turned to see her standing in the doorway.

"What the hell is that?" Matt breathed, scrunching his brow.

"My cat. Petunia."

"That is not a cat." He jutted a finger at her, and she growled. Matt stepped back and cast a sideways glance in my direction. "That is a gremlin. A hideous, terrifying gremlin."

"She's just cranky because I haven't given her breakfast yet. Well, actually, who am I kidding? She's always cranky."

"Why does it look like that?" He choked on his laughter. "What's wrong with it?"

I looked down at Petunia who only glared back up at me. Admittedly, she wasn't the most affectionate cat in the world, and certainly not the most beautiful, but her odd looks had grown on me. "Petunia here has had a rough life." I stepped back into the house and grabbed the bag of cat food. "When I moved in here a few months ago, she was living under the porch. Over a few weeks, I coaxed her out with food and eventually she started to come near me." When I poured the food in her dish, she trotted over and started eating.

"Where are its ears?" Matt covered his mouth, but it didn't hide the smile he fought to suppress.

"Well, when I found her, she'd been an outside cat her whole life. I didn't want a cat, you know, because I'm a dog person." I shrugged, and he nodded, knowing full well I wasn't a cat lover. "But I didn't want to leave her alone, so I got her friendly enough with me I could get her into a kennel, and I took her to the humane society. They gave her an exam, and they said her ears had frozen off from frost bite. Most of her tail, too." I pointed to the odd stub she flicked while she enjoyed her morsels. "And the patches of missing hair are some kind of kitty alopecia. She doesn't have mites or fungus or anything, they checked, so you don't need to worry about that. Nothing contagious."

"Wow. I see." He chuckled. "Good to know. Because it certainly looks like it could bring on the start of the plague or something. So, if you took it to the humane society, how the hell did it end up back here?"

"*She,*" I corrected, "turned out she's not exactly

adoptable. They tried for a few days, but she scared everyone with the way she looks. And she's not exactly an affectionate cat with most people. In fact, she attacked several of the workers."

"Jesus," he whispered.

"So, they called and told me they would have to put her down or release her as a barn cat since no one would ever adopt her. I couldn't have that, and she seemed to get on with me okay, so I drove back down and picked her up. She's been with me ever since."

"I... I just... wow." Shaking his head, he exhaled a deep breath. "That is the ugliest cat I have ever seen in my life."

"You'll get used to it." I shrugged. "I think she's cute now."

Petunia looked up at us, and another low growl forced Matt to take a step back.

"Just don't make eye contact with her. Or touch her. Or get too close when she's sleeping. Actually, just don't get too close at all."

"Is that all?" He laughed with a touch of fear. "There isn't a lot of room in this cabin to avoid her."

"Just stay out of her way and you'll get on just fine. She and I are buds now. She's even started sleeping in my bed."

"I'm scared for you, Jo. It might try to kill you in your sleep."

"*She* won't hurt me. We're kind of the same. A little rough around the edges, picky about who we let near us, and absolutely lethal if you piss us off." Waggling my eyebrows, I gave Petunia an appreciative smile. Not many people got her, but then again, not many people got me either. "We're both an acquired taste. She loves me now."

As if on cue, Petunia hissed at Matt and he crossed his arms.

"Not so much you, but who can blame her," I jibed.

"Ouch."

"Just stay out of her way. And mine, too." I pointed a finger at him. "Cabin rules. Don't wake me up. Don't leave your shit laying around. Don't invite anyone over. Don't leave dishes in the sink. Don't eat my food."

"Anything I *can* do."

I put a hand on my hip. "Yep. You can try not to piss me off."

"But you're already pissed off. So, you mean try not to piss you off more than you already are? Because I can't unpiss you off it seems, so that rule is pretty much already permanently broken."

Pursing my lips, I fought the smile that tugged at the corners of my mouth. Instead, I stared at him, blinking.

"Don't piss you off more. Got it." Lifting his hand to his head, he gave me a salute. "Aye, aye, Captain."

"Oh. And don't leave the toilet seat up. I don't want to go ass diving in the middle of the night."

"Wouldn't dream of it. Grew up with three sisters, remember? They'd burn me alive for that transgression."

"Good."

"Good."

We stood in a silent stand-off. So many emotions swirled inside of me while I tried to process this turn of events, and the fact that Matt would no longer be a person I avoided at all costs, but instead would be a fixture in my home and my life. This set-up, us living together, was once something I would have considered a dream come true, but now I just hoped I hadn't turned my happy life into a living nightmare.

CHAPTER FOUR

MATT

The soft waves lapped at the shore, and I picked up a smooth white rock and flicked my wrist, watching it skip across the water before disappearing into the bay. Glancing back at the cabin, I wondered if Jo was awake yet. Not wanting to start off our first morning on the wrong foot by waking her up too early after she'd gotten in late from bartending, I'd kept myself scarce and spent the morning doing a little fishing off the Sister Bay dock and enjoying the serenity of her backyard on the water. My presence here already had her riled enough, and I didn't need to give her any ammo to toss me out on my ass.

After I'd done what I'd done, fallen for Nikki's charms and crossed the line like a dumbass, my entire world had tipped upside down. Not only had Nikki bolted from town when word got out and left me to deal with the aftermath alone, but I'd become a pariah.

A castaway from our little Baileys Harbor society left to slink around the shadows, bolting out from beneath one scornful gaze after another.

A town that once treated me like a favorite son quickly closed ranks around Jake and left me on the outside... a place I probably deserved to be, but not for the reasons people thought. Living in a small town meant rumors spread like a game of telephone. What was a kiss grew into a make out session, and then that make out session grew into a hook-up, which then grew into a full-blown affair that went on behind Jake's back for years. Even when I told the truth, that Nikki and I had just kissed *one* time, no one believed me. And finally I stopped trying. A betrayal was a betrayal after all, and even though I hadn't slept with her, I may as well have.

I'd betrayed my best friend.

And because of it, the entire town had betrayed me.

After months of agony, I'd finally gotten to explain myself to Jake, and he'd seen the truth in my eyes and forgave me. Only in that moment did the angry town take a breath and that scorching heat from everyone I knew turned down to a low simmer. Finally, after Jake and I rekindled our friendship, one by one the snarls and disappointed headshaking stopped when I entered a room. One by one they followed suit and forgave me, just like Jake had. And now, a little over a year later they'd all forgiven me... all but one.

Jo.

I'd received a lot of scornful gazes since the incident, but the anger that darkened Jo's chocolate eyes when she looked at me hurt the worst. Those same eyes that used to smile when we were together now narrowed any time they drifted in my direction. Whenever her glare clapped onto me, it felt like my soul ripped open a little bit more. The looks from Jo weren't just disappointment or judgment like they'd been from the rest of the town. Fury lurked in the depths of her eyes. Like I'd fallen out of favor with her forever. And it killed me that I couldn't turn the light back on in those eyes that used to shine so bright.

I'd attempted to beg her forgiveness more times than I could count, but one thing I knew for sure. Jo wouldn't easily be swayed by a sob story. And as one of the most loyal people I'd ever known, she wouldn't easily forgive a betrayal. And my out of character display of disloyal behavior had stripped away all the years of good I'd done. All the years of being a supportive friend, a shoulder to cry on, and her biggest cheerleader. With one whiskey-fueled bad decision I'd shattered the man she had always thought me to be. And I'd shattered my own confidence in my ability to be that man for her.

I was Matt. The friend. The brother. The one you could count on to swim you a paddle when you were up Shit Creek without one. But after years of battling the feelings I had for my best friend's girl and fighting to be happy for him, when her attentions had turned to me that night I'd finally given in to temptation. As my thoughts drifted back to the woman, my stomach clenched. I'd never told Jake about the times she'd tried to seduce me in the past... the times I'd been strong enough to resist her. To put my best friend first. But that night, that one night, I'd succumbed to my desires when she'd pressed her lips to mine, and I'd regret that fateful moment for the rest of my life. And now Jo might never forgive me for my moment of weakness even after I'd forgiven myself.

Last night when I'd gotten the idea to crash in her spare bedroom, it wasn't just that I wanted a room to stay in that made me push her harder during the last round of bar dice. It was that I wanted a chance to be near her. To force her to see me as the same Matt she'd always known... the one she thought no longer existed. I knew in my bones if I could just force her stubborn ass to be in a room with me, she'd see through the shadow of my mistake.

Looking at my phone, I checked the time. Ten o'clock. She should be getting up soon. Pushing up from the rocky seat, I brushed off my shorts and grabbed the Piggly Wiggly bag and tray of coffees from the ground. When I got to the cabin, I cringed when the door creaked as I opened it. I heard Jo shift in her bed, and then the low growl of that nasty cat. Damn hideous thing creeped me out so much I'd pushed a chair in front of my door before I went to sleep last night.

Tiptoeing across the tattered wooden floor, I carefully set the coffee and groceries on the counter, flinching when the paper bag crumpled. I glanced toward her door, but it didn't open, and an irate Jo didn't burst through the door, storming out here to give me a lecture about the cabin rules. I'd already received several of those during our brief encounters when I moved in yesterday. She'd avoided me most of the day, then went off to work last night. The few times we'd crossed paths hadn't been any more pleasant than that time I got a fishing lure stuck in my cheek.

Torn between wanting to surprise her with breakfast and not wanting to wake her up with the sounds of my cooking, I decided to wait until she was conscious before preparing her favorite meal. I shuffled over to the ripped-up couch and settled into the old cushion that no longer offered any support. My weight continued sinking until I dipped so low I didn't know if I'd ever get out.

Buy Jo a new couch. Check.

Another item on my growing to-do list. And one I hoped would help show her I was still me. Still the guy she could count on no matter what.

A stack of books was propped on the end table, and I saw two of our high school yearbooks at the bottom of the pile. I pulled out the one from our freshman year, smiling as memories flooded into me while I flipped through the pages. Halfway through an old picture of Jo, Jake, and I as kids caught my eye. While Jo rode me piggy-back, Jake had me in a headlock. A typical day for the Three Amigos. When I looked at the picture, I remembered that day vividly... Andrea's fourteenth birthday party. The swallow I forced down my throat burned as an ache spread through my chest. I'd given up on my lifetime of unrequited love for Jo that day. A childhood crush that I had realized would never turn into reciprocated feelings since Jo only looked at me like a brother. It was the day I'd finally forced myself to accept that fact and move on. Something I often needed to remind myself of when she stepped into a room. Jo was just a friend... a best friend. Or at least she used to be.

"What are you doing?" Jo's voice startled me, and I slammed the yearbook shut.

"Good morning, sunshine!" I chimed, turning to see her standing in the doorway of her bedroom, rubbing her eyes. The sight of her startled me. She looked softer in her light pink pajamas. Sweet. Approachable. A vast difference from the tough-as-nails chic who usually sported a black leather coat and tackled the world head-on. The woman who could send a grown man twice her size hightailing it for his life if he crossed her. Today she looked less lethal, those intense brown eyes heavy from sleep instead of penetrating the world around her with their intensity. Her features, while feminine and breathtakingly beautiful, were often masked by the attitude she wore with such pride. An attitude that warned anyone in her vicinity that messing with her would end badly. But not today. Today she looked soft and vulnerable in her little pink pajamas.

She ignored my chipper greeting. "Why do you have that?"

I glanced down at the yearbook then set it back on the table. "Just trying to keep myself occupied so I didn't wake you up. Reminiscing to a time when you didn't hate my guts." Flashing her my sweetest smile, I waited for her to return it. Instead, her face only tightened.

"Don't touch my shit. Cabin rule."

Without another word she stumbled past me toward the bathroom. Tucking up my legs to get them out of the way, I tried to fight the pain searing into my gut from her callous words.

It will take time, I reminded myself.

With the slamming of the door I exhaled a deep breath and struggled to climb out of the sinkhole this couch had sucked me into. Once I managed to free myself, I marched into the kitchen with my newfound purpose of winning Jo's affection back. I dug out the frying pan and pulled out the bacon and eggs I'd grabbed during my quick stop at the grocery store this morning. When I dropped the bacon into the pan, it sizzled and crackled. The smell I knew she adored, and wanted to turn into a perfume, wafted up and filled the tiny cabin.

The door cracked open and her head popped out, her smooth dark hair knotted in a messy bun on top of her head, and a toothbrush clamped between her teeth.

"Is that bacon?" she asked, the words jumbled as she talked around her toothbrush.

Grinning, I pushed the bacon around in the pan. "Bacon and eggs. Your favorite. Oh!" I skipped to my left and grabbed a coffee from the tray. "And coffee. Regular, one cream, one sugar, just how you like it. I grabbed it on my way back from the grocery store."

Her face twisted while she bit down on her toothbrush, a contemplative narrowing of her eyes taking in all my offerings. Without another word, she disappeared back into the bathroom and slammed the door.

Was that a good narrowing of the eyes or a bad

one? Knowing her deep love of bacon, I hoped it was the good kind. After I cracked the eggs and tossed them in the bacon grease, the door opened, and Jo walked out.

"Coffee?" I held it up again, a sheepish grin accompanying my offering.

With a heavy sigh, she stepped forward and took the cup. "Thanks."

Thanks. A simple but powerful word. There was no "Thanks, asshole" or "Thanks, dickhead". Just "thanks", and I considered that a small victory in my battle to win back Jo.

"Have a seat. Take a load off. Breakfast will be ready in two minutes."

She slumped into the couch, and I watched her struggle to find a comfortable spot.

"I'm going to grab us a new couch if that's okay? I'll pop around the thrift shops or look on Facebook. That thing is like a deathtrap."

"Sure. Why not?" She shrugged then kicked her feet up on the makeshift coffee table constructed of two wooden crates and a board.

"And I'll make us a new coffee table, too."

Glancing at the contraption she must have hastily tossed together when she moved in, she shrugged. "Whatever you want. Just don't touch anything in my room. Or my stuff."

A dark eyebrow contrasting her soft, ivory skin rose in a warning.

"Don't touch your stuff. Got it." I flipped the eggs onto a plate and scooped on a pile of bacon beside them. "Here. Breakfast of champions."

Wary eyes watched me approach, and just before I reached her, that mangy cat came around the corner. I stuttered to a stop and took a healthy step back when it hissed and growled at me.

"He's got bacon, Petunia. Don't attack him." She looked back at me. "Yet."

Biting my lip and digging into my courage to close the distance between myself and the cat that looked ready to launch at my face any moment, I pushed forward. "Here." I handed her the plate then scurried a safe distance away. Petunia's eyes followed me for a moment and then moved to Jo's plate. A raspy meow paired with pleading eyes prompted Jo to break off a piece of bacon and give it to her.

"Is that the trick? Do I just need to feed it bacon every day, so it doesn't kill me in my sleep?"

Petunia chomped on the bacon, and Jo shoved a piece in her mouth. "Bacon helps. For both of us."

"Bacon. Check. I'll keep feeding you both bacon until one, or hopefully both, of you decides I'm not the devil."

"It's gonna take a lot of bacon." She arched her

brow and stuck another piece in her mouth.

"I'll buy out the Piggly Wiggly every week. Whatever it takes."

"Mmmhmmm," she mumbled then went to work on her eggs.

Progress.

While Jo ate, I cleaned up my mess in the kitchen. I actually enjoyed cooking and having someone to cook for this morning was fun. A nice change from waking up alone every morning in my bachelor pad. I'd cleared out the last of my boxes last night while she was at work, and everything I owned was now piled into my new tiny bedroom with the single bed that had already been in there. A bed with a mattress as old as this cabin that I had to move to the top of my list of things that needed updating. The crick in my neck was just the beginning of what would be a long, painful summer if I didn't get a more comfortable mattress soon.

Jo finished her bacon, and I hurried over to take her empty plate. Petunia hissed when I got close, but she didn't lunge at me or swipe at my legs like she had last night when I wandered too close.

More progress.

"Did it work?" I asked as I took her plate.

She furrowed her brow. "Did what work?"

"The bacon. Am I forgiven?" I gave her my most

charming grin, but it dropped when I didn't see amusement return to her eyes.

Jo tapped her chin, faking a contemplative face. "Hmmm. What do you think, Petunia? Does a few slices of bacon undo the fact that the man I thought I knew better than anyone in the world turned out to be a selfish asshole?"

Petunia didn't answer, but the scowl on Jo's face told me what I already knew.

"So, more bacon?" I sucked the air through my teeth.

With an eyeroll, Jo pushed herself out of the pit she'd settled into and stood.

"Come on, Jo. Are you seriously still going to be pissed at me? Can't we get past this?" I knew I shouldn't push it. Just like Jo had tamed that nasty cat with slow, methodical moves, I should take my time chipping away at her wall constructed of well-placed anger. But like I always did, I charged right in with no tact or timing.

"Really? I'm barely awake, it's your first morning staying in *my* cabin... the one I didn't want you in, and right away you expect that all is forgiven?"

Realizing the error of my ways, I pressed a finger to my chin. "Not so much *expect*, but more like *hope.*"

"Well quit hoping. This is temporary, and only happening because unlike you, I'm not a complete asshole. But just because I took pity on your homeless ass doesn't mean I'm going to forgive and forget. What you did..."

She closed her eyes and the agony of my decision slammed into me again.

"I know," I breathed. "It was stupid. Selfish. But you have to find a way to forgive me. You have to. I miss you. I miss us."

For a brief second, I saw her anger slip. Her eyes flashed for only a beat without the heavy emotion that had filled them ever since that fateful day. But only for a second, and then they hardened again.

"Just try to stay out of my way, Matt. I'm taking the day shift today, so I'll be home by nine. Try not to screw anything up. And stay out of my room."

Giving up the fight, for now, I nodded and stepped out of her way. She marched back into her bedroom and closed the door, sealing me into the living room with Petunia. The cat and I shared a look before I crept out of its way, careful not to get too close while I moved back to the kitchen to wash off Jo's plate.

Feeling defeated by my first attempt at patching up the biggest crater left from when I'd exploded my entire life, I went in my bedroom and grabbed my fishing pole from the corner and headed out for some fishing therapy. As I went out the door, I didn't notice Petunia crouching beside the couch, and I let out an embarrassing shriek when she launched out and swiped at my legs.

"Jesus!" I shouted as I scooted out the door, grateful it slammed shut behind me. "Fucking cat."

Shaking my head, I marched back to my truck and climbed in, pausing to shoot Jake a text. I'd called him yesterday morning to tell him I was moving in with Jo, and his snort and answer of "Good luck with that" only shook my confidence more.

Me: *It's not going well.*

Jake: *Did you think it would, dumbass? Jo hates your guts.*

I blew out a breath, trying to dig into the resolve I needed to ride out this storm.

Me: *How can you forgive me but not Jo? It just doesn't even make sense.*

Jake: *It's Jo. Have you ever known her to forgive anyone? She holds a grudge like nobody's business. I hope she doesn't kill you in your sleep.*

Me: *You and me both, bro.*

Jake: *If she does, make sure you have it written down somewhere I get your fishing stuff. I want that new rod you just picked up.*

Laughing, I shook my head.

Me: *Dick.*

I put my phone on the seat and pulled out to head to the Sister Bay Marina. Fishing had been good this morning, and I wanted to get a couple casts in to help shed off the tension that tightened my shoulders. When I got to the dock, I parked and hopped out, grabbing my pole from the bed of the truck.

"Hey, Matt! What are you doing on this side of the county? I thought you only fished in Baileys Harbor."

When I turned, I saw an old fishing buddy leaning against the boat rental kiosk.

"Hey, Ted. Yeah. I'm staying up the road now so looks like Sister Bay will be home base for a while."

"Oh yeah? Where you working?"

That was a good question. With the season in full tilt, fighting the slow-moving lines of tourist traffic to Baileys Harbor and back five days a week would be a real pain in the ass. "Working for Baileys Harbor doing maintenance right now. Why? You know of something?"

"Hell yeah! I'm desperate for employees. I could use someone with your boating skills to rent out boats and teach the tourists what they're doing so they don't kill themselves."

Pursing my lips, I contemplated it. Though it wouldn't be a long-term job since it shut down every fall when the Wisconsin weather forced everyone off the water, it could be a good gig while I figured out what the hell I wanted to do with my life. Spending my days on the water with boats and jet skis? Not a shabby way to spend the day.

I gave the water an envious glance. "Can I fish when it's not busy?"

"Yep. You can almost cast right out of the kiosk." He tapped on the side of the small wooden building just a stone's throw from the water's edge.

Now that was something I could work with. "Hours?"

"Pretty flexible. We can work around your schedule."

"Pay?"

"I'll beat whatever you're making in Baileys Harbor."

"You've got yourself a deal!" Tucking the fishing pole beneath my elbow, I stepped forward and grabbed his hand.

"Great! Come in on Wednesday when it's slower and I'll give you the tour and show you around the rentals."

"I'll let the town know to start looking for a replacement, and as soon as they have one, I'm all yours."

"Looking forward to working with you, Matt!"

With a grin as wide as if I'd just hauled in a big fish, I marched over to the side of the dock and cast my lure into the water.

Place to live. Check. Fun job in Sister Bay. Check. Winning back Jo's forgiveness...

No check yet, but with the way my luck was going, it was only a matter of time.

I hoped.

CHAPTER FIVE

JO

The day shift at JJ's provided a welcome reprieve from the insanity of the night shift. I'd agreed to switch out today so Valerie, the day bartender, could go to a friend's wedding. The day shift consisted of mostly burgers, sandwiches, and sodas, making my job a hell of a lot easier.

Even though I couldn't see my cabin from behind the bar, I still glanced out the window in that direction. I wondered what Matt was up to today. He hadn't been back before I went to work at noon, and I wondered if he was there now. Hopefully if he was, he was keeping his mitts out of my underwear drawer. I'd never had a roommate before, much less a guy, and I had no idea what kinds of trouble they could get into home alone. I valued my privacy, and the thought of someone pawing through my belongings sent a shudder through my body.

Especially someone as untrustworthy as Matt.

Untrustworthy. Now that was a word I'd never thought I'd utter about Matt. But now... now it was the first word that popped to mind when I thought about him.

"What up, sis!" My sister's voice pulled my attention away from thoughts of my cabin.

I turned to see her waltzing up to the bar with a leggy blonde in tow. A bride, no doubt. Jenna was a wedding planner who had a thriving business up here in Door County.

"Hey, Jenna. What are you doing here?" I walked over and leaned on the bar while she and her companion settled in.

"Wedding planning. And we got a lot done, so we earned ourselves a margarita." She grinned, her white teeth gleaming in the ray of sun that leaked in through the window. "Darcy, this is my baby sis, Jo. Jo, this is Darcy, the beautiful blushing bride whose phenomenal wedding I have the honor of planning."

"Nice to meet you." Darcy extended a hand and my eyes bulged at the size of her ring. I could have slapped on some ice skates and taken a few spins around that bad boy.

"Nice to meet you, too." It took everything I had to lift my eyes from the rock on her finger. Not that I would ever want one that big, that wasn't my style, but it was near impossible to ignore it.

"Can we get some margaritas, JoJo?"

If she hadn't been with a client, I'd have ripped her a new one for calling me JoJo. At least she didn't say Josephine. Only my grandmother could get away with that unscathed.

"Sure thing, JennaJenna," I answered, and she gave me a coy smile.

"I love that you work here now." She dropped her expensive handbag on the bar. "Like I needed another excuse to drink margaritas, but I'll take it."

"You two could be twins!" Darcy said, snapping her head between us.

It was true. Even though Jenna was two years older than me, we shared just about every feature possible. The same long dark hair, the same brown eyes, our mother's dainty nose and chin. We were even the same height. But even though we looked like twins, our personalities couldn't be any more different.

Jenna loved the finer things in life. She drove nice cars, wore designer shoes and clothes, and indulged in regular manicures and massages. Spending time outside for her meant sunning herself by a pool. Then there was me who loved the outdoors, rarely painted my toes, barely knew how to pronounce the designer names, and drove an old blue Jeep I'd gotten in high school and refused to put down. I was as attached to it as I was the leather jacket I'd been wearing for as many years.

Though she lived a pampered lifestyle, she'd busted her ass to achieve it. She'd put herself through college, worked for a few years as an understudy barely scraping by, and then finally branched out to open her own event planning service in Door County. And crushed it. Her impeccable taste and hyper-organization had made her the most sought-after planner in the area. Now she enjoyed the fruits of her labor, but she never took it for granted.

"We get that all the time. Considering my baby sister is a knock-out, I take it as the highest compliment there is."

"Aw," I teased as I filled up their margarita glasses. "Right back at ya."

Darcy glanced between us. "Seriously. You're both gorgeous. Good genes!"

"It's our mom. We can't take any credit," Jenna said. "And what about you? You're a freaking bombshell! Bill is a *very* lucky man."

"And he'd better never forget it." Darcy waggled her brows while she flipped her blonde hair over her shoulder.

"So, you two are working on wedding plans today?" I set the margaritas in front of them.

"Yep. We just got done going over the ceremony site so we could decide on chair arrangements.

She's getting married at a gorgeous barn out in the countryside. Very shabby chic." Jenna pursed her lips and nodded. "It's gonna be to die for."

"Sounds amazing. You're in good hands with Jenna. She plans the most incredible weddings."

"Don't I know it," Darcy said after taking a sip of her drink. "We postponed our wedding date since she was booked the weekend we wanted to get married. I wasn't walking down the aisle unless Jenna was the one organizing the event."

Jenna pulled her in for a hug. "I'm the luckiest wedding planner in the world."

"So, plans are going well?" I asked.

"So well. It's crazy good." Jenna released her hug and took a swig of her drink. "So good we earned a margarita break. What about you, sis? What's new with you? I haven't talked to you all week."

With an eye roll, I groaned and leaned forward on the bar. "A lot is new with me."

"Ooh. Dish!" Jenna leaned in closer.

"So, I was working two nights ago, and Tony, Aaron, and Matt came in." I snarled when I said his name.

"Her friends from high school." Jenna narrated to Darcy. "And Matt was her best friend, but she doesn't talk to him anymore."

"Gotcha," Darcy said, leaning in with the same expectant eyes.

"So, it turns out Matt lost his place to people renting vacation houses and was homeless. And my tequila-soaked idiot of a self, gambled away the extra bedroom in my cabin. And lost."

Jenna's eyes went wide. "And..."

"And... Matt moved in yesterday."

"Holy shit!" She laughed then turned to Darcy. "Let me catch you up. Jo hates Matt because they were besties and they had a third bestie, Jake. Well, Matt got hammered and kissed Jake's fiancé."

Darcy's eyes widened to the point of popping out of her head. "No!"

"Yes," Jenna went on. "Jo was so furious with Matt because he betrayed Jake. It's been a year, and she still isn't talking to him. Well, I suppose if he's living with you that's changed?"

They both turned to stare at me, and I shrugged. "Barely, but since he's living with me it's impossible to avoid him completely."

"So," Jenna said, turning back to Darcy. "Jo was really upset because not only had Matt betrayed Jake, but Jo has been in love with him since like... forever."

"What?" Darcy and I echoed, and our gasps merged into one.

Leave it to Jenna to overshare... and miss the mark completely. "I am *not* in love with Matt!" I shouted too loud and caused the few customers scattered throughout the restaurant to look over. Lowering my voice, I leaned back in. "Why the hell would you think that?"

"Ummm... maybe because it's *true.*" She rolled her eyes and tapped me on the forehead.

"You're in love with him?" Darcy's slack jaw remained open as she fumbled to get the margarita back to her lips.

"No." I returned the tap to Jenna's head with a little extra force, and she swatted my hand away. "I am not in love with Matt."

"Is that so?" Jenna said, her brows raising to her hairline while she pursed her lips in a challenge.

"Yeah. That's so."

"Then you don't think he's crazy hot?"

"Well," I stumbled for words. "I mean, I'm not blind, Jenna. But just because he's hot doesn't mean I'm in love with him. I know a lot of hot people that I'm not in love with. You're hot. I'm not in love with you."

She tapped her fingers on her chin. "Then riddle me this. If everyone else, including *Jake*, has forgiven him for his transgression... you know, the one against *Jake*... then why haven't you?"

My mouth opened and closed like a fish out of water while I searched for an answer. I had one. It just wasn't coming out.

She leaned back in triumph. "See. It's because

you love him, and he made out with that whore and it pissed you off."

"That's not it!" I shouted too loud once again. "I'm still mad because he's not who I thought he was. He's not the stand-up guy who would never betray his friends. I was duped. And let's not forget it was me who cleaned up the mess with Jake he left behind. Jake was destroyed."

"And Jake is madly in love with an heiress and living a life better than any of us could fathom." She quickly turned to Darcy. "Jake, the other hottie best friend who got screwed over, met and fell in love with... get this... Cassandra Davenport."

"Shut the hell up!" Darcy spat. "*The* Cassandra Davenport? The billionaire playgirl from the gossip magazines?"

Jenna threw her hand up in an oath. "Yep. One in the same. Though it turns out she's actually a super cool chic and they're engaged. She lives up here with Jake now. I'm planning the wedding, and it's going to be epic. Right on Kangaroo Lake."

"Damn. Talk about an upgrade." Darcy nodded.

"Yep. So..." Jenna turned back to me. "Thanks to Matt and his inability to keep his tongue in his mouth, Jake ended up meeting the woman of his dreams and got a happily ever after. Shouldn't you all be thanking Matt for helping Jake get rid of that tramp he'd been stuck with for like, a decade?"

Her eyebrow rose in a challenge, and I clenched my teeth while I struggled for another answer.

"No. Just because it turned out okay doesn't mean we need to throw him a parade. He's still a backstabbing asshole."

"A backstabbing asshole that you *love.*" Her lips puckered up while she made kissing noises at me.

"If you weren't here with a client, I'd grab you by the hair and yank you over this bar."

"Bring it, sister," she challenged with a grin.

"Then you're not in love with him?" Darcy asked.

I shook my head so hard my teeth rattled. "No. Of course not. I can't stand the man."

"It's a thin line between love and hate. Just remember that." Jenna pointed her finger at me, but I swatted it away.

"I'm not in love with him."

"But you were."

"But I'm not anymore."

Darcy's head twisted to keep up with our back and forth.

"Ha!" Jenna slapped the bar. "*Anymore.*"

"What?" I pressed my fingers into my temples.

"You said, 'But I'm not anymore.' Anymore implies you were at one time in love with him. Anymore implies that I was right all along." She turned to Darcy.

"I've always known but even as a kid she denied it until she was blue in the face."

"Fine!" I tossed my hands up. "When we were kids, I did have a crush on him. There. Are you happy?"

"A little." Jenna sat back and crossed her arms. "But not anymore?"

"No!" Exasperated, I slumped forward. "No. Not anymore. I realized in middle school he was never going to see me as anything but tomboy Jo. And then *Nikki* moved into town and he and Jake practically fell at that whore's feet."

Nikki moved up to Door County from Chicago our freshman year. Since we only had fifty people in our grade, the beautiful new girl had turned every guy in high school into bumbling idiots when she was around. Even the seniors had a thing for Nikki, but it was Jake who'd caught her eye.

Jenna scoffed. "Oh, I remember when she moved to school. I was a junior and that chick seriously threw off my game when she arrived. I mean, I had it going on, but fresh meat and all."

Darcy nodded her understanding.

"So," Jenna pressed on. "You *were* in love with him. And you're *sure* you're not still in love with him and that's why you're the *only* person who can't find it in their heart to forgive him?"

"I'm sure."

Was I? Suddenly her words struck a little too close to home. I'd questioned myself often this past year, wondering why I *was* the only one hanging on to my animosity with both hands. Sure, I had one good reason to hate his guts, but I also had a list a mile long of all the incredible things he'd done for me throughout our lives. All the things that made him one of the best guys I'd ever known. *The* best if I was being honest. And yet, there was a hurt so deep inside me over his indiscretion with Nikki I still couldn't bring myself to forgive him. A hurt I realized I couldn't identify.

"Just think about it, baby sis. There's a reason you can't forgive him, and I don't think it's the reason you think it is." She tapped on her temple then licked the last of the salt off her margarita. "We've got some wedding planning to do. But you better keep me posted about how this goes down."

"I will."

She leaned over the bar and pulled me in for a hug. "Unless you're in love with him, you'll forgive him. And even if you are... forgive him anyway. Forgive him, Jo. Harboring all this anger toward him only hurts you. He's a good guy. A great guy. He fucked up. Once. It's time to let it go." She lowered her voice and whispered, "I know what dad did to mom—to us— makes us both a little less likely to forgive men who betray people, but it's time. Matt didn't betray you. Matt's not dad.

Forgive him." Those words felt like a sledgehammer to the stomach. *Matt's not dad.*

And he wasn't. In fact, Matt was the guy who'd filled in around the house for my dad when he'd cheated on my mom and ran off with that hussy. But that unforgiveable action from my father had sent me on a path that took any form of betrayal as a mortal sin. It had broken me. Changed me. I couldn't forgive him for what he'd done, and I couldn't forgive anyone who broke my trust again. No one. Not even Matt.

After pecking me on the cheek, she pulled away and grabbed her purse, tossing a twenty on the bar.

"It was nice to meet you," Darcy said as she stood up. "Good luck with everything."

"Text. Me. Everything." Jenna pointed to her phone. "I want deets. Since I have no love life of my own, I'm living vicariously through you."

"I have no love life either, Jenna, and this isn't going where you think it's going."

"We'll see." She winked and blew me a kiss.

After they left, I was stuck in this empty bar with nothing to do but overanalyze her observations. I mean, I'd harbored feelings for Matt over the years. Yeah, of course. How could I not? He was gorgeous, kind, funny, and the guy who was always there for me. Perfect, really. But each time those feelings reared their head I just reminded myself that he thought of me like a sister and I shoved them away.

Just friends. That's what I always reminded myself. A mantra I recited in my mind each time he walked into a room looking too good and smiling that way that used to make my stomach do cartwheels.

But now we weren't even that. *Just friends* no longer applied since he'd gone and blown up our friendship last year.

"Jo?" Maggie, the waitress called and shook me from my spiraling thoughts.

"Yeah?"

"Did you get that drink order I put through?"

"Huh?" I spun around and saw the white paper hanging out of the drink printer. "Oh, shit. I was zoned out. Sorry. Just give me a second."

Once again, I shoved my not-so-friendly thoughts about Matt back into the pit they'd called home for over twenty-five years and I got back to work.

When I walked up the path to my cabin, I stopped when I saw the living room glowing with the colored lights of the television. It was strange to see my cabin alive in my absence. Normally I had to turn on my cellphone flashlight to find my way up the stairs when

I got home. But tonight, the warm glow lit my way, and I took a deep breath before I continued my way up. With Jenna's words, "forgive him", ringing in my ears, I opened the door.

Matt was sprawled on the couch in a position that made my bones ache just looking at it. He was right. We needed a new couch.

"Hey, Roomster! Welcome home. How was work?" he asked, clicking the remote to mute the TV.

"Fine," I snapped, then closed my eyes and took a deep breath.

Unless you're in love with him, you'll forgive him.

Determined to prove my sister wrong, I forced my lips up into an unnatural smile. "It was good. A lot easier than the past two nights. And I got cut early."

Wide eyes met mine while he undoubtedly processed the fact I'd willingly spoken to him. And smiled. Well, kind of smiled.

"Uh, good. Great." He tried to sit up but the bow in the couch thwarted his attempts. "Sorry. Let me just," he grunted, "get out of this. Jesus! I'm throwing this thing out tomorrow."

The sight of him struggling caused a real smile to start on my lips, but I bit my lower lip and forced it away.

Petunia came out of my bedroom and rubbed up against my legs. "Hey, Petunia." I leaned down to scratch her.

"Great. I'm stuck in the couch and that damn cat has the upper hand if she decides to attack me right now."

The smile started again, and this time I let it rise for a full second before forcing it away.

With a grunt, Matt rolled out of the hole and landed on the floor, quickly leaping to his feet and stepping out of Petunia's swiping range.

"Ha!" He pointed at her. "Not this time."

The smile got the best of me and I let it grow. Even showing my teeth this time.

Matt stood staring at me, then pointed at my face. "Is that... is that a smile?"

"Don't push it," I grumbled and pulled it down into a frown.

"Right. Don't push it."

Awkward silence settled between us. Having spent our lives in easy conversation and endless laughter, it was painful to feel the tension between us. Tension that I continued to put there. Tension I was going to try to ease up on. A little.

Maybe.

"Whatcha watching?" I sat on the arm of the couch to avoid getting sucked into the endless pit.

Matt took a few cautious steps toward me and then sat on the other arm. "Uh, reruns of *Family Guy*."

"I love *Family Guy*."

"I remember." He smiled; a shy smile unnatural for the guy who usually lit up the room with his grins.

"Yeah." I shook my head. "Of course you do. We used to watch it together all the time."

"I remember that, too." His smile grew a little more.

The silence seeped into the space between us again, and I shifted on the couch arm.

"Should I turn the volume on? You wanna watch?"

Forgive him, Jo.

With a shrug, I nodded. "Sure."

While I sat on the uncomfortable ledge, I tried to force my eyes on the screen. Tried to keep from staring at Matt like he'd sprouted three heads. Vegging out watching *Family Guy* was something we'd done a hundred times, but right now it felt like the most unnatural thing in the world. It'd been over a year since I'd sat in a room alone with him. Over a year since I was even in a room with him and not glaring at him or telling him to get the hell out.

Everyone else has forgiven him, Jo. He's not dad. He didn't betray you.

We watched the show for the better part of an hour, our quiet laughter the only conversation between us while we shifted over our uncomfortable seating arrangements.

I shifted again, grimacing as the backache I'd

earned from a long day at work only amplified from my perched position.

"Are you okay?" Matt asked, and my gaze slid sideways to meet his.

When our eyes met, I quickly shifted mine back to the TV. "I'm fine. Just a little sore."

A groan escaped his lips. "Are you as uncomfortable as me? This couch freaking sucks."

Glancing back over, I saw his smile growing, and it softened me a little more. "Yeah. It super sucks. I've had it since I was nineteen and it's long past its prime."

Standing up, he stretched, and I couldn't help but take notice of the abs that peeked out from beneath his t-shirt.

Just friends. No. Not even that. Not anymore.

It wasn't the first time in my life his impressive physique had me reminding myself of our platonic relationship. And this time we weren't even platonic. Now we weren't really even friends, more like frenemies.

"So, at the risk of pushing it." He dropped his arms and turned to me, the definition of his abs disappearing again. "Do you want to head up to The Garage and grab a drink? There's a band playing tonight, and it's really nice out."

Biting my lip, I let Jenna's accusations bounce around in my head.

Just forgive him, Jo.

He worked his jaw back and forth as he waited. "Unless you don't want to. We can just sit here on this busted ass couch in pain all night."

With a deep breath, I closed my eyes for a beat, then opened them and nodded. "Sure. Why the hell not?"

The spark that had always lived in his eyes flickered back on. "Really? You'll come out with me?"

Shrugging, I stood up, grimacing from the pain now searing through my ass. "I could use a drink and you're right... we need a new couch."

"Drinks are on me."

"Damn straight they are." I looked up, and we exchanged a brief smile.

Forgive him, Jo.

Baby steps. Though I wasn't ready to forget everything that went down, I was making baby steps. Teeny, tiny baby steps. And right now, those steps were taking us out for drinks.

CHAPTER SIX

MATT

Jo followed me through the crowd that had gathered outside at Husby's Garage Bar. I tried not to overwhelm her with my excitement that she'd agreed to have a drink with me. It had taken all my willpower not to sweep her into my arms and spin her around when she'd said yes.

Take it slow.

The folk music floated up through the open-air bar, and the small crowd gathered in front of the three-piece band swayed to the sounds. The Garage Bar was just that... a garage that had been turned into a bar. Situated halfway down the steep hill heading into downtown Sister Bay, Husby's was the busiest bar around, and what had started as a simple idea to use the empty garage to expand the space, making room for visitors to sit outside and enjoy the fresh Door County air, had taken on a life of its own. Now the garage had been transformed into a charming wrap around bar, ample tables dotting the outdoor space and giving guests plenty of places to sit. They had also constructed a small stage for the bands who played here a few nights a week. The Garage was now one of the most happening spots in Sister Bay on any given summer night.

I saw two bar stools open, and I bee-lined toward them so I could get them before the other couple I saw heading their way.

"Quick. Sit." I yanked out the stool and nearly pushed Jo into it. When I looked over my shoulder at our competition, they met me with two mirrored glares.

Not this time, folks. I was a man on a mission and that mission involved having a nice evening with Jo. Prime seating at the bar was a good start.

I slid into my stool beside her and pulled out my wallet. "Whatever you want."

She arched a brow. "Anything?"

"Yep. Anything."

"Well, in that case, can you order me a cabin without a pain-in-the-ass roommate?"

"How about a cabin with an unbelievably handsome, hilariously funny, devastatingly charming guy who makes a mean side of bacon. Oh wait! You have that, you lucky son of a bitch." I grinned, trying to ease the tension between us more.

Jo closed her eyes and squeezed them tight, a deep breath lifting the shoulders covered by the black leather jacket she loved and had worn for years. "Damn it. I'm supposed to be forgiving you or something and I can't stop my mouth from making snarky comments."

"I've always loved your snarky comments. Granted they normally weren't aimed at me but some other poor chump who'd pissed you off, but I can take it. Fire away."

When she looked at me, regret churned inside her eyes. "I'm trying. Honestly, I am. It's just going to take a little time to stop my forked tongue from spitting out insults at you since it's been all I've done for over a year. Habits die hard."

"Why the change of heart?" I asked. "Why are you ready to try to forgive me?"

Her face tightened, and she turned away with a slight shake of her head. "Just something Jenna said today when she stopped in at JJ's."

"Oh, yeah? So, I have Jenna to thank for the reduction in glares? What did she say?"

A pink flush crept up into her cheeks while she pushed a piece of hair behind her ear. "No biggie. Just... she just said it's time to forgive you. I mean, we're stuck living together, so I'm going to at least *try.*"

"Thank you. I won't fuck up again. I promise. Me and these luscious lips are gonna keep far away from

Jake's lady, and I'll definitely never betray you by making out with your guy, so you're safe."

She chuckled and rolled her eyes. "We'll see."

"Well, unless you date Henry Cavill. I may be a straight dude, but even I have a bit of a mancrush on him. I mean, seriously. Have you seen that guy's abs?" I jokingly bit the back of my closed fist and moaned. "I'd fight you for him."

"Would you shut up!" Her small smile started to widen. "You're terrible."

As we exchanged a little laughter that started to feel natural, the bartender arrived in front of us. "Hey, Jo."

"Hey, Angie. Can I get a beer? Do you have Door County Brewery's Pallet Jack?"

"Absolutely. And for your... date?" The blonde bartender raised a brow as her gaze slid to me.

Jo's head shook so hard I worried it may fly off and roll down the Sister Bay hill. "God, no. Not a date," she said, and even though I hadn't expected a date, for some reason the intense denial stung a little. "This is Matt. He's my... roommate."

Roommate. I could handle that. Better than "this guy I hate."

Angie's eyes lit up and narrowed into seductive slants while she leaned on the bar in front of me, as if Jo's rejection just opened a door she intended to waltz on through. "And what are you having... *roommate* Matt?"

Not wanting anything to do with the pretty young thing batting her thick eyelashes at me, I crossed my arms and leaned back. "I'll have what Jo's having."

"You got it, hun." With a quick wink she turned and walked away.

Jo rolled her eyes and snorted. "Some things never change."

"What the hell is that supposed to mean?" I leaned forward on the bar and craned my neck to get into her line of sight.

"You. Girls. They're always throwing themselves at you. It's obnoxious."

"Obnoxious?" I laughed. "Well, I can say the same about you and guys. How many times have I had to toss gropey guys out of the bar for you?"

"Whatever." She shrugged. "I can handle touchy randoms myself."

"No doubt about that, but I've always been happy to come to your rescue. Now, the question is, if this bartender gets too handsy with me, are you going to save me and toss her down the hill?"

Her lips pressed into a thin white line and I welcomed the smile begging to be let free. When she gave in, the soft sounds of her laugh, her full laugh, were more melodious than the music playing behind us.

Because you haven't heard it in over a year.

"I could take her," she said between laughs.

"Damn straight you could. Hell, you could take me and I'm like twice your size."

Her laugh deepened, and she flexed her small bicep then faked a snarl. "And don't you forget it. Next time you mess up it's not going to be Jake pummeling you into a bloody pulp. I'll happily take my turn."

My laugher sputtered off and regret crept back over me like a shroud I couldn't seem to shed.

"Sorry." She grimaced and her laughter sputtered out. "Force of habit."

"It's okay."

"No." She shook her head. "Jenna is right. I have to find it in my heart to forgive you. I mean, you have been an incredible friend for the majority of my life. Then you made a mistake. A big mistake – but only one."

The unexpected information swirled between my ears. "Yeah? You really think you can forgive me?"

"I'm going to try, Matt. I promise I am."

I basked in her words, feeling the tug of hope in the center of my chest. "Good. I missed this, Jo. Us. Just hanging out."

"Yeah," she said on a sigh. "I suppose I did, too."

Angie arrived with our beers and slid mine in front

of me with a seductive grin. "Just let me know if you need *anything* at all."

Jo's groan rolled out of her full pink lips before she shoved her bottle of beer between them to stop it.

"Thanks, Angie." I took my beer and turned away from her as quickly as I could, hoping it gave her the hint. Tonight was about Jo... and only Jo.

"Anything at all." She winked again.

Nope. Still didn't get the hint.

"So," I said, changing the subject. "I have news."

"Yeah? What kind of news?" Jo asked.

"I got a job offer today. Down at the Sister Bay Marina. I'll be renting boats and jet skis."

"Seriously?"

"Yep. Ran into Ted Anders when I went fishing there today. Remember him?"

"Yep. Jill's dad, right? Your old fishing buddy."

Noise buzzed around us, so I leaned in closer. "That's the one. Well, he's managing the boat rental and needs a body who knows their way around boats."

"You certainly fit the bill."

"Yeah. I think it will be good. I called my boss in Baileys Harbor today and gave him the news. Turns out I got lucky and there are a few people lined up who want my job, so I can start the new one by the end of the week."

She angled her torso toward me, and I fought the

itch to drape my arm around her. "That's awesome, Matt. Driving to Baileys Harbor every day is a serious pain in the ass. That's why I left the Blue Ox for JJ's."

"Exactly. And now I can spend my days on the water and fish when it's slow."

"That's pretty perfect for you. Lucky you went fishing today."

"Right?" I grinned. "Who knew it would land me a job instead of a fish."

"What's your plan for the winter, then? Don't they shut down by Fall Fest."

"They do, so I'm not sure." I swiped a hand along the back of my neck. "I mean, I know your place is only temporary, so I guess I'll figure out where I'm moving to full-time and then figure it out from there."

"Always swinging like a monkey from one career to the next."

"I know." I took a sip of my beer, then sighed. "When am I going to realize I'm not twenty-one anymore, buckle down and find a permanent job?"

Jo shrugged. "Eh. How many of our friends do we know who went off to college, got the 'dream job' and are absolutely miserable cooped up inside, sucking down lungfuls of stale air?"

"A lot." I laughed.

"Exactly. You were one of them. But you realized office life wasn't for you, so you went after a life that would make you happy. I think that's something to be proud of, not ashamed of. Most people aren't brave enough to give up the security of a nine to five to find happiness. To go against the normal standards of society and do what makes them happy. You're brave. Be proud of that."

My focus started to waver as the intoxicating sensation of her sliver of forgiveness weaved through me. "Wow. Thanks, Jo. That means a lot to me that you don't think I'm just a lazy, meandering bum."

She chuckled, another layer of darkness evaporating from her expression. "Not at all. People are always asking me when I'm going to get a 'real job', and I just smile and laugh. When I tell them I make more in four days bartending than most of them make in a week, even with their college degrees and fancy jobs, it shuts them up pretty quick. Not to mention I have almost every day off to enjoy the sunshine, three months off every winter when we close down, and a lot of fun most nights... well, when I'm not getting my ass kicked. I love bartending. It suits me. I wish people would get that and not think it's my 'fallback', or something I'm doing because I don't have another option. I've got plenty of options. Just none that are a better fit for my life."

"Right?" I sighed. "People don't get that there's a lot more to life than making six-figures sitting in a stuffy office. Some things in life are worth more than money. I may float between careers, but at least I'm not dreading going into work every day and counting the hours until I can leave. I like what I do, until I don't... then I pick something else."

"Since you get bored with jobs easily, you need to be challenged regularly. So why lock yourself down to one thing and be miserable for all your days just because you 'should'? I think it's good you change it up."

Her ability to recognize my values felt like someone punching the gas on my emotions, flooding an ache into my limbs. An ache that wanted more Jo. "I'm glad someone understands my need to keep life interesting."

"You've always been that way. And I don't think it's a bad thing at all. It's just who you are."

Of all the people that had come and gone from my life, none understood me better than Jo. It was part of why losing her friendship had torn my soul to shreds.

"Thanks, Jo. That means a lot. But I do think I should try to find a career I can enjoy and stick with for more than a few seasons."

"What about being a handyman? You're so good at it. And it's always something different."

"You know, I've been trying to figure out how to do something with that. I love puttering around with different projects. Maybe after I'm done with your cabin, I'll look into how one becomes a professional putterer."

Jo laughed, and this time it came out more naturally. "Professional putterer. I like it. Maybe we can make that your business name."

Holding my hands out like I framed a sign, I grinned. "Matt's Professional Puttering Services. It has a ring."

Pursing her lips, she shook her head and laughed. "I take that back. No one will ever hire you."

Feigning my disappointment, I swung a fist through the air between us. "Damn. I'll keep working on it."

As I watched her struggle, the air between us crackled with all the words that remained unspoken. I held my breath, waiting for her to regress back into her anger, but then she surprised me. "And about my cabin. I don't actually expect you to do all that work on it."

Scoffing, I sat back. "Are you saying you don't trust me to turn your crappy cabin into a kick-ass beachfront getaway?"

"No." She lifted an eyebrow. "I'm saying that I was wicked pissed at you and wanted you to suffer if you insisted on living with me. Since I'm working on this whole forgiveness thing, I just want you to know

I don't expect you to basically give me thousands and thousands of dollars of free labor."

"Well, too bad. Because I've got my heart set on fixing that place up. So, don't try to stop me."

"Only if you're doing it because you *want* to, and not because you think you have to."

"Jo," I said, my smile sliding away as I looked into her eyes. "I *want* to help you fix up your place. You deserve an awesome place to call home, and I am so very grateful you opened your other room to me. Even when you wanted to smack me."

A smile played across her lips. "Okay. But only if you're sure."

I nodded. "I'm sure. And I'll try to do my work when you're bartending, so I don't drive you bananas."

"Deal." She lifted her beer in a toast, and I paused, realizing the significance of the small gesture.

A peace offering. A sign of friendship. A sign of her forgiveness. The ringing of our bottles together echoed deep in my soul, and I let loose a grin so wide I worried my face would rip.

"Deal."

As we sat there for an hour sipping our beer and listening to the music, Jo continued softening toward me, her knee-jerk insults diminishing with each interaction. Seeing her smile again, and having it directed at me, felt like the first day in spring after a long winter. The first rays of sunlight illuminating a dark, grey world. I'd known I had missed her... God how I'd missed her, but even I hadn't processed just how much until tonight. There'd been a hole in my heart when she'd vacated it, and I hadn't realized until now just how big that hole was. I was surprised it'd managed to keep beating with the few slivers she'd left behind when she'd walked out of my world. But tonight, with each smile, each laugh, a little bit of my heart returned.

"No. Way!" a familiar voice echoed behind us and we spun in our seats.

"Hey, Andrea," I said, giving a little wave to one of our high school classmates.

"Jo? Matt? It *is* you!" She pushed through the crowds and tossed an arm around each of us, pulling us in for a group hug.

Her high-pitched squeals caused me to grimace.

"Oh my God, it's been years!" she continued, and her squeals got louder while her grip tightened.

When she finally let us go, Jo and I exchanged a quick glance. No doubt her thoughts mirrored mine. We'd never been close with Andrea in high school, yet she was acting like we were all the best of friends reunited after ages apart.

"Honey! These are my friends from high school, Matt and Jo." She pointed to us while she gestured to the little man in glasses who followed through the crowd she'd parted. "This is my husband, Allen."

"Nice to meet you." He extended a hand, and I shook it.

"I can't *believe* you two still hang out together. Honey, Jo and Matt were *best friends* since like..." She looked between us. "Well, *forever!* And I guess some things never change, because here they are all these years later and they're still besties! I love it!"

Jo and I shifted in our seats, an awkward glance passing between us while she chewed on her lower lip. Last year that observation would have been accurate. Tonight, I was just grateful to be this close to Jo without getting an elbow to the face.

"Andrea and I are up visiting for a week this summer," Allen said. "We live in Dubuque now."

"That's right." Andrea grinned. "Met this handsome stallion in college and we moved there a few years ago. But I told Allen it had been too many years since I'd been home, so we hopped in the car and came up. And here you both are... and nothing has changed. Just love it, love it, love it!"

"Yep. Nothing changed at all," Jo said, sliding another glance my way.

"Just the same old Jo and Matt," I added, glad Jo was playing along and not dishing that I'd kissed Jake's fiancé, broke up the band, and was just now tonight poking my head above water.

"Well, it has been so fun seeing you both. I've got to show Allen all around town, but I'm sure I'll see you two around before we head back next week. Small towns and all."

"Looking forward to it," I lied.

"Nice to meet you, Allen. And good to see you again, Andrea." Jo forced a smile.

With one last awkward group hug, Andrea said goodbye. Jo and I blew out a mirrored breath of relief and spun back to face the bar.

"She hasn't changed at all." Jo laughed. "You'd think she was still leading the pep squad with all that energy and excitement."

"Does she ever not smile? Ever?" I shook my head. "It must be exhausting always being that perky."

"No fucking thank you." Jo shook her head.

"Agreed." I lifted my beer and Jo clinked hers against it. "It's so weird we saw her. I was just looking at a picture of us in the yearbook from her fourteenth birthday at Nicolet Beach. Do you remember that day?" I asked, the memory flooding back to me like it was yesterday.

"You mean the birthday party when her parents rented the entire beach, pretty much brought in a freaking carnival, and had that big band come and play? Oh yeah... I remember. My fourteenth birthday consisted of a couple of cards and some cupcakes."

"That day was crazy. Everyone was there. Not so much because we liked her, but the party was off the hook."

"Oh my God!" Jo almost spit out her beer. "That was the day we went jet skiing, and I flipped you off the back." Her eyes squeezed shut while she tossed her head back and dissolved into laughter. "You flew so far!"

Her laughter was contagious, and I joined it while I remembered the moment vividly. "No warning. No 'hang on'. No nothing. You just gunned it and cranked it left, and I did a full-on airshow for everyone watching at the party. Man, that hurt!"

"So funny!" She continued cackling at my expense, but her genuine smile eased my pain.

"Says you... the one who didn't get a face wash in front of the whole eighth grade class."

"Ahhh, the good old days. That was fun. I don't think I've been jet skiing since that day."

"Probably a good thing, considering you almost killed me."

Jo flicked a wrist at me. "Ah. You're tough. You lived."

"My body, yes. Not so much my pride. Everyone teased me for weeks."

With a shrug, she smiled "You should have held

on tighter."

The other memory I had from that day remained hidden, but now that the gates had opened on memory lane, it hit me like a brick. It was the reason *why* I hadn't been holding on tight. Andrea's parents had provided jet skis for the party, and when Jo had asked if I wanted to go, I'd said yes in a heartbeat. After she'd insisted on driving, I'd realized I would have to ride behind her. When she'd hopped on wearing nothing but a life jacket and her bikini, I'd had to wrap my arms around her waist. The minute I'd slid my hands across her bare skin, all those feelings I'd been harboring for her had exploded like a bomb inside me.

We're just friends, we're just friends, I had chanted in my mind while she drove off with me skipping across the waves. Unable to withstand the torture of having her so close, of holding her in my arms like I'd done only in my dreams, I'd pushed myself to the back of the jet ski and let go of her... the girl that had sent my fourteen-year-old hormones into overdrive. It hadn't taken long for Jo to get ballsy with her steering skills, and soon me and my hormones had been cooling off in the bay after she'd sent me flying.

"I'm never riding behind you on a jet ski again."

"Whatevs," she teased. "I had mad skills."

"Remind me not to let you teach the tourists how to jet ski this summer when I'm at work. It's my job to make sure they have fun and get back safe. With you at the helm they'll all end up in the ER."

Jo laughed, shrugging her shoulders. "Fair enough."

We both let our laughter trickle off, and silence settled around us again. But this time it didn't feel awkward. The silence wasn't the product of her anger, her actively ignoring the best friend she could no longer stand. This time the silence was comfortable, a silence shared between friends while they reminisced about a lifetime of memories together. Good memories.

"You working tomorrow?" she asked, and I shook my head.

"Nope. Day off. You?"

"Monday Funday for me as well."

"Sweet. You got any plans?"

She shook her head. "Nope."

"Me neither. I might get started on your place, if that's okay."

"Fine by me. I'm planning on finding a spot in the sun and soaking up the summer rays."

"You certainly earned it after how hard you busted it at JJ's this weekend."

She nodded and lifted her empty beer. "So, since neither of us need to get up tomorrow, we staying for another?"

She wanted to stay out with me. In my eyes, that

was another mark of the success I was making in repairing the rift between us.

"Absolutely. You up for a round of bar dice?"

Jo grinned wide. "You really want to get your ass kicked again?"

"Let's not forget, you do lose sometimes. If you didn't, I'd be sleeping in my truck." Waggling my brows, I taunted her with a smile.

"You're on."

We flagged down the bartender and argued over who shook first.

Just like old times.

We're back.

CHAPTER SEVEN

JO

That smell. It tantalized my nostrils and forced my eyes to blink open. My favorite smell in the world.

Bacon.

Pushing off my blanket, I stretched and then tossed on my robe. Petunia meowed from her perch at the foot of my bed, then looked to her partially full bowl, but this time I ignored her pleas.

"Finish up what you have. Starving cats in the world and all." I shook a finger at her, but those pleading eyes met mine and I remembered how thin she was when I'd found her. A mangled ball of fur hanging off her emaciated frame. "Ugh. Fine. But this is the last time. The *last* time. Starting tomorrow you have to finish all your perfectly good food before I fill it again."

When I grabbed the bag of cat food, she chirped and hopped down, rubbing against my legs as I filled it back up.

"So spoiled." I petted her head and then marched

out my bedroom door, following my nose to the smell that made my stomach grumble.

When I stepped into the living room, Matt stood in the kitchenette pushing bacon around in the pan. He looked up, and that bright white smile stretched across his face.

"Morning, Roomster! Breakfast of champions coming right up."

A handsome man cooking me bacon. Again. Okay, maybe Petunia wasn't the only spoiled one in this cabin.

"Morning, Matt." I smiled, and this time I didn't have to force it. By the end of our evening at The Garage, the anger and hurt I'd carried around the past year had sloughed off, and we were starting to find our groove again.

We weren't us yet... not by a long shot, but we were stepping in the right direction. We'd been like an old married couple before last year. A comfortable way of existing together, finishing each other's sentences, and knowing what the other was thinking even before they did. But now, even though we were moving toward each other again, it felt different. Fresh. Not unlike dating someone new.

But we weren't dating, I reminded myself. Never had, never would. Our rekindled friendship may bring with it the same nerves and uncertainty that came with dating someone new, but our destination was different. Our destination was friendship. Plain and simple. I'd realized that years ago, and I wasn't going to start letting other ideas flood into my mind again. It'd been hard enough to accept it the first time. No sense in going through *that* agony twice.

"I got a lead on new couch," he said.

"Yeah? What's it look like?"

"A sweet distressed brown leather. It will look perfect in here. Kasey is selling it. Saw it on Facebook."

"Works for me. How much money do you need?"

He scoffed. "Fixing up your cabin is my treat. Consider it part of my rent."

"Matt, I told you last night—"

"Shush." He raised a hand and then clamped it shut. "My treat."

Not ready to argue with him this early in the day, I just shrugged and kicked my feet up on the boards I called a coffee table.

"Oh, and I've got an idea for a coffee table, too. It's gonna be baller."

"Whatever you say, handy man."

Matt scooped a pile of bacon onto the plate, walked around the small island, and handed it to me. "Eat up. You're going to need your energy today."

"Energy? For what?" I popped a piece of bacon in my mouth. Cooked to perfection. Extra crispy. Just how I liked it.

"Just eat your bacon and put on your suit. I've got a surprise."

Arching a brow, I finished chewing. "What kind of surprise?"

His charming smile stretched wider and mirth danced around in his eyes. I knew that look. I'd seen it hundreds of times and it usually prefaced us getting into a boatload of trouble as kids or running from the cops as adults.

"If I told you the details, it wouldn't be a surprise."

"Is this one of your 'it's going to be fun' ideas that ends up with one or both of us needing to get bailed out of jail? Because they told us last time, they wouldn't let us go with just a warning again."

Matt tossed his head back and laughed. "Oh, come on. That was fun and you know it."

Pursing my lips, I shrugged. "Yeah. I guess it was. But no cops today."

Clamping a piece of bacon between his teeth, he lifted his hand and extended three fingers, mumbling, "No cops. Boy Scout promise."

"You weren't a Boy Scout." I gave him a knowing glare.

"Don't you trust me?" he asked, and the simple question held more weight than I was prepared to comprehend only several minutes after waking up.

Do I trust him? The short answer was no. Not anymore. But the long answer was more complicated than that. The long answer was once I trusted him more than any human being on this planet. Once I trusted him with my life. But now... now I was just starting to move toward forgiveness and trust. But full trust... that was still a ways away.

With a shrug, I smiled. "You haven't gotten me killed... yet."

That disarming grin grew again and took down more of my dwindling defenses. "Then you're in. Good. It's a Roomster bonding day."

"Would you quit calling me Roomster?" I laughed as I finished my bacon.

"Nope." He popped the last piece in his mouth and put his dish in the sink. "I'll clean them when we get back. Now hurry up and put on your suit."

"Jeez. Slow down there, Speed Racer. Just give me a few."

"Chop, chop," he teased and clapped his hands as he blew by.

After he disappeared into his bedroom, I went in the bathroom to wash my face, brush my teeth, and get ready for the day. When I was done, I grabbed my suit that had been hanging from the shower and tossed it on along with my coverup.

When I came out, Matt leaned against the screen

door, his mirrored sunglasses hiding the trouble dancing in his eyes judging by the smile playing across his face. The day-old scruff wrapping around his jaw gave him that extra edge of mischief, and I tried to force away the thoughts fighting their way to the front of my mind.

God, he looks hot.

Damn it. That one slipped by.

Just friends.

My mantra. The one I'd had to recite on occasion over the years when I'd caught those not-so-friendly thoughts slipping into the forefront of my mind. Times when I noticed just how handsome he was. When I'd notice the way his square jaw ticked as he struggled to suppress his laughter. How the tiny flecks of gold in his brown eyes sparkled in soft lights. The way his biceps flexed when he'd snag a fish and crank the reel. The times I wondered what his lips may taste like.

Times like this one.

Chasing the thoughts from my mind about how hot he looked in his board shorts and t-shirt that fit oh-so-well, I took a breath and grabbed my beach towel hanging from my door.

"Ready?" he asked, pushing open the screen door.

"I have no idea where we're going, but I could use a beach day."

I grabbed my purse off the couch and headed

out the door. Petunia meowed and trotted out of my bedroom, sending Matt scampering out after me, slamming the door to separate him from the cat who bid him goodbye with a hiss.

"You still scared of her?" I snorted.

"It hates me, Jo."

"*She* hates you. But she'll get used to you... as long as you stop running away from her screaming like you're starring in some B-rated horror movie and she's an axe-wielding psychopath."

Shuddering, he shook his head. "If I *was* starring in a B-rated horror movie, I'd be the s*mart* one. The one that lives to the end. That thing would kill me in my sleep if I didn't push a chair in front of my door at night."

"Try the bacon. It worked on me." I smiled and slid my sunglasses into place. "Where to?"

"Come on." Matt ushered me down the stairs and we climbed into his truck. We both rolled down our windows, and he drove down the road toward downtown Sister Bay.

The warm summer breeze blew in through our open windows as I rode along in silence, wondering what his goofy brain had concocted today. Matt was the king of adventures, always planning something that would have my cheeks hurting by the end of the day from all the laughter. Life was filled with fun when

I was at his side, and I only realized now how boring my life had been without him in it. Lonely even. With Jake and Cassie shacked up together, and me not wanting to be a third wheel, I'd spent most of my time bartending and watching Netflix. But like the breeze blowing in through my window, Matt had whooshed back into my life and shaken it up again.

In a good way.

"We going fishing?" I asked when he pulled up in front of the Sister Bay Marina.

"Better."

"Better than fishing? That's saying something when it comes to you." I peeked over the top of my sunglasses.

"Come on."

The excitement radiated off him and I felt it building up inside of me. What were we doing? Grabbing my purse and towel, I followed him down the sidewalk to the boat rental kiosk.

"Hey, Ted!" Matt called, waving at Ted who was reading a book behind the little glass window.

"Hey, Ted," I echoed.

"Hey, Matt. Hey, Jo." Ted set his book down and pushed himself off the chair. "Try to have it back by five." He tossed a set of keys out the window and Matt caught them with ease.

"You got it, Ted. Thanks for letting me borrow it."

"If you're going to work here, you need to know the ins and outs of all the equipment. Consider it training."

"My kind of training! We'll be back later."

Ted gave a little wave. "Have fun, kids."

"Thanks, Ted."

I walked behind him not knowing why he was thanking Ted. When we reached the dock below, a white and blue jet ski bobbed in the water and answered my question.

"No way." I laughed, looking over the sleek machine.

"Yes way." Matt looked over his shoulder and grinned. "You. Me. A whole day jet skiing around Door County."

"Okay... this is a pretty good idea. I seriously haven't been on one since we were kids."

"We're long overdue."

We reached the smaller dock the jet ski was tied to, and Matt held out his hand. "Hand me your purse and towel. I'll put it in drybag in the cubby, so they don't get wet."

After handing him my stuff, he shoved them in the waterproof bag. Nerves crackled inside my stomach, and I tried to quiet them down. Just yesterday I'd never wanted to talk to Matt again, and now I was about to spend the day in close contact with him. *Very* close contact.

"One big difference this time. I'm driving." He

waggled his eyebrows, and I scoffed my response.

"Hell no. I'm driving," I protested, but he shook the keys in my face.

"Not this time, Jo."

Before I could argue, he grabbed the bottom of his shirt, yanking it up over his head. Those tanned muscles came into view, and I swallowed. Hard.

Shit.

There was a reason I'd insisted on driving the jet ski all those years ago. The thought of wrapping my arms around the boy I'd wanted to kiss since I'd discovered kissing had been more than this girl could stand. Especially since I'd been trying to convince myself of Matt's friend-zone status. And now that he was all grown up, so were his muscles. If I'd thought it would be difficult to suppress my attraction when I was wrapped around him back then, one look at him today had me quaking in my flip-flops.

Just friends, just friends, just friends.

"I think I should drive," I said, trying to force the saliva to return to my mouth.

"Not a chance in hell." He shoved his t-shirt inside the bag and gestured to my turquoise coverup. "You want to wear that, or do you want it in the drybag?"

Though I had no interest in any more skin-to-skin contact than necessary, I also didn't want my only clothing for the day soaked if I needed to wear it later.

Swallowing hard, I slowly peeled it over my head and handed it to him. His mirrored sunglasses hid his eyes, but a slight tip in his chin told me he may have just peeked at my goodies as well.

"Cute suit," he said, and shoved my dress into the bag.

Cute suit. Never mind. He wasn't eyeballing my goodies after all; he was just taking note of the army green bikini I sported.

Doesn't matter. Just friends.

After a lifetime of getting good at pretending I had no feelings for Matt, Jenna's words yesterday had reignited those emotions I'd long thought gone. Well, perhaps they'd never been totally gone, but they'd been much quieter. Maybe the time spent apart had flamed my feelings to the point of incinerating me from the inside. The year apart had amplified all those feelings, and I was out of practice at shoving them back down. What had become a quiet reflex anytime they had tried to surface before was now a struggle akin to folding up fitted sheets and getting them back into their original packaging.

While I watched his toned, tanned muscles flex as he put our dry bag in the cubby beneath the seat, I continued my mantra and hoped soon it would burn back into my brain.

Just friends. Just friends. Just friends.

"Life jacket. Here." He tossed me a blue jacket and then strapped on his own. Grateful for the lessening of our upcoming close contact, I clicked on my straps and pulled them tight.

He climbed onto the jet ski, patting the seat for me to jump on. Swallowing my groan, I climbed on behind him. The muscles in his broad back twitched while he started it up, and I glanced back at the dock wondering what excuse I could spit out for launching back onto dry land and running for my life. After a lifetime of pretending my feelings for him were nothing more than a childhood crush long passed, I hadn't realized how easy this last year had been away from him. A whole year of not having to chant my mantra when his smile threatened to turn my world upside down.

"Hold on, Jo. Don't want to send you flying... although I suppose you deserve some payback." He smiled over his shoulder.

With a groan I didn't bother to suppress since he couldn't hear it over the humming of the engine, I scooted forward and wrapped my arms around his waist. Actual agony radiated from the tips of my fingers when I brushed against his skin. Why? Why couldn't I just get rid of these feelings once and for all? I'd thought after his betrayal that finally, *finally*, I would be free of the rogue attraction to him that continued rearing its head at the most inopportune times.

Like this one.

But it would seem my luck in that department had all but run out.

Matt gave the jet ski some gas, and we puttered through the marina and out past the Sister Bay beach. Children leapt off the long, concrete dock and I remembered being one of them myself once upon a time. As kids, Matt, Jake, and I had played there a number of times, and our squeals had echoed through the summer air when we'd plunged off the dock hand-in-hand. Today it wasn't our squeals coming off the dock, but howls of joy from the children enjoying their summer vacations. The shrieks of their happiness traveled across the water and blended with the sound of our engine as Matt gave it more gas.

"You'd better hold on tight," he said as we made it out of the no-wake zone.

With willpower that rivaled keeping The Incredible Hulk at bay, I bit my lip and wrapped my arms around his waist even tighter. As sensations spiraled through my body, I understood this was the reason I'd insisted on driving the jet ski all those years ago. This agony of being wrapped around him and feeling him between my thighs. Although, at Andrea's birthday party when he'd climbed up behind me and I'd felt his grip tighten around my waist it had ended up being just a different kind of agony. But shortly into our ride he'd let go of me, scooting back as far as he could, like I repulsed him and he couldn't stand the thought of touching me. I'd gotten pissed at the insult, and my temper had gotten the better of me, so knowing he had nothing to hold onto, I'd intentionally tossed him off that day.

Matt gunned it and we lifted in the air, skipping across the waves cresting along the bay. As we reached our cruising speed, the jet ski settled into its plane and we zipped along the shores of Sister Bay. The breathtaking bluffs helped me focus my attention on something other than the man between my legs. Something other than the feelings that were replacing the rage I'd felt this past year. Something other than the not-so-friendly feelings his return to my life had amplified. What had been reduced to a barely audible whisper over the years was now like having someone screaming in my ear with a megaphone.

Instead of listening to it, I tried to drown it out.

Just friends. Just friends. Just friends.

CHAPTER EIGHT

MATT

Wow. That was a bad idea of epic proportions, I thought while I guided the jet ski between all the boats anchored around Nicolet Bay.

I'd thought I was being so smart forcing Jo to sit behind me, ensuring I'd avoid the unfortunate incident that had happened last time we'd gone jet skiing. I'd thought I'd be safe up here and we could enjoy a nice day on the water reconnecting again. As friends.

I'd thought wrong.

The minute those long legs had slid against my hips I'd reverted to that fourteen-year-old boy again... and there weren't enough baseball images in the world to push away the anything-but-platonic thoughts that invaded my mind.

What the hell was wrong with me? I'd gotten past this. I'd moved on from Jo years ago.

Hadn't I?

Sure, I'd suffered an occasional flare up of feelings over the years, but for the most part I'd been successful. Okay, more than occasional flare-ups, but they were at least manageable. Today was no mild flare up. Today, the moment I felt her body wrap around mine, the closeness brought on a raging inferno. I'd spent the past thirty minutes wrestling with the fire scorching me from the inside out, but I was anything but successful in extinguishing it. I was failing. Miserably. Apparently spending a year apart had been like shoving my bottled-up feelings into the bottom of a champagne bottle and giving it a shake. Now the desperate pressure dared me to pop the cork.

But there would be no popping of the cork and expressing my deepest desires. Not with Jo. I needed to keep those feelings contained in the bottle until they fizzled out... just like I'd done all those years ago right here on this beach after we'd played spin the bottle and it had ended in a most unfortunate kiss.

Now here we were again, back at the scene of the crime. Back at the beach we'd come to for Andrea's fourteenth birthday party when I'd finally given up on my unrequited love for Jo.

When I'd spun the bottle and it had landed on Jo, every nerve in my body had twitched with excitement. Finally... *finally* I would get to kiss her. And when I had leaned across the circle of cheering friends and pressed my lips to hers, my world had flipped upside down. After years of coveting her lips and wondering what they tasted like, I'd finally experienced a kiss with the girl who'd held my heart since we were in preschool. Pulse racing. Breath stalling in my lungs. That moment became the culmination of every fantasy I'd ever had.

And then she'd demolished my fantasy like a wrecking ball. The moment our lips broke apart, she'd wiped her mouth, spitting into the sand with a face twisted in disgust.

A face I'd never, *ever,* forget. The face that told me Jo would never see me as anything other than a friend.

And I'd do well to remember that disgusted expression right now.

Just friends.

Glancing at the spot in the sand where my dreams had been dashed all those years ago during Andrea's birthday party, I repeated the process of shoving my confusing emotions about her back into the closet I'd stored them in. We were just friends, and I needed to drill that back into my mind. Last night I'd been thrilled she'd even cracked open the door to friendship, and I wasn't going to do anything to stretch the already frazzled tether between us.

Didn't matter how good she looked in that green bikini.

Or how amazing her arms felt wrapped around my waist.

Or... nope. Ignore it, damn it.

Just friends.

She tapped my shoulder and pointed to the sandy spot off to the side of the swimming area. "You can pull up over there." Desperate to get off this jet ski and out from between her legs, I maneuvered us through the boats dotting the quiet water. Families and friends sprawled across the bows of their boats and yachts, and I tried not to get caught in their anchor lines while I twisted and turned between them. When I reached waist deep water, I killed the engine and flung myself off the side.

"What the hell!" Jo shrieked, shielding her eyes from my splash.

"Sorry, I was hot," I lied.

"You could have at least driven us up closer to shore. It's a jet ski, you know. You can pretty much beach it. Now I've got to swim in."

There was a reason I'd needed to jump into waist-deep water, and I didn't need her getting a glimpse at the effects of having her body wrapped around me.

"I'll just pull you in," I said, hoping the cold water would have things in my shorts sorted out by the time I needed to emerge. A plunge into the lake had cooled me off the last time riding a jet ski with her had my emotions and hormones in overdrive.

With Jo perched on the seat, I grabbed the line and tugged her and the jet ski up to the shore. Much to my relief, things below settled down, and I rose out of the water exhaling a deep breath of relief. She climbed off, landing in the knee-deep water at my side.

"I haven't been here for years," she said.

"Me neither. But I bet they still have ice cream. You want?"

Arching a brow, she placed a hand on her hip. "I know we haven't really spoken in a year, but have you ever heard me turn down ice cream?"

Grinning, I shook my head. "Nope. Bacon and ice cream... always a good idea in Jo's world."

"Exactly."

"Grab my wallet out of the dry bag."

When she leaned over the jet ski to open the cubby and retrieve my wallet, my eyes took on a life of their own and raked across her figure. Feeling like I was violating our friend oath, I slammed them shut and inhaled a stilling breath.

"What are you doing?" she asked, and I opened my eyes to see her staring, my wallet clutched in her hand.

"Uh, sand or something. Maybe a bug. Just got in my eye."

"You good?" she asked, and I nodded.

"Yep. All better."

"Good. Then let's get this girl some ice cream." She smiled at me and I almost dropped to my knees.

Why in the hell was she having this effect on me again? Frustrated with myself for sliding so far back in the progress I'd made putting Jo in the friend zone, I grabbed my wallet and waded through the water, hoping these feelings would wash away with the waves. And soon.

Bodies soaking up the warm summer sun flooded the sandy beach. While we wound between them, I ducked to avoid a football being passed between a father and son, and I smiled watching them interact. My father had marched out the door when I was fifteen and I hadn't seen him since. But even when he'd been around, tossing a football wasn't something he'd ever made time for.

When the football came flying at my head a second time, a botched throw by the son, I leapt in the air and caught it, tossing it back with a grin. "Catch!"

"Thanks, sir!" he called, and I gave him a wave.

Lucky kid. I'd have killed for a dad to toss around that football with me.

"You're so good with kids," Jo said, trotting up to my side.

"I'm a sucker for kids. Someday I'd like to have some of my own."

"Yeah?"

"Definitely. And since I had a shit for a father, I'm going to make it my goal to be the best dad ever. Breakfast every morning, tossing around footballs, fishing... you name it and I'm doing it."

"I hear you about shit fathers."

Part of what solidified Jo in my life as my best friend was her understanding the situation with my father. Her dad had cheated on her mom and walked out, too. When she was a kid, he'd started a new family with his mistress and never even bothered to send her a birthday card. It was like she and her sister had ceased to exist.

She was the only person I knew who understood the damage done by a parent deciding they didn't want you anymore. That you weren't worth it to stick around. That kind of abandonment messes with your head, and Jo had been the one person I could open up to about it. The one person who got it, because she'd lived it, too.

"You're going to be a great father someday." She smiled, and just like it had the day she'd sat at my side and held my hand when I found out my dad had left us, it soothed every crack in my soul.

"Thanks, Jo. You're gonna be a kickass mom."

"You think?" She chuckled as her gaze washed over the playing kids around us. "I can't picture it."

"A kickass mom. For sure."

"What makes you so sure?"

"Well," I said, stepping between the sunbathers. "If you can love that mangy cat of yours, then you've got that motherly unconditional love thing down pat, and that's the most important thing."

She slapped my arm and burst out laughing. "You leave Petunia out of this. She's beautiful."

"See? Mom eyes. You're gonna crush it in the mom love department. And you're the most loyal, dependable person I know. And funny. Smart. Caring. All top-notch mom qualities."

"Hmmm." She pursed her lips and tipped her head. "I guess maybe I won't totally suck."

"Not a chance."

We bumped shoulders and shared a smile before we padded up the stairs to the concession stand. After snagging the soft serve twist cones we'd both loved as kids, we strolled along the pathway toward the volleyball court.

"Is that your sister?" I asked as we approached the court.

"Huh?" Jo mumbled with her mouth full of ice cream, her eye following my pointing finger. "Well, hell. It is."

As we walked toward the sand volleyball courts, we cut across the grass lawn where some kids raced around in an aggressive game of tag.

"What up, sis?" Jo called to Jenna, her right arm back as she prepared to serve.

Jenna glanced over and her face lit up with excitement. "Shut up!" she said, tucking the ball under her arm. "Time out!"

Jenna trotted off the court and ran up to us. A coy smile tugged at her lips while her eyes darted between me and Jo, and then I caught Jo impaling her with a warning glare.

Having no idea what had just transpired between the Parker sisters, I took another lick off my cone while I watched their silent showdown.

"I didn't know you'd be here," Jo said, ending the standoff.

"Yep. Couple of the groomsmen from the wedding this past weekend wanted to hit up the courts, so I brought the whole bridal party down here for a little after wedding get-together."

"Sounds like fun." I eyed up the group making the most of their time-out by sipping on beer.

"And what are *you two* doing here?" Her eyebrow rose as she and Jo slid back into another sister standoff.

"Nothing, *Jenna*." Jo stiffened, and I furrowed my brow, wondering what the hell kind of unspoken conversation they were having. "Just out for a jet ski ride. Matt moved in with me and we've made up. We're friends again."

"Is that so?" Jenna smirked.

"Yep." Jo crossed her arms. "Friends."

"Am I missing something here?" I finally asked.

"Nope." They mirrored, and I popped the last bite of my cone in my mouth and shrugged.

Sisters. I had three. I knew they had a language of their own, and apparently, I wasn't invited in on their conversation.

"So anyway," Jenna said. "We're just playing some volleyball and having a few well-earned post wedding beers. You guys want in?"

"Hell yeah!" I grinned. "I'm game. Jo?"

"Two-time state high school volleyball champion here. Remember?"

Of course, I remembered. I had been the guy sitting front row at every single one of her games cheering her on. "Yep. I remember. So, you want to resuscitate those mad skills?"

A smug smile lifted her lips. "You know I'm in."

"Three-time champion for me." Jenna waggled her brows.

"I only played two years so..." Jo stuck out her tongue and Jenna giggled and returned the playful gesture. Jo pulled her tongue back in her mouth. "Are we going to team up against them, or are we planning on kicking each other's asses?"

"Well, normally I would say let's team up and

cream them, but since they just paid me a boatload of money to plan that wedding, I don't want to embarrass them. How about two on two. Me and Blake, the best man who's pretty good, against you two."

Mirth danced in Jenna's eyes again, sparking another one of those silent standoffs. After a few moments of watching the showdown, I tossed an arm around Jo's neck and put an end to it.

"We're in. You're going down."

"Bring it, Michaelson." Jenna flexed her muscles and then trotted back to the courts. "Blake! You ready to help me kick my sister's ass?"

"Hell yeah!" He slammed his beer and crushed the empty can in his hand before tossing it in the trash bag. "It's on!"

"We got this?" I asked, glancing down at Jo.

When she looked up, I saw the fire burning in her eyes. "Oh, yeah. We got this."

We bumped fists and then marched over to the court.

Jenna met us at the edge of the sand court with her partner, and I tried not to be intimidated by his size. Though I stood six-foot and was no slouch in the muscles department, this guy looked like he could crush me as easily as he'd smashed that can of beer.

"Jo, Matt, this is Blake. Blake, this is Jo and Matt."

His eyes never moved to mine. They locked onto

Jo's and remained fixed there while his smile grew.

"Hey, Jo. Really nice to meet you," he said. I watched him flex his pecs, his biceps tightening in an obvious show while he reached out to shake her hand.

The guttural growl echoed deep in my stomach and I struggled to keep it from rumbling out of my mouth.

"Hey," she said, and I watched her face for signs she was impressed by this roided-up muscle head.

Nothing. Just her game face.

Good.

I'd seen Jo with her share of men over the years, and it stung a little every time. But I'd reminded myself we were just friends, and her happiness meant more to me than my own. So, I'd stood at her side while she dated different guys, and I'd comforted her when it inevitably went south. With Jo's abandonment issues, her finding a guy who could hold on while she pushed him away had proved difficult. They didn't know what I knew. That she was just testing them to see if they'd bail. Deep down she wanted them to stay, but she couldn't help it. She pushed them away. Hard. And I was always there to lean on when they gave up the fight and left her.

If only they knew she just wanted to feel safe. To know they weren't ever going to leave her and let her down like her father did. To be there for her every day, no matter what.

Like I was. And always would be.

"Rocks, paper, scissors for serving?" Jenna asked and Jo nodded.

The two sisters pounded their fists in the air, Jenna tossing a scissors to Jo's paper.

"Ha! Already winning!" Jenna hopped up and down.

"Enjoy it while it lasts!" Jo taunted, and the two of them air boxed for a moment before busting into laughter.

"All right, Rocky." I grabbed Jo by the hand and pulled her onto our half of the court. "Save it for the match."

"Matt," Jo whispered, "that dude is *huge!*"

A surge of jealousy churned inside me again.

Just friends.

"Yeah. He's a beast."

"But he's a total dumbass meathead, and probably slow, so we just need to be quick and we've got this."

Dumbass meathead? That's not the kind of thing a girl says about a guy she's hot for. Of course Jo wouldn't go for a guy like that. I couldn't suppress my smile.

"What?" she asked as we got into position.

"Nothing. Just pumped to win," I said, my smile refusing to wipe away.

"We need a name."

"Huh?"

"You and me. A team name. What are we going to be called?"

"Roomsters?" I shrugged.

Jo grinned and shook her head. "Roomsters are gonna kick some ass!"

We slapped hands and I still couldn't tear the smile off my face. And this time it wasn't because Jo had dissed ol' Meathead. It was because we were here together. As friends again. She'd forgiven me and let me back into her life and I was back at her side. Right where I belonged.

Jenna served the ball and Jo leapt into action. The sound of her hand hitting the leather echoed through the summer breeze, and she sent the ball sailing back over the net. Blake lifted his giant hand and tapped it back over, and this time it was mine. Refusing to let that muscle-head score on me, I rose in the air, spiking the ball down with so much force my hand exploded in pain. For a second, I thought my palm was on fire.

"Yes!" Jo shouted, and she jumped at me, hands raised for a double-high five. We slapped palms, and the pain in my hand from my overly enthusiastic return seared through my skin. My grimace didn't go unnoticed.

"Seriously, Sally? Don't tell me you huwt youw

wittle hands." She pushed out her lips in a fake pout.

"Shut up, Parker!" I laughed. "I'm out of practice!"

"Well suck it up, Sally! We got a game to win, and Jenna's gonna be fired up now!"

"We got this." I gave her a sharp nod and wiped my palm against my shorts, hoping it would soothe the throbbing.

As expected, Jenna came back with a vengeance. For several rounds Blake and I could have sat back and had a beer while the Parker sisters slapped the ball back and forth, each showing unrelenting determination and mirrored skill. But even with their competitive streaks visible from a mile away, their laughter could be heard just as far.

With the score tied, Jo served over the ball. Blake leapt up and sent it back, spiking it down toward the base of the net.

"Got it!" Jo shouted, diving into the sand and saving it just before it touched down. I sent it back over as she leapt to her feet. When the ball came flying back with breakneck speed from another Meathead spike, Jo and I leapt toward it.

"Got it!" she called again. As she leapt toward the ball, I saw the thin string around her neck securing her suit top snap. While her body flew through the air, the thin green material covering her assets started its slide down. I'd eat a smorgasbord of sand before I'd let Meathead get an eyeful of Jo's goods, so I changed my trajectory and launched myself at her. Wide eyes met mine when she saw me flying toward her. Those eyes widened even more when she glanced down just before her breast popped out.

Before it made its break for freedom and gave everyone watching a show, I threw myself against her body, the force of my protection sending us both to the ground.

After we rolled to a stop, I blinked my eyes, squinting against the sand clinging to my eyelashes. As my vision came back into focus, Jo's face popped into view. My body pressed down on top of hers, and even though I knew I should push myself off, every muscle in my body revolted, forcing me to stay pressed against her. Our eyes locked as I felt her quick breaths match my own, our chests moving as one while we panted together.

Just friends, I told myself while I gazed deeper into her eyes.

Just friends, I tried to chant while my gaze drifted to her parted lips.

Just friends, I reminded myself when I looked up and saw my own desire reflected in her eyes.

Not just friends.

I wasn't sure if it was my push or her pull, but my mouth moved toward hers, the inches between our lips disappearing as every muscle in my body demanded I claim her kiss. Demanded I give up my fight; extinguish my agony by tasting her tongue and catching her breath in my mouth. A demand I no longer wanted to rage against as I felt her breath ghosting my lips.

"You guys okay?" Blake called.

Our bodies froze, the world I'd forgotten about racing back like a runaway train. A runaway train I was powerless to stop.

"Um, yeah! We're fine!" Jo called, her wide eyes now devoid of passion stared up into mine.

And just like that our moment evaporated.

Fucking, Meathead!

"Blake!" Jenna shouted, and we turned to see her kicking sand at him. "What the hell!"

Jo and I slowly looked back at each other, and a long gulp slid down my throat. "Sorry, I, uh— your top..." I stuttered, words refusing to form on the tongue I desperately wanted in her mouth.

"Yeah... um... did you see anything?" She bit her lip... the one I wanted to be kissing.

"Uh, no. Nothing. Sorry. I didn't mean to tackle you."

"It's fine. Thanks, I guess."

"No problem. Just didn't want, uh, you know... anyone to see or anything."

"Yeah. Thanks."

We remained locked in our position for a few moments longer before my body finally responded to my pleas to move. Jo slid her hands between us and held her top up as I rolled off her, but I couldn't stand yet. I flopped onto my back and stared up at the swirling white clouds while I tried to regain the senses she'd stolen from me.

What the fuck just happened?

"Really sorry, guys!" Jenna called, and I looked over to see her mouthing something to Jo.

"It's fine, Jenna. Just... let's just finish this." Jo tied a double knot in the string, properly securing the suit before trotting back into position.

Another silent conversation went down between the Parker sisters, but I was too disoriented to try and interpret it.

Did we almost kiss?

"We finishing this or what?" Blake grumbled.

If it wasn't for the fact it'd be like running into a rhinoceros, I'd have tackled him into the sand and pummeled his face for interrupting what I was pretty sure was a moment with Jo. A moment where we almost kissed.

It was, wasn't it?

Or was I hallucinating that desire I could have sworn pooled in her eyes?

And thanks to Meathead, now I'd never know.

With a groan in part from my disappointment, and in part from the pain of our collision, I rose to my feet. "We're finishing it."

Jo and I avoided all eye contact while we finished the round, and I never felt better slamming that winning spike at that moment-ruining Meathead's feet.

"Good game," he said, then stumbled off the court for another beer I was certain he'd smash on his thick skull.

"Great game, guys!" Jenna trotted over and moved into the gap between Jo and me. A gap saturated with awkward silence. "So..."

"So." Jo pursed her lips.

"So." I clucked my cheek.

After a few moments, Jenna let out a breath. "Do you guys want to stick around? Have a beer?"

"No. We need to go," Jo blurted. "Bye."

Without another word, she spun on her heel and hurried back toward the jet ski.

I lifted a shoulder and let it fall. "Uh, I guess we're going."

"Bye, Matt."

Jenna's sympathetic smile admitted she'd seen what had happened. Or what had *almost* happened. But I couldn't figure out the meaning behind the expression. Was it a "sorry we interrupted your moment" smile, or a "poor Matt, she only thinks of you as a friend, you dumbass" smile? I glanced over my shoulder and saw Jo disappearing into the trees on her way back to the jet ski. It was time to go.

And I'd never know which sympathetic smile Jenna had given me.

"Bye, Jenna. I'll see you later."

The sympathy in her face only deepened, and with it my confusion.

With the weight of my disappointment heavy on my shoulders, I slunk after Jo and went back to the jet ski. When I got there, she'd already pulled the anchor and was sitting up front, her hands on the handles and the engine running.

"Ready?" she asked, but her eyes looked everywhere but mine.

Her icy cool expression gave me the answer. And it wasn't the one I was hoping for. My overactive brain had turned an innocent moment into one with meaning. But only to me.

Just friends.

"Ready." I climbed up behind her, and this time I knew I wouldn't have the same issue I'd had the last two times I'd been on a jet ski with her.

This time I didn't feel anything but devastated.

Friends. We're just friends.

But at least I had her as a friend again. At least she was in my life. Trying to remind myself I'd managed to survive her rejection once before, I wrapped my arms around her waist and shoved my feelings for her back inside the dark hole where they belonged. And where I hoped they would finally stay.

CHAPTER NINE

JO

It'd been three days since Matt had taken me jet skiing. Three days since we'd played volleyball. Three days since we'd... almost kissed.

We had almost kissed, hadn't we?

For three days I replayed the moment over and over in my head, trying to determine if his lips had actually been headed for mine, or if mine had been headed for his.

Or both?

Groaning, I pulled a pillow over my face. For three days I'd been living that moment on repeat and I still had no idea what to make of it. Part of me thought I'd finally lost my senses and leaned up for a kiss... a kiss he no doubt wouldn't have wanted.

Because we were just friends.

But he'd leaned toward me. *Hadn't he?*

And the look in his eyes. That wasn't in my imagination. Or was it?

With more confusing thoughts cluttering my mind, I pushed the pillow off my face and willed myself to get out of bed. Even though three days had passed, Matt and I had successfully avoided each other. With him working all day, and me heading off to work at night, it hadn't been hard to steer clear of him. Each morning when I woke up, he was already gone, and each night when I came home late from work, he was tucked safely behind his bedroom door. I'd tiptoe into my room and close Petunia and I inside.

Two doors between us were better than one.

But today he had the day off. And tonight I was off early. So, unless I planned on abandoning my cabin and making for Antarctica to live out the rest of my days avoiding him, today was the day we had to put an end to our successful evasions.

Actually, the chill of Antarctica looked pretty good.

Did we almost kiss?

No. Definitely not. Matt had always been, and would always be, just a friend.

I stood up, and without taking off my tank top, I slid a bra on underneath it. A skill I'd perfected since Matt moved in. After that first morning he'd shown up and caught me in less-than-appropriate clothing, I'd been certain to cover all my goodies before opening my door each morning.

Petunia chirped and trotted to her mostly full food

bowl, but this time I refused to cave in and fill it up again.

"No. That's over. Finish your food, you ungrateful feline."

Her eyes widened when she saw me heading toward the door without stopping to fill up her bowl.

Meow.

The sweet, sad tones stopped me in my tracks, and I made the mistake of glancing down at her. Even though she had no ears to flatten to her head and improve on her pitiful gaze, I caved to the big blinking eyes staring up at me.

"Last time, Petunia. I mean it this time."

With a shake of my head, I reached up and grabbed her cat food bag. Happy chirps filled the small room while she wove between my feet, her body pressing against my legs.

After Petunia's bowl was topped off to her satisfaction, I put the bag away and went to my bedroom door. Closing my eyes, I took a breath and prepared for the inevitable encounter with Matt.

The door creaked on rusty hinges when I opened it, and I peeked out into the empty living room.

Nothing. No Matt. Good.

As I stared into the empty space, I noticed my absent couch and coffee table. Furrowing my brow, I walked through the void on my way to the bathroom.

Still jumping at every creak of this old cabin and expecting Matt to appear at any time, I finished washing my face, brushing my teeth, and getting ready for the day. When I came out of the bathroom, I did so with the same tentative moves I'd mastered over the past few days.

Peeking out into the living room, I once again saw it vacant.

Hmm. Maybe today wouldn't be the day I had to face him again. The day I needed to look him in the eye and suppress all those feelings I had been scrambling to shove back inside. And if I did see him, maybe, just maybe, today would be the day I succeeded once and for all.

Maybe.

The sound of waves crashing at the shoreline drew me to them, so I made a cup of coffee and headed out onto my back porch. Pushing open the screen door, I paused, inhaling the intoxicating blend of coffee and the smell of fresh water. A perfume I'd bottle up if I could... just like how I felt about bacon.

A loud pounding jarred me from my tranquil moment and caused my eyes to snap open. My gaze skated across the rocky beach below and then slammed to a stop when it landed on Matt, hammering nails into a heap of driftwood.

A shirtless Matt.

A sweaty, shirtless Matt.

A sweaty, shirtless, impossibly sexy Matt.

Yeah. About those feelings...

Damn it!

Matt swiped an arm across his forehead, and I felt the lump sliding down my throat while I swallowed... or *tried* to swallow.

Just friends. Just friends. Just friends.

He turned, his eyes lifting to the porch and locking onto mine. "Hey, Jo! I hope I didn't wake you."

Sweet Jesus. Has he always been this hot?

When a smile tugged up his lips, deepening his dimples, my knees wobbled, and I reached for the now non-existent railing. My hand swiped through the empty space and I teetered forward, catching myself before I plummeted off the edge.

"You okay?" Matt yelled, dropping his hammer and jogging across the rocks toward me.

"Uh, fine!" I called down, stepping safely away from the edge. "Just forgot that railing fell off."

He arrived at the bottom of the stairs, and the sunlight glistening on his sweaty skin only amplified the definition of his muscles.

Antarctica. It looked like I'd be getting a couple parkas, some huskies, and hunkering down in an igloo for the rest of my life. No way in hell the feelings searing through my body would go willingly back into the hole where they used to reside. They were alive and well and enjoying their newfound freedom by doing cartwheels inside my stomach.

"Careful, Jo. I'm going to work on that railing today. My order for lumber just came in at Lampert's Hardware."

He came up the stairs, and with each step toward me, those feelings busted out new gymnastic moves in my belly.

"Did you notice the roof?" he asked, pointing above my head. My eyes tried to follow his finger, but instead they skated across every plane of his body, finally drifting along his tanned bicep and moving to where his finger insisted they go... which was in the opposite direction of where they'd spend all day staring if I let them.

When I looked up, I saw all the old shingles were missing, and a shiny layer of material covered the peaked roof.

"I figured it was dark when you got home last night, so you hadn't noticed. I got all the old shingles ripped off and disposed of, and I got the underlayment down, so today I can finish putting up new shingles. You'll have a new roof by tomorrow!"

"Holy shit, Matt." My jaw dropped open when I realized just how much work he'd put into my cabin while I'd been slinging drinks. "You did all that last night?"

"Yep. I got home at four thirty and went at it until eleven. I just stuck some lights up there after it got dark. Luckily, it's a small roof, and those shingles were barely hanging on, so they came off without much fuss."

"I'm literally speechless. The contractor quoted me like several thousand dollars."

"Matt's Professional Puttering at your service." He grinned wider, and the nerves I'd been feeling in anticipation of this reunion started to quiet down.

Matt seemed normal. Relaxed. Maybe it *had* all been in my imagination, and for three days I'd been hiding for no reason and building this molehill into Mount Everest.

But suddenly realizing that almost-kiss must have been all in my head stung a little deeper than I'd expected. If he wasn't feeling awkward, then that meant the kiss hadn't almost happened. And if the kiss hadn't almost happened, then I'd been imagining that there was anything between us other than what I'd known my whole life.

Just friends.

With a deep breath, I tried to get my feelings for him to stop their Olympic gymnastics tryouts in my stomach. With the realization that kiss existed only in my mind... or only *my* lips had been moving in for the kill, I felt their antics subside.

"I can't thank you enough, Matt. Seriously. This is the greatest gift ever."

"You're welcome, Jo." His smile softened before spreading back out into a goofy grin. "Wait! If you think this is cool, just hold on."

With that he trotted back down the stairs and disappeared around the side of the cabin. A minute later he reemerged, this time with a brown leather loveseat balancing on his back.

The sight of his muscles flexing beneath the weight of the loveseat sent the gymnastics team in my stomach hopping back into their floor routine. But after a second of soaking in the sight of him, I realized standing around staring while he schlepped a heavy piece of furniture solo was just poor manners. Even if I enjoyed the sight of it... a little too much.

"Oh my God, Matt!" I said, hopping into action. "Let me help!"

I ran down the stairs, but he just smiled and kept on walking, that couch looking like it gave him no more trouble than the Superman backpack he'd sported every day of elementary school.

"I got it, Jo. Just grab the door."

Racing up the stairs ahead of him, I pushed open the screen door. When he got to the doorway, the couch bumped into the doorframe.

"Shit. It's too wide. Gonna take some finagling.

Can I get a hand?"

"Yep. Of course."

I stepped out onto the porch and watched his eyes narrow in thoughtful contemplation while his creative mind went to work.

"Okay. I got it. You take that end, we'll flip it on its side, spin it around, then slide it in."

Despite the innocence of the comment, my mind plunged into the gutter when I thought about the ways I wouldn't mind him flipping me on my side, spinning me around, and sliding it in.

Ugh! Just friends!

Pushing the incredibly pleasant visual from my mind, I nodded and took ahold of my end of the couch. "I'll follow your lead."

We worked together to squeeze the big piece of furniture into the living room, both panting while we scooted it into place.

"Eh?" He smiled, stretching his arms out to showcase the new loveseat. "Not bad, huh?"

He hopped in the air and landed on it with a bounce, then patted the seat beside him. "Sit. Try it. It's awesome."

I slid onto the couch beside him and he leaned back, stretching his arms out along the distressed brown leather behind our heads.

"It's great, Matt. Again. Thank you."

"Sit back. Really get in there."

Choking on my groan, I leaned back into the comfortable couch. His forearm brushed against the back of my head, and I tried not to close my eyes and inhale his salty, masculine scent. But when he threw his arm around my shoulder and gave me a squeeze, it was impossible to keep it from invading my nostrils.

He smelled like pure man.

So sexy.

"Whaddya think, Roomster? Not too shabby, right? We'll be having *Family Guy* marathons without needing a walker to get around after."

"It's awesome."

Petunia slunk around the corner, her tail puffed up like a raccoon while she examined the new addition to her cabin.

"Hey, evil cat." They eyed each other up as she slunk away, hissing at him before she disappeared. "And the best part? It's springy, so when she attacks me, I can leap to safety."

Matt bounced up and down on the seat beside me, and my mind climbed into the elevator that went straight back down to the gutter.

"You like it? Really?"

"It's perfect."

"I've got one more surprise for you. Come on." He sprung up with ease from the couch that didn't insist on holding us hostage, and I popped up behind him. Matt led me outside onto the beach, and we walked up to the intriguing clump of driftwood he'd been working on earlier.

"Check it out." He waved a hand over the driftwood. "I'm turning this into a coffee table."

Tipping my head, I looked it over. "It looks cool, don't get me wrong, but where are we supposed to set our drinks? It's all twisty and stuff."

"Oh, yeah. I should have explained better. This is just base. I've got a piece of glass coming that will attach to the top. Then we'll be able to look down through it to this driftwood base I'm crafting."

My eyebrows shot to my hairline. "Okay. Now *that* is seriously cool. You're making this?"

A proud smile lifted his lips while he puffed out his chest. "Yeah. I got the idea when I was walking on the shore the other morning. I've been collecting the driftwood ever since."

"You could sell these. Like, seriously, Matt."

He'd always been creative. It was part of why he had such a hard time sticking to one job. His mind was always demanding a challenge, and new and interesting stimulation. But this... this was a perfect combination – taking advantage of all his creativity and talent with his hands.

"You think?" He stepped back and stared at it.

"Yeah. I know. It's beautiful. Like art. And I bet people would be falling over themselves for handcrafted Door County driftwood furniture."

He scrubbed a hand down his face, and I saw those wheels turning in his mind. "You know... I bet I could figure out how to make more custom driftwood styles. Like chairs, tables, lamps, and other house décor."

"Matt. You should do this." I turned and looked at him. "Like, for real. This could be your thing. You get to use your creativity, your building skills, and you'd never get bored always getting to come up with different designs."

Pursing his lips, he looked back over at his creation. "Jo, I think you may be on to something. I could start up my own handyman business and make furniture as well."

"I got your back." I bumped him with a hip.

"What would I do without you?"

"Try not to fuck up again and let's hope you don't ever need to find out."

His smile softened, and he nodded. "You have my word, Jo. Never again. I know how much you value honesty, loyalty, and friendship. And God knows I know how you feel about cheating after..."

His voice drifted off.

After my dad.

He didn't need to say it. I knew he understood

how badly that had fucked me up. I hadn't needed a therapist to tell me I had abandonment issues since my dad had walked out at a crucial time in his daughter's life. Instead of a therapist, I'd had Matt. And though I was still a far cry from being capable of healthy relationships, I'd always had Matt to lean on when that scared and scarred little girl inside me had tossed a stick of dynamite into my relationships. It'd always been him who'd been there to help me deconstruct what I'd done. To support me and help me recover from each catastrophe.

And after all these years, he was still the only man I'd ever completely trusted. I trusted Jake as well, but Matt and I shared a different connection. After his dad left too, he understood the searing pain of a father's rejection. He was the only one I'd ever been able to open up to about my dad and how messed up I was on the inside. To feel safe and secure sharing even the most painful parts of me with someone I trusted with my whole heart.

Until last year when even he'd shaken me to my core. And with one whisper of betrayal, my safety net had been yanked away.

Matt hadn't exactly *cheated*... that honor belonged to Nikki, but he'd been a willing participant. He'd been the hussy who'd stolen my father away and broken up my family. The dirty mistress whose selfishness destroyed a relationship and affected everyone within blast range. And once again that someone had included me.

And maybe that was part of why my anger for him had lingered on as long as it had. My dad's betrayal had damaged something deep inside me I didn't think would ever be whole again. And though I'd never forgive my father for what he'd done, I was willing to forgive Matt. I had to. Not having him in my life was too painful.

"Yeah. Shitty dad issues rearing their head again," I said on a sigh. "But you aren't going to do that again, so it's a moot point."

"Exactly." He gave me a sharp nod.

"Exactly."

Silence settled over us, the waves lapping at the shore the only sounds surrounding us. Matt looked back at his driftwood coffee table base.

"You really think I could make a business out of being a handy man and making these for people?"

Nodding enthusiastically, I blew out a sigh. "Yes. Seriously. So much yes."

He rubbed his chin for a moment, and then turned to me, eyes lit up like the sun. "Matt's Manly Masterpieces!"

"What?" I snorted.

"The name of my business!"

"Oh, God no! Terrible!" I burst into laughter.

"Terrible?"

"So terrible. Keep trying."

"Damn it. Thought I had it." His laugh merged with mine.

"We'll think of the right name."

His laughter petered off, and a shy look softened his face. "Do you... do you want to get a drink together after work? I feel like I've barely seen you in days."

"Yeah. That sounds good. I should be done by nine."

"Okay." He smiled, and I tried to put a halt to the cartwheels starting up in my stomach again.

Settle down, Jo. It's just friend drinks, not a date.

"Okay." I returned the smile and then turned back toward the house. "I need to get some water. Want anything?"

"Nah, I've got water out here, but thanks. Back to work for this guy. I've got a new business to start and I need some products to display!"

"Don't hurt yourself, Bob Villa."

"Shut it. I could run circles around Bob Villa."

"Just don't lop off a finger. I've got errands to run today, and I'll hit the grocery store and get us some supplies. Text me a list. You've certainly earned whatever the hell you want after all of this work you've done." I waved a hand at my roof.

"Captain Crunch!" he shouted after me. "And

Doritos! And maybe some ice cream!"

"How the hell are you not five hundred pounds?" I shouted back as I made my way up the stairs.

"And bacon!"

"I'd never forget the bacon. Just text me the damn list!"

With one last wave I went back into the cabin, pressing my back against the wall once I'd made it safely out of his sight line.

Drinks with Matt tonight. No big deal. We'd done this hundreds of times. But everything felt different now after what I'd *thought* was an almost kiss. What I'd thought was maybe the start of something new. But seeing the nonchalant way he acted around me today only drilled home the fact that my feelings remained one-sided. That kiss on the court held all my desires, and none of his.

Even though the thought of spending an evening at his side seemed like torture at the moment, I knew if I was going to get past this again, I had to rip it off like a band-aid. Force myself to stay at his side until the feelings subsided and my brain accepted what I'd always known.

Just friends.

CHAPTER TEN

MATT

"Dude. What is up with you?" Aaron asked.

I stared at the old drink ring stain on the wooden bar at the Sister Bay Bowl and shrugged. "Nothing."

"Nothing? This is the least amount of words I've ever heard from you in a five-minute span. Like ever."

I looked up to see his blue eyes boring into me, a quizzical look scrunching up his face.

"Nothing, man. Just tired. Been working hard on Jo's place is all."

The same scrunched look remained while he stared me down.

Laughing, I lifted my hand. "Promise. All good."

His eyes narrowed a little, and he stroked the long red beard that swallowed up most of his face. "Mmmhmm."

"Just tired," I lied. I couldn't very well tell him the real answer.

I almost kissed Jo, and she bolted away and then avoided me like I had the plague for three days.

"All right, then," he said, but his tone lacked conviction.

Attempting to pretend like everything was normal between us, like she hadn't shattered my soul when she'd run off from our almost kiss, I had done my damnedest today to act unaffected. I'd put on a performance worthy of an Oscar while I'd played the part of the old friend. The old friend who wasn't dying to press her back into the sand and cover her lips with mine.

But if keeping her in my life meant spending the rest of mine pretending we were just friends, then that's exactly what I planned to do. Would it be painful? Oh God, yeah. Excruciating? For a while. Okay, a long while. But eventually I'd grow numb to it and being next to her without pulling her into my arms wouldn't feel like a task more difficult than scaling a rocky cliff with my bare hands. It would be painful, yes, borderline unbearable, but I would endure it until I could quiet the screaming inside me.

I'd done it when I was fourteen, and I could do it again.

I hoped.

Inviting her to drinks tonight had been part of my ruse to act normal, to keep from spooking her into avoiding me again. But the minute the words had rolled off my tongue I'd wanted to shove them back in. A night of just the two of us sipping on cocktails was more than my body could endure this soon after I'd almost gotten to kiss her. A temptation too strong while I still felt the power of her pull.

So, I'd called in reinforcements. Tony and Aaron. Jake and Cassie were out of town for a couple nights or I'd have dragged them here, too. The more bodies I could keep between me and Jo the better. And I'd decided to take our evening up to the Sister Bay Bowl, the local bar and bowling alley, because if anything could douse the attraction I had toward Jo, it was bowling shoes.

My gaze drifted over to the door again, then up to the clock hanging on the wall. She should be here any minute. When I looked away from the clock, I saw Aaron's interrogating stare boring into me.

"What?" I defended against his silent accusation.

His eyes narrowed into slits. "Nothing." But his gaze remained, and I worried any minute he'd figure out what thoughts were running a marathon through my mind.

The door opened, and I whipped around to see Jo walking in.

My God is she beautiful.

And not in that overdone kind of way like so

many girls I saw these days. Her beauty was natural. Effortless. No harsh makeup chiseled lines into her face masking the features I didn't think could ever be improved. When she looked over and saw me staring, I forced a smile and waved. It was time to step back out onto the stage and put on another performance where I starred as the platonic best friend. Too bad it had quickly become my award-winning role.

"Hey, Jo!" I called.

She smiled back and walked over, sliding into the stool beside me. "God, I need a drink. My feet are killing me."

"Hey, Jo!" Aaron leaned around me and rapped her on the shoulder.

"Hey, Aaron! Didn't know you guys were coming out tonight."

"Hell, yeah! Now that you two have a sweet pad in Sister Bay we're planning on coming to town more often."

"No complaints here." She smiled and gave him a fist bump.

"Jo! You made it!" Tony came in from the bowling alley part of the building and wrapped his arms around her shoulders, giving her a tight squeeze.

"Hey, Tony!"

He sat down beside her. "You guys want to split a pitcher?"

"In," Jo answered, and Aaron and I nodded as well.

"Sweet." Tony flagged down the bartender and ordered a pitcher. When it arrived, we filled our chilled pint glasses and raised them for a toast.

"To old friends," Aaron said.

"To old friends," we echoed, and I felt that anxiety wind the knot in my stomach.

Friends. Ugh. That was not the title I wanted for the perfect woman sitting beside me. But I smiled and sipped on my beer with the rest of them, forced to endure my silent torment.

Since returning to her life, I'd seen Jo in a new light, and it was like someone had ripped open the curtains in a dark room. And this new light was blinding. And now that the curtains were open, I was desperate to yank them back shut and hope I could forget how amazing everything looked bathed in the light.

When we finished our cheers, I snorted when I saw the white foam clinging to Aaron's mustache. "Man. You have got to shave that thing." I laughed. "Not only do you look like a yeti, but now you look like a yeti with rabies."

Aaron pushed out his upper lip and looked down at the remnants of beer still hanging out on the bushy beard.

"Can't shave it," he said, then wiped the foam away. "Chicks dig it."

Jo snorted, then covered her nose. "Oh my God. You almost made beer come out my nose."

"What? They do," Aaron defended.

Jo shook her head. "No, Aaron. Chicks may dig some facial hair, but this is straight up swallowing your head. Have you ever made out with someone sporting a rough, scratchy mop on their face?"

She pulled a face, and I tried to keep mine from following suit. Not from the vision of Aaron sucking face with another yeti, but the thought of Jo kissing someone with a beard. Someone who wasn't me.

"Agreed," Tony answered. "They like us smooth as a cue ball." He swiped a hand across his shaved head then scrubbed it down the smooth skin on his face. "*This* is what chicks dig."

"I look tough. Like a Viking warrior." Aaron frowned.

Jo leaned across me and placed a hand on his shoulder. "You look like a hipster, Aaron. Hipsters aren't known for being tough." Jo chuckled. When she retreated back to her seat, her breasts brushed across my arm and I leapt up off my stool.

"What the hell?" she said, wide eyes staring at me while I bumped into the juke box behind me.

"Sorry, I uh..." I struggled for an answer. Any answer that didn't end with "your tits touched me, and my fourteen-year-old-self invaded my body."

"You okay?" she asked.

"Yes. I just... leg spasm. Charlie horse!" I said it too loud, excited for an answer that made sense. Well, kind of made sense.

"I hate those!" Tony clenched his fist. "I had one for almost an hour last week. Torture. They're like torture!"

"You need more potassium," Aaron said decidedly. "Bananas. You should eat more bananas."

"What the hell are you talking about?" I reached down and rubbed the fake cramp in my hamstring.

"Potassium prevents muscle cramps, and bananas are high in potassium. Therefore, you need to munch on some bananas, dude."

Wondering how in the hell my life had crumpled into a faked injury and a conversation at the bar revolving around my consumption of bananas, I just shook my head. "How in the hell do you even know that?"

"Saw it on Facebook." He shrugged, then took another sip of his beer.

When he set down the pint, I rolled my eyes and gestured to his lip. "Seriously, man. Shave that thing. You look like you've got rabies."

Aaron just shrugged and wiped his mouth with his sleeve. "Whatever. You're just jealous you can't grow a beard like this."

"That is *not* what's going on here." I laughed.

Jo jutted a finger at me. "Don't you ever, *ever* grow a beard, Matt. I'll throw you out on your ass."

"Deal, Roomster." I smiled, trying to regain my coerced composure. When she crossed her legs and flipped her long hair over her shoulder, I felt myself sliding back down the time warp to eighth grade. And there was only one thing that could stop my mind from doing things to Jo that I knew she'd smash my head into the bar for thinking.

Bowling shoes.

"Who's up for bowling?" Clapping my hands, I rubbed them together.

"In!" they cheered in unison.

Desperate to get Jo into a hideous pair of brown and orange bowling shoes to help me simmer down, I grabbed my pint and the pitcher and hurried into the bowling alley. The shoes were stacked along cubbies in the wall; the way our safe, small town did bowling shoe rental. Just help yourself and don't steal them. The Door County way.

We each grabbed a pair of bowling shoes and picked out our balls from the assortment along the wall. When Jo sat down to put on her shoes, I counted the seconds until she'd be wearing what would most certainly be the kryptonite to my raging hormones. But after she tightened the Velcro and rose, I struggled to suppress my groan.

Damn it!

Even in her hideous bowling shoes, she still looked gorgeous. Her ripped skinny jeans clung to her curves, and when she pulled off her leather jacket, my gaze raked over the breasts filling out her white tank top just right.

Why would I have expected anything less? Hell, Jo would look cute even if she was rocking an orange beard like Aaron's.

Okay... maybe not that far, but she'd look cute in just about anything else.

"Who's up first?" Tony asked, sliding into the chair at the scoring table.

"One roll each and whoever gets the most pins goes first." Jo cracked her knuckles and stretched.

The sight of her body flexing and bending in front of me almost had me hightailing it out the door.

"I'll start." Aaron grabbed his ball, lined up and tossed it down the lane. "Eight! Boom!" He shot at us with his fingers, then blew away the invisible smoke from his imaginary guns.

Tony went next, clipping two pins and returning with a scowl.

"I'm up." Jo pursed her lips, and I could see the competitive fire igniting in her eyes.

Always the tomboy, she'd kicked our asses at most

sports since we were kids. Even though she was half our size growing up, she'd still managed to knock us on our asses in football, score the most shots in basketball games, and hit more home runs in baseball than I could even begin to count. Jo was a natural athlete, and when I saw her line up to roll the ball, I waited to hear the sounds of the pins smashing after she inevitably took them all out.

As she eyed up her shot, I watched her wiggle her ass, and I closed my eyes against the assault to my sanity. I heard her ball trucking down the alley and the pins exploding from her hit.

"Hell, yeah! Strike!" she cheered.

When I opened my eyes, hoping the ass shaking was over and it was safe to do so, Aaron was staring at me, those red eyebrows furrowed while he once again appraised me with a contemplative glare.

"Nice job!" I cheered, ignoring Aaron and hoping he didn't catch on to what had me so undone. If Aaron figured out it wasn't just our friendship we'd rekindled, and that my old feelings for her were consuming me like wildfire, I'd never get him to shut up about it. And if he got a few shots in him, he'd no doubt go blabbing it to Jo in some ill-conceived drunken attempt to help me.

Desperate to keep that from happening, I vowed not to slip up again. No groaning, no gawking, no dumping a pitcher of beer on my head to cool down the fire she'd started inside of me.

Just friends.

That's what I needed to remind myself tonight... even if I had to do it with every single breath.

"You're up." Jo gave me her signature cocky victory grin, and I pushed off my chair.

After grabbing my ball and lining up, I exhaled a deep breath and tried to focus my attention on the pins at the end of the lane. With determination to knock them down as if they were my feelings for Jo, I strode toward the line, drawing my arm back and preparing to unleash my fury.

But instead of a perfect shot to topple my imaginary feelings, I overstepped the shot line, hit the slippery alley and flew up into the air.

Oh shit, I thought just before I landed on my ass with a thud. Wishing the alley would swallow me whole, I laid my head on the wood and licked my wounds for a second while I listened to my ball plunk into the gutter.

Well, if there was even the slightest chance of a mutual attraction, I had just successfully ensured my ass headed straight back to the friend zone.

Forever.

"Are you okay?" Jo called, and I could hear the laughter peppering her words.

"Fine," I grunted as I rolled to my knees. "Totally

fine."

When I stood up, I stared at the floor for a second before forcing my eyes up to Jo. Her face was a mosaic of reds while she pursed her lips into a tight white line.

"Go ahead. It's cool." I tossed my hands in the air and let the assault of their laughter wash over me.

Jo collapsed on the floor, clutching her stomach while she rolled onto her side. Tony and Aaron clung to each other, tears glistening in their eyes as their laughter rolled a hell of a lot farther than my bowling ball... the one stuck halfway down the gutter.

"Get it out, get it out." I sighed. But as mortification over my debacle blazed my cheeks, I couldn't help but let the sounds of Jo's laughter ignite my own. It was contagious, and it was a sound I had missed so much this last year. Bending over, I pressed my hands to my knees and choked on my laughter, tears forming in my eyes as well.

"Dude! You fell down!" Aaron spit between waves of laughter.

"I totally fell down." I laughed harder, replaying the memory in my mind. "I fucking fell down."

"You fell down!" Jo called up from the floor, laughter shaking her body.

"You *fell* down, and you're never going to *live this* down!" Tony pressed his head into his arms, and his shoulders lifted with each airy laugh.

While we gasped for air, our faces glistening with tears, I shook my head and did the walk of shame back to the scoring table. One by one our laughter trickled off, heavy sighs refilling the air the prolonged laughter stolen from our lungs.

"So, I guess there's no way we can pretend that never happened and erase it from our brains?" I asked, giving them a sheepish smile.

"Not a chance." Aaron chuckled then pointed to my ball in the gutter. "You gonna go get that?"

"I'm gonna throw another ball at it to knock them both in, then go back to pretending this never happened."

"You do that, Matt." Jo rose from the floor, her face still as red as a rose. "You forget all you want, because we won't. And we'll just keep reminding you. You know... that you fell down."

Their laughter exploded again, and I couldn't help but join them. While they continued mocking me, I tossed another ball in the gutter with enough force to send both balls slamming into the catch.

"I'm going again," I said as I walked back.

"Oh yeah?" Tony said. "Is that like a rule we don't know about? You fall on your ass and you get a freebie?"

"It was... my hamstring." I grinned as I leaned down and rubbed the perfectly fine muscle. "Another cramp."

"Bananas, man. I'm telling you. Bananas." Aaron pointed the short wooden pencil at me. "I eat a banana every day. And you know what? No cramps." He tapped the pencil on his head.

"I'll pick some up this week," I lied, then grabbed my ball as it came back down the return. This time I wasn't going to embarrass myself in front of the girl I could still hear snickering. The girl I had intended to impress with my bowling skills before I landed on my ass. The girl who looked so damn good tonight I just wanted to...

Damn it! Just friends.

Narrowing my eyes as I pushed my frustration into my ball arm, I strode toward the lane, releasing my ball before I stepped over the line this time. It shot down the center of the lane, and when it hit the center pin, there was an explosion of sound as the pins went flying.

"Yes!" I shouted, pumping my fist at my side.

Vindicated.

Turning around, I pointed my index fingers at Jo. "It's on."

"Bring it, Sir Falls-a-Lot."

When I arrived at her side, I checked her with a hip. "You know, I'm surprised you waited to find out if I was okay before you started laughing. I'm well aware that you think people falling down is the funniest thing on the planet."

Her cheeks swelled while she smiled. "Because it *is* the funniest thing on the planet! I love it when people fall!"

"I know you do," I said, smiling. "I'm glad I could entertain you."

"You sure know how to brighten my night. Best friend ever."

Ugh. There it was. That phrase. That word. Friend. I'd hated it when she called me that as a kid, gotten used to it as an adult, and now I wanted to erase it from the English language.

"All right, you two are tied for who goes first." Tony gestured to Jo and me.

"Nah," I answered. "Jo can go. Ladies first and all."

Her brow rose as she crossed her arms. "If its ladies first, doesn't that mean you're up?"

Our smiles mirrored each other while we faced off. "Well, if you insist." I curtsied and watched her smile grow.

There was nothing I wouldn't do to see that smile on her face. Even if it meant spending the night flat on my ass just so she could watch me fall. And the more I stared at her, the more I realized that while there were lots of things I could do to make her smile, there was one thing I couldn't do... not anymore. As hard as I tried, I couldn't ignore the feelings for her that were anything but friendly.

Just like my attempt at knocking down those pins had landed me on my ass, my attempts at knocking down my feelings for Jo were headed in the same direction... with me flat on my ass and not a single pin on the ground.

CHAPTER ELEVEN

JO

The vision of Matt flying through the air and landing with a grunt last night invaded my mind again, and I chuckled while I punched another dinner order into the computer at JJ's.

"What's so funny?" Hanson asked as he reached over my head to grab a margarita glass.

"Nothing. Just my friend falling down on the lanes at the Sister Bay Bowl last night." I chuckled again.

"I love when people fall down!" He grinned, and it caused my chuckle to explode into a full laugh.

"Me too! I can't stop laughing!"

"I wasn't even there and already... laughing," he said as he joined me. "Nothing better than people eating it."

"And this was a good one. He took one step on the lane, legs flew out from under him, at least a second of airtime before he crashed back down. It was amazing."

Hanson tossed his head back and closed his eyes. "I can totally envision it, because I've seen other people do that on the lanes. Priceless."

My laughter petered off while I tried to get composure. "I'm glad we can share in a love for people falling down."

"Nothing better." He chuckled again as he walked over to make another margarita.

With a smile that kept popping up each time the memory came back to me, I tried to focus on placing my order. But each time I pushed the buttons to select different dinner sides, the memory returned.

And then old memories joined that one. Memories of Matt, Jake, and I bowling back in high school. I remembered how cute I'd thought Matt had looked in his bowling shoes... not unlike my thoughts last night. How cute his ass had looked in those jeans... and once again the same thought I'd had last night. But as I walked back down memory lane, an unwelcome visitor invaded my memory.

Nikki.

Jake had invited her bowling with us one night, and even though he hadn't seen it, I had. I'd seen the way she flirted with Matt, stolen looks that slid to him when Jake would look away. I'd hated her then, and not just because I didn't trust her. I also hated her because every now and again, I'd see Matt get confused.

Like a fish in a net, he'd squirm around, and I'd see him struggle with what he should do. But before Jake could turn around, he'd shake it off and go back to ignoring her attempts. He'd go back to being the good friend... the loyal one. The one who didn't fall into her temptations—well, until he made one regrettable mistake.

Visions of him and Nikki in some passionate lip-lock last year forced themselves into my mind, and I cringed while I tried to push them away. I never wanted to imagine that vision again. I suppose I shouldn't have been surprised that Matt gave in to her seduction last year... she'd been at it since high school. And he'd probably been fighting his attraction to her for as many years.

Not his attraction to *me*. What man could resist a sexpot that just kept coming at him? At the end of the day, Matt was only human

Maybe that was what had stung the most about his betrayal. That I'd been here the whole time. *I* was single, available, and not his best friend's fiancé... and yet he'd still chosen to kiss *her*. My thoughts tumbled around in my head, and I didn't even care that I'd never given him a clue that I liked him in that way. That *I* desired him. I'd never given him a better choice. As that realization hit home like a bowling ball smashing the center pin, I finally understood the depths of my anger and why I'd felt so hurt when he had done what he'd done.

He could have picked me.

But he didn't. Instead he'd picked her, and at the expense of everyone around him.

While I shoveled ice into a glass, I tried to fight the anger seeping back into me. Anger I'd finally gotten control of since he forced himself back into my life. Anger I didn't want anymore.

The shadows of the past – they were always behind you. Now I just needed to figure out a way to let them go.

You're just friends, Jo. And you've forgiven him. You have.

Taking a deep breath and exhaling the tension the realization had driven into me, I closed my eyes for a beat and forced all the hurt back out of me.

Matt was my friend. Always had been, always would be. And just friends.

"Hey, JoJo!" My sister called, and I turned to see her climbing into a stool.

"Hey, JennaJenna!" I taunted back.

She smacked her lips and I cringed. "You've been avoiding me. I've texted. I've called. Time to dish."

She was right. When I'd gotten off the jet ski the day of the non-kiss, she'd been blowing up my phone asking me what the hell had happened. Demanding an update.

But I hadn't known what to say. And I'd blown her off and stalled by answering "call you in a bit" and "Nothing happened. You need glasses." But she'd kept on, and I guess I shouldn't be surprised she'd shown up here. She knew damn well I was trapped and couldn't avoid her when I was stuck behind the bar.

"I've just been busy. Sorry!" I answered, hurrying around behind the bar to look too slammed to admit to my innermost feelings. The dinner crowd was picking up, and I hoped they would flood in soon, so I really *was* too busy to talk to her.

"Dish, sis. What the hell is going on with Matt? I *definitely* saw you two almost kiss. I do not need glasses."

When I looked up, she pursed her lips and her eyebrows lifted in a challenge.

"Jenna. It was nothing. He was just trying to prevent a little wardrobe malfunction. We fell down, we were a little stunned, and nothing is going on with Matt and I."

"Mmmhmmm." She crossed her arms.

"Jenna." I stopped in front of her, placing my hands on the bar. "Nothing is going on. We're just friends. Drop it."

Hoping by convincing her I could convince myself, I waited for her submission.

With an eye roll, she unclamped her crossed arms. "Fine. Just friends. But—"

"No buts. Just friends."

"Ugh. Fine!" She flung her arms up in defeat. "Can I at least get a marg?"

"That I can do."

Giving gratitude for her immediate surrender, I took a deep breath. I'd convinced Jenna I had no feelings for Matt, and now just one non-believer remained.

Me.

I made Jenna her margarita and as I dropped it off, the doors opened, and the bar flooded with bodies.

Dinner rush.

Hanson and I jumped into action and slid into fifth gear while we took orders and made drinks. Jenna, always the outgoing one, made some new friends with the couple seated next to her and continued sipping on drinks as I raced around the bar.

While I struggled to keep my head above water, I reached into the beer cooler to grab a bottle, and when I looked up, Matt was sitting next to her.

"Matt!" I gasped and almost dropped the bottle. Luckily my nimble fingers regained control before it hit the ground.

"Hey, Jo," he said with a smile.

Startled by his sudden appearance, I struggled for

a second to respond. "Sorry. You just startled me. I didn't see you come in."

My gaze slid to Jenna's, and a knowing smirk lifted her red lips.

"Yeah. I needed something to eat, so I thought I'd come in here and grab a bite."

"Yeah. Good, uh... good idea. I'll grab you a menu."

"No need. Pork Torta all the way! Best sandwich ever."

"Good choice!" Hanson called as he raced past. "Pork Tortas all the way!"

"Got it. Yeah." I stood there holding the beer, my mind still churning to catch up.

Why did he have to look so good? I stared at him for a few moments too long. After he caught me gawking, I dropped my gaze down. Then I noticed the beer still in my hand, and realized I had no idea where it belonged.

I looked up from the bottle clutched tight in my hands and started scanning the bar hoping a familiar face would remind me who'd ordered it.

"Jo?" Jenna asked, shaking me back to my senses. "You okay?"

"Huh? Yeah." My gaze darted to Matt for a second, and I felt heat rush into my cheeks.

Oh shit. That's not good.

Aware of the feelings written across my face, I shot a look to Jenna. When our eyes met, I saw it... that look in her eye that confirmed I could deny it until my face turned blue, but she knew.

Her eyes narrowed as a smirk lifted one side of her lips.

Oh, yeah. She definitely knew.

Please don't say anything, Jenna, I pleaded with my eyes.

It was bad enough Jenna knew the secret I'd been hiding, even from myself, but now I could only hope Matt hadn't caught onto the reason I'd suddenly come undone.

Jenna and I locked in a silent standoff, and I pleaded with her again, a soft shake of my head begging for her silence.

"You okay, Jo?" Matt asked, glancing between the two of us.

"Yep." I forced a smile, spinning on my heel to stalk down the bar with this beer hoping I remembered where it went before I got to the end. And hoping by the time I had to go back by Matt these feelings would be back under control... or at least they would be off my freaking face. I swiped an ice cube from the bin as I hurried past and pressed it to my scalding cheek.

CHAPTER TWELVE

MATT

What the hell? Jo looked like she'd seen a ghost when she'd seen me sitting here.

"So," Jenna said, and I turned to see her grinning at me. "How's it going?"

"Um, good I guess. And you?"

"Good. Very good," she answered, and trouble brewed in her eyes.

I furrowed my brow while she stared at me, her hand propped under her chin as her smile lifted one corner of her lips.

I'd known Jenna my whole life, and I knew that look. She'd worn the same one when she'd told Jo and I that monsters lived in our closet when we were six, causing us both to sleep with the lights on for months. She'd worn the same one when she'd told me I had permission to take the cake from Susie's ninth birthday party… just before I'd gotten reamed out for trying to steal it.

Trouble. What was brewing in those amber eyes was nothing but trouble.

"What?" I asked, and she pursed her lips tighter.

"Nothing."

"It doesn't look like nothing. It looks like something. And if I know you, it's trouble. What?"

"Nothin'." She grinned.

"Okay. You're starting to freak me out." I chuckled while Jo paced behind the bar, staring at her bottle of beer and searching the faces of the customers.

"Over here!" A man said, and I saw the recognition flash in her eyes while she hurried over to give it to him.

"So," Jenna said, pulling my gaze off Jo.

"So."

"So…" She smiled again, and I waited for more.

Jo appeared with a bottle of beer and held it in front of me. "Spotted Cow good?"

"Perfect. Thanks, Jo."

"You got it." She set it on the coaster but missed the edge and it almost toppled over.

"Oh shit!" She caught it and set it upright. The soft pink bloom in her cheeks deepened to crimson while she gave me an unnaturally shy smile before spinning and hurrying off.

"So..." Jenna said again, and I looked over to find her smile so wide she could have been the Cheshire Cat. Or from the looks of her, the cat that ate the canary at the very least.

"Why do you keep looking at me like that?" I took a sip of my beer.

"No reason."

"Jenna, I know you. You're up to something. What the hell is it?"

"Nothing." She kept grinning.

I heard glass shatter and then Jo's curse words punctuating the din of the bar crowd. When I turned to look, she knelt on the rubber mat picking up the remnants of a margarita glass.

"Jo seems off tonight. I wonder what's going on with her?" I asked.

"I wonder... What could be wrong with Jo tonight? What, what, what?" Jenna's voice trailed off, and she placed a finger to her chin, tapping on it.

"What does that mean?"

"Nothing."

"Jenna! What the fuck?" I laughed.

Tossing her hands up in the air she huffed. "Seriously? Are you legally blind?"

"What are you talking about?"

"Ugh! I can't take it anymore! You!"

"Me what?"

"Y-O-U are what is wrong with her tonight, dumbass! She's crazy about you!"

I choked on the sip of beer I'd just taken, almost spitting it out in her face, but I managed to gulp it down. "What?" I gasped.

Jenna tapped me on the forehead with each word. "Are. You. Stupid?"

"No. I'm not... what? What the hell do you mean she's crazy about me?"

The bar spun around me while I tried to digest her words.

"Jo is in love with you. She's been in love with you *forever*. And you're in love with her. It's like, HELLO!" She flicked me on the head. "Dumbass."

Jo is in love with me?

Impossible.

"No way. Jo thinks of me as a friend. *Only* a friend."

Jenna shook her head. "You really are as dense as a door. Jo *pretends* to think of you like a friend, the same way you *pretend* to think of her only as a friend."

Was it that obvious? My feelings for Jo weren't a secret? Desperate to keep up the ruse I'd been playing for the better part of my life, I shook my head.

"No. We're just friends, Jenna. You're way off."

Crossing her arms, she shook her head. "Nope. I'm not off. Not even a little. I'm dead freaking on."

"Jo doesn't like me like that."

194

With the roll of her eyes, she placed her hands on my shoulders. "Do you know what I do for a living?"

"Um, yeah. You're a wedding planner."

"Do you know what that means, Matt?"

"Um, that you plan weddings?"

Where is this going?

"It means that I spend every day, day in and day out, with couples who are in love. I know love. And I can determine with 100% accuracy which couples are going to make it and which ones will be having a date in divorce court based on one thing."

"What thing?"

"The way they look at each other. The energy that moves between them. It's palpable. And you and Jo?" She scoffed. "I could do a freaking polka on the connection between you. It's there. And it's real. Even if you dumbasses won't admit it."

She flicked my head again.

"Ow! Stop it!" I laughed, swatting her hand away.

"I'm telling you; I know what I know. This is my skill. My gift. My *superpower*. And I'm telling you that my superpower is certain you and Jo are totally and completely in love with each other. I'm never wrong. If I was a baseball player, I'd be batting a zero."

I arched a brow. "A zero? That means you suck."

"What? Oh. I thought zero meant the number of times I struck out."

"No. Zero means the number of times you hit the ball. I think you mean you're batting a thousand."

"Oh. Well, *whatever!*" She tossed up her hands again. "Then I'm the batting a thousand player. I kick ass at this."

"I... it's not possible, Jenna. She doesn't like me like that."

Visions of our awkward kiss in eighth grade flooded back to me, followed by memories of the way she'd reacted just the other day when I'd almost kissed her again.

Jenna propped an elbow on the bar and leaned forward. "You keep saying 'Jo doesn't like me like that', instead of 'I don't like Jo like that', which tells me two things. One, that you are crazy about Jo. Two, that since I'm right about your feelings, I'm right about hers. Boom." She faked a mic drop.

Words rattled around in my brain, but my mouth only opened and closed while I struggled for an argument to explain away her very accurate accusation about my feelings. But one look in her eye and I knew she had me backed into a corner.

Busted.

With a sigh, I leaned forward. "Okay, fine. You caught me. I'm fucking crazy about Jo. Always have been, always will be."

"YES!" she shouted, pumping her fist in the air.

Jo passed by and slammed to a stop. "What's up?"

"Nothing!" we echoed, and our unnaturally high-pitched response caused Jo to furrow her brow.

"What's going on?" she asked again, but her eyes bore into Jenna's. Another silent standoff between the Parker sisters went down.

"Jo, that guy's waiting for a drink. Chop, chop." Jenna clapped her hands, ending the telepathic conversation.

"Just... Jenna." She pointed a finger in Jenna's face, and I tried to grasp what the hell they were arguing about.

Me?

Was it possible Jenna was right and Jo was warning her not to say anything?

More memories of Jo running back to the jet ski in disgust after I'd almost kissed her flooded my mind.

Nope. Definitely not what was going on here, because Jo was *not* into me.

With a final glare, Jo spun on her heel and marched back to work.

"So," Jenna turned back to me. "As you were saying?" She propped her chin in her hands and batted her long lashes.

"Nothing. Just forget I said anything."

She slapped my shoulder and then gave me a shake. "No way. Not backing out of this now. You were *saying* that you've always been in love with Jo. And I was saying that meant if I was right about one of you, I'm right about the other."

I leaned in. "Jenna. I almost kissed Jo at the beach the other day. You saw it. I know you did. And you know what she did? She ran. And then avoided me for three days straight. I'm trying like hell here to keep my feelings for her in check, and you're not helping. At all. I won't mess up our friendship, Jenna. I can't. This last year without her was torture. I won't risk ruining things again. I need her in my life."

Jenna's shoulders lifted with her heavy sigh, and her face softened. "You need her in your life because you *love her.* And she ran off because, well, she's Jo. And you know better than anyone that Jo doesn't do feelings well. She may be tough as nails on the outside, but on the inside, she's got that melty, gooey center. She's scared, Matt. Probably of the same thing you are. Of ruining the friendship. And she's also gotta be so scared of getting hurt."

It *was* something Jo would do... running away from something that might get serious. Might cause her to risk getting hurt. But was Jenna right? Was it possible the reason she took off after our almost-kiss involved fear instead of disgust?

The possibility almost melted my mind.

"I'm telling you, Matt. What you're feeling is not

one-sided. But one of you needs to take the leap and get this thing going. You've spent twenty-plus years doing this dance together, both of you too chicken-shit to admit how you feel. You're a grown-ass man now, and you know what grown-ass men do?"

"Pretend they aren't in love with their best friend for all eternity?" I gave her a sheepish grin.

In turn she flicked my head again. "No, dumbass. You man up and tell her how you feel!"

"I can't, Jenna. What if you're wrong? What if she doesn't feel that way about me and she ends our friendship? I'm still on very thin ice with her."

"She won't."

"But what if?"

Jenna blew out an exasperated breath. "Fine. Let's say on the zero percent chance she's not into this, what is the worst thing that happens? You tell her, she says no, and it's a little awkward for a while. But you two are Jo and Matt... you'll get through it."

Shrugging, I took a sip of my beer.

"And what if she says yes?" Jenna placed a hand on my shoulder.

What if she says yes?

Images of life with Jo in my arms flashed through my mind. Her touch. Her kiss. Her laugh in my ear when we woke up in the morning. Like a whirlwind of happiness, emotions flooded through me and permeated every inch of my soul. Images I'd never dared to let loose in my mind galloped free as I pictured a life together if she said yes.

A life filled with more happiness than I'd ever imagined possible.

"So?" Jenna prompted.

"So..." I stalled. "So, I'm freaking scared, Jenna."

"Matt. That's my baby sister." She pointed to Jo as she flew past carrying a plate of enchiladas. "Her happiness means more to me than my own. If I didn't *truly* believe that she felt the same way about you, I would never say anything. Because if I was wrong, it would mean I would hurt her by damaging your friendship. I would never hurt her, Matt. Never."

I tried to let her certainty dissolve my fears.

"Matt, you need to tell her. You need to tell her *tonight*... before you chicken out. You're M.F.O.E."

I scrunched my brow.

"Made for each other." She went to flick my head again, but I caught her hand in mine, bringing it down onto my lap and giving it a gentle squeeze.

"Are you sure, Jenna? Like a million percent sure? Because if I do this there is no going back."

She returned the squeeze and smiled. "I'm sure. Tell her, Matt."

Fear like I'd never known coursed through my veins when I looked up at Jo. She turned and locked eyes with me, a soft smile lifting the lips I was desperate to taste. Thinking of living a life beside her as only a friend and never knowing what could have been, I knew what I needed to do now.

Jenna was right. It was time.

"Okay. I'll do it."

Jenna's squeal rang my eardrums, and she pulled me in for a hug. "Yay! It's gonna be great!"

"Just hold on to your celebrating there, Meddlypants. She hasn't said yes yet."

"She will," Jenna whispered in my ear and then sat back.

God, I hope so.

Jo appeared holding my sandwich and just the sight of her sent my heart racing faster than if I'd flung myself out of an airplane.

"Here you go." She set the sandwich down in front of me.

Normally my mouth would water when I saw my favorite pork sandwich covered in cheese, onions, and peppers, but one look at it and my already queasy stomach turned.

With the nerves I had right now, eating had gone from the first thing on my mind to the last. Not to mention if there was even a one percent chance of a kiss with Jo tonight, those onions weren't my friend. "You know what? So sorry to be a pain, but can I get this to go?"

Jo shrugged and pulled the plate back. "No problem."

Jenna kicked me under the bar, and I let out a deep sigh. "Hey, Jo?"

She stopped and turned back. "Yeah?"

"Um, what time are you off tonight?"

"Probably midnight?"

"Okay. Um... do you want to like hang out or something? With me?"

She shrugged and nodded. "Sure. If you're still up."

"Yeah. I'll wait up."

"Okay, I'll see you at home then?"

"Yeah. Sounds good."

When she walked away, Jenna gave me an appreciative nod. "Atta boy. Rip it off like a band-aid."

"You'd better be right, Jenna."

"I'm right. You'll see." She bopped me on the nose, then settled back into her seat. "I'm a fucking professional."

Even if she wasn't right about Jo's feelings for me, she was right about one thing. I had to try. To miss out on the chance of having Jo in my life as more than a friend was a risk I'd regret forever if I didn't at least try.

And now I had to come up with the perfect way to turn our friendship upside down.

CHAPTER THIRTEEN

MATT

"Wine, check. Blanket, check. Balls, no check," I mumbled to myself while I paced the little cabin waiting for Jo to get home. Petunia watched with cautious eyes as I burned a hole through the floor. "Don't judge me, Petunia. I'm freaking out. I could use some support here. A little camaraderie, you know."

A warning growl and her hiss were my only encouragement.

Normally I didn't lack confidence when it came to women. Honestly, asking out women had always been easy for me. A little coy smile, some flirty lines, and they seemed to melt into a puddle of goo. But the women from my past weren't Jo. Melting Jo into goo would take more than flashing my signature smile. It would take something as hot as molten lava, and I worried I couldn't crank my temperature up high enough.

The moment of truth had arrived, hurried along by an unlikely messenger. Over twenty-five years of pining for Jo and tonight I was going to confess it. Put my heart out on a platter and hope she didn't pummel it into smithereens.

I looked at my phone. Only fifteen minutes until midnight. Fifteen minutes to get my shit together and figure out the perfect thing to say. Why the fuck had Cassie picked this week to take Jake up North fly-fishing and out of cell-phone range? I could use them right now and they wouldn't be home until tomorrow night. If they were here, I'd be making Cassie run lines with me while I begged Jake to talk me off the ledge.

But they were gone, and I was alone.

Alone with my runaway thoughts of seeing Jo's face twist in disgust when I told her that I didn't want to be what we'd always been. The same face she'd made when I'd kissed her in eighth grade.

I cringed just thinking about it.

The face that said we were *just friends*.

Footsteps drummed up the stairs, and with them my heart beat faster. Jo appeared in the doorway, pushing it open and tossing her purse on the couch.

"You're early," I blurted.

Damn it. I needed those extra fifteen minutes to compose myself.

"Yep. You and Jenna took off, things stayed crazy

at the bar for a bit, but then they slowed down. So, I'm a little early."

"You're early," I repeated, panic turning my brain to mush.

Jo's eyebrows snapped together. "Yeah? Is that a problem?"

"Um, no. No not at all. It's great. Yep, totally great. You're early."

"What the hell is wrong with you?" She tugged off her hairband and her ponytail turned into long, flowing waves of hair brushing across her back. The sight of her hair swaying as she ran her fingers through it nearly took me to my knees with screams of "I love you!" rolling off my lips.

Keep it together.

"Nothing. Just... I'm fine."

"So, we're hanging out? *Family Guy* or do you want to do *Sons of Anarchy* or something? I spent all night in a bar so I'm not really up for going out."

"I, uh... I actually had a different idea."

"Oh yeah?" She flopped down on our new couch. "What's that?"

"Well, I remembered that tonight is the start of the Perseids meteor shower."

Her eyes lit up. "Oh, yeah! That's right! I love the Perseids!"

Part of the joy of living in Door County was the

lack of urban lights. It was why people flooded up here from the cities, to enjoy our skies filled with millions of stars, and the Northern Lights that danced across the sky many nights in the summer. And on a few August nights every summer, hundreds of meteors would streak across the sky like our own private intergalactic light show. The Perseids meteor shower. It was something that Jo had loved when we were kids, and I was glad to hear that hadn't changed.

On the right track. Keep it together.

"I know. I remember. We used to watch them every year when we were kids, remember? Begging our moms to let us stay up late and see them?"

"I remember." She smiled. "I haven't seen them in a couple years. That sounds awesome. Wanna crack a couple beers and sit on the porch in the dark and watch them?"

Swiping a hand across the back of my neck, I shifted my weight. "I, uh, had a different idea. I thought we could get away from *all* the lights so we could see them really clearly."

"How so?" She kicked off her shoes.

"There's a little rowboat I noticed just up the beach. I thought we could take it out a little way then watch them from the water."

"A little rowboat?" she asked, the concern heavy in her voice. "Do you mean you want to *steal* a rowboat?"

"Borrow." I grinned. "The house has been dark all week. They aren't even up here right now, so what's wrong with borrowing a perfectly good rowboat from next door?"

"This is one of those ideas that gets us thrown in the slammer, isn't it?"

"It's midnight, everyone is asleep, and we'll have it back in no time with no one the wiser. Come on, Jo... you chicken?" I hit her soft spot.

"Am I chicken? What are we, ten again?"

"So, you're chicken." I crossed my arms and watched her face tense up.

"I'm not chicken."

"Prove it."

"I'm not falling for that anymore. I'm not a kid. You can't convince me to do stuff I don't want to do just by calling me chicken."

"Okay then... chicken." I let out a bawk and her face turned red.

"Get the boat."

"Ha!" I clapped and laughed. "I knew you couldn't resist."

She cocked a hip. "Just hurry up before I change my mind. I'm changing my clothes."

"I'll paddle it up front. Meet me on the beach."

Jo headed into her room, and I grabbed the blankets and the bottle of wine and raced out the door.

The boat was just a short jog down the beach, and when I got to it, I tossed in my shoes, the blankets and wine, then looked around to make sure no one was watching. After rolling up my pants, I pushed it toward the water, and it ground against the rocks, the sound echoing through the still night. I cringed, pushing it slower and hoping no one heard all the noise. When it slid into the water, the loud clanking of rocks subsided and all I heard were the gentle waves lapping along the shore.

The cool water sent a chill through me as I waded out a little farther before climbing over the edge. As I settled into my seat, the tiny boat rocked beneath my weight, and I almost dropped an oar into the water.

"Don't screw it up now," I breathed as I re-situated the oars and started paddling toward the lights of our cabin.

When I got there, Jo stood on the beach in a pair of jersey pants and a sweatshirt. Even in the casual clothing, she'd never looked more beautiful.

"We'd better not get busted," she said as I pulled up on the beach.

"Your chariot awaits." I hopped out and held the boat steady while she climbed in and sat on the small back bench seat. When she looked settled, I pushed the boat back out and then hopped inside.

"Careful!" she laughed, holding onto the edges

while the boat teetered back and forth.

"Sorry." I sucked the air through my teeth as I took my seat and waited for the rocking to stop. "Little boat."

"Little *stolen* boat," she added, and then chuckled.

"Borrowed." I smiled and started paddling.

Jo leaned back, staring up at the sky as I paddled us away from the lights on the shore. When we were far enough out that the lights from shore dimmed, I fumbled for the anchor at my feet then tossed it overboard. I felt it hit bottom, and I gave it a tug to make sure we wouldn't float off and require a rescue from the Coast Guard. Getting busted in a stolen boat wasn't exactly part of my perfect romantic evening.

"There. Perfect." Careful not to rock the boat, I leaned down and pulled out the folded blankets.

"What's that?" Jo pointed to them.

"Blankets. So we can lay back and watch the meteor shower."

"Oh," she answered, and I saw something flash across her face.

I searched her expression, analyzing it. If I had to put money on it, I'd pick concern. Did she not want to lay next to me? Did the thought revolt her? Was Jenna wrong?

Trying not to lose the gumption I was barely hanging onto, I pushed forward. With a wave of my arms, I flung the blanket into the air and let it settle onto the floor.

"Go ahead. You get situated and then I'll join you."

Jo bit her lip then nodded. The boat teetered as she shifted to the floor, and I braced against it while I waited for her to get settled. Once she was lying down with her feet on one seat and her head at an awkward angle on the seat beside me, I climbed down beside her.

"Here. We can use this blanket as a pillow." I lifted the other thick blanket and gestured to her head. Jo sat forward, and I placed the blanket behind her, then laid my head back beside hers and kicked my feet up on the other bench. "Not bad! Pretty comfy for a tiny boat!"

"Not bad at all." She glanced over at me and the close proximity of her lips sent a surge of excitement and panic flooding back through me.

The usual chant of *just friends* started up in my head, but this time I told it to get lost. Tonight, that taunting voice wasn't welcome here. Tonight was about confessing my feelings for her... the ones I'd harbored since before I'd learned to ride a bike. And I couldn't remember a time in my life I'd been more terrified.

Jo looked away and then up to the sky. Millions of stars dotted the black canvas, but none were dancing across the sky yet.

"They should start soon. I googled it while you

were getting the boat. Peak should start in about fifteen minutes."

"Cool. I haven't seen them in years." I folded my arms behind my head and stared up at the sky with her.

"When was the last time we did this?" she asked.

"You and me together? Middle school, I think."

"That's the last time I remember, too. I've seen them other times, but just by myself."

"Oh good, I thought you were going to say you cheated on me and watched the Perseids with someone else. Meteor showers are our thing."

I glanced over and caught her smile. But as soon as our eyes met, she quickly looked away.

My nerves crackled inside me, and I struggled not to blurt out what Jenna got me so desperate to say.

Timing. It was all about timing.

"Oh!" I sat forward, and the boat rocked with my movement. "I brought wine."

"Wine?" She arched an eyebrow. "Whoa. When did we get so fancy?"

With a shrug, I pulled the bottle out of the blanket. "Figured wine went better with stargazing than beer."

"I can dig it."

As I stared at the bottle, I cringed when I realized it wasn't a screw top and I hadn't brought a corkscrew. "Shit."

"What?"

"Um, no corkscrew."

"You dumbass." She laughed.

Shaking my head, I started to put the bottle down. "If the shoe fits."

"Ooh!" She lit up and sat forward beside me. "Hold on!"

Jo grabbed my discarded tennis shoe and opened her hand for me to give her the bottle. I watched in awe as she placed the bottle upside down between her knees and then smacked it repeatedly with my shoe. After some impressive whacks, she stopped and lifted the bottle. A triumphant grin spread across her face when she hoisted it up to show the cork halfway out.

I shook my head. "That's awesome!"

"Bartender trick." She grabbed the top of the cork, grunting and grimacing while she tried to pull it the rest of the way out.

"Allow me to do my part." I opened my hand, and she handed it over with some resistance.

"Normally I could do it, but my hands are tired from opening beer bottles all night."

"I got you." I yanked the cork the rest of the way out, grateful I'd been successful and hadn't had to hand it back in defeat.

"And... no glasses, either." I grimaced.

Really crushing it, Casanova.

"Do I seem like the kind of girl who requires a glass

to drink wine?" Jo pressed the bottle to her lips and took a swig.

God, I love this woman.

"Nope. Not the Jo I know." She handed me the bottle, and I took a much-needed swig.

She leaned back against the make-shift pillow and I followed, resting my head beside hers.

"This was a pretty good idea." She pulled the wine bottle from my hand and took another sip.

"I'm full of them."

"You're full of something..."

We turned toward each other, our noses almost touching and laughed.

Don't kiss her. Don't kiss her. Don't kiss her.

It seemed I had a new chant now that *just friends* wasn't valid anymore.

"Look!" she jerked her head away and pointed at the sky.

I caught the tail end of the white streak before it disappeared. "Cool. It's starting."

We lay back quietly and passed the wine back and forth while the sky awakened. First one, then another, and with each passing minute more streaks shot across the sky.

"I love the Perseids. Seriously. It's so cool, isn't it?" Jo sighed.

"It's pretty amazing."

The boat bobbed along the water, and I listened to her breathing and the soft lapping of the waves on the hull.

Just tell her.

"I'm glad we're friends again," I started, hoping the speech I'd been preparing would come back to me. At the moment, that was the only line I could remember.

"Me, too."

"Yeah. I'm glad you forgave me."

"As long as you stay the hell away from Nikki and never touch another taken woman again, we're good."

"Never. Never ever. I still don't know what the hell came over me."

She snorted. "Ah, come on. I'm not stupid. I saw the little hussy flirting with you for years. I didn't think you'd *go there,* but it's not like this was all on you."

"Yeah. Hindsight is twenty/twenty. I should have told Jake the first time she flirted with me. I didn't want to hurt him."

"You did a bang-up job with that." Jo scoffed, then smiled.

"Yeah. Really bang-up job."

"Well, I guess since you were..." her voice drifted off for a beat, "in love with her, I can kinda see the predicament you were in."

"I only *thought* I had feelings for her. More like a long-standing infatuation which was actually just a distraction."

"A distraction? From what?"

You.

An in. I should take it. Blurt it out. But instead my tongue tied up in knots and I just shrugged.

This was impossible.

As a wave of fear gripped me, I wondered how the hell was I supposed to tell Jo how I felt? What if she said no? What if she laughed at me, threw me out of her cabin and out of her life? Then what?

And what if she doesn't?

Still struggling to blurt it out, I shrugged. "Just things."

"What kinds of things?"

"Well," I swallowed hard.

Now or never.

"When Nikki came to school, she was the girl who helped me get over my broken heart."

"A broken heart from who?"

With a sigh, I forced the truth out of my mouth. "From you."

"What?" Jo whipped her head toward me, but I kept staring at the stars, too scared to make eye contact. "What are you talking about?"

With a deep breath, I rolled my head to face her. "Jo, I was totally and completely in love with you since… well, since my first memories. And then there was that kiss where you dissed me and…"

"Kiss? What kiss? We never kissed!" Wide eyes stared into mine. "I would remember if we kissed."

Chuckling, I nodded my head. "Oh, there was a kiss. Two in fact."

"What are you talking about?"

"Well, my mother has a picture of us pecking when we were about five."

"Okay, that I can see. But what other kiss?"

"The one at Andrea's fourteenth birthday party."

Her face lit up in recognition. "You mean spin-the-bottle? That didn't count as a kiss! That was a game!"

I snorted. "Not to me! That was the day you shattered my little teeny tiny boy heart."

Confusion danced across her face. "How? What? I don't understand."

"Well, up until that day I held out for the fact that maybe, just maybe, you'd see me as more than a friend. Then when the bottle landed on you, I thought that was finally my chance. I was so excited when I leaned over to kiss you. Like, probably the most excited I'd ever been in my whole life." I laughed. "But then I kissed you. And instead of the fireworks and sparks I was sure would explode around us, you scrunched up your face, wiped your lips and spit repeatedly into the sand."

"Oh my God." She clasped a hand over her mouth. "I did do that."

"Yep. You did. That memory is burned in my mind for all eternity. And so that day I vowed to force myself to get over you, and a couple months later Nikki waltzed in, so I threw everything I had into my fake infatuation so I would get over my feelings for you."

"Holy shit," she breathed.

"Yep."

She fell silent for a moment, chewing on her lips while worried eyes searched mine. "There was a reason I acted like that," she whispered.

"Yeah. The reason was I disgusted you!" I laughed. "Maybe I still..."

"No! That wasn't the reason at all. I was crazy about you and I didn't want anyone, especially *you*, to know. So, I pretended to be disgusted to ensure no one caught on to me."

My mouth fell open as I struggled to find the words. "Wait... you liked me, too?"

She sucked her lip between her teeth and nodded. "Um, yeah. A lot."

"Holy shit. You mean you shattered my little boy heart for nothing?"

She grimaced and nodded. "Apparently. I'm so sorry. I had no idea you liked me and that my response to our kiss was so heartbreaking. You never showed it! I had no idea, Matt! My God!"

She cupped her hands over her face, and I struggled

to breathe. All these years. All these agonizing years and she'd liked me back. If only I'd been braver then. If only she'd been braver. If only we'd been so many things.

But the timing hadn't been right. And life was all about timing.

"Holy shit, Jo. I had no idea you liked me, either. I really thought you just thought of me as good buddy Matt."

"Well, I did. But I also felt a whole helluva lot more than that."

Silence passed between us while my brain went into overdrive analyzing every interaction I'd had with Jo when we were kids. Searching for those signs I'd missed. Signs that could have saved me a whole lot of pain. How had I missed it?

Now I knew she'd liked me then, but that didn't answer the big question.

The most important one.

Did she still feel the same way?

I took a deep breath and watched another meteor streak across the sky. "You were my first kiss, you know."

"And you were mine."

"And..." I swallowed hard as I pressed forward. "I've never stopped wanting to kiss you since."

Our heads turned, and our eyes locked. My breath

quickened along with my heart. They were right there. Her lips. They were there for the taking, but fear roared inside my chest, my anxiety tearing me apart from the inside.

Her eyes drifted to my lips, then rose again, and when I looked in her eyes, I dug into my resolve. We'd wasted all those years hiding from the truth, and this time I wasn't going to let fear stand between us.

Not this time.

I slid a hand along her face, pausing to give her time to shove me away. A moment to tell me we were just friends.

But the argument against my intentions didn't come.

Instead she leaned forward, and I pulled her mouth against mine. Our lips connected, and I sighed into her mouth. I exhaled years of agony, torture, and desire now satiated with every swirl of her tongue. While I closed my hands around her face, I pulled her closer, every inch between us too many. My lips burned as I kissed her harder, and they finally claimed what they'd craved all those years.

Her taste.

Her touch.

Her passion.

This time she didn't push me away, spitting out my affections. This time she wrapped her arms around my neck and melted against my body. Emotions I'd long suppressed raced each other to the surface, rejoicing in their freedom as she pulled me in closer, our kiss slowing as it deepened.

With every swirl of her tongue and brush of her lips, I felt our connection crackling to life. The walls we'd built between us came crumbling down, and for the first time in our lives, nothing stood between us. Finally, it was just us.

As our kiss softened, her lips ghosted mine. I captured her soft sigh in my mouth, then pressed my forehead to hers.

"Jo," I whispered. "I've wanted this my whole life."

Her ragged breaths danced across my skin.

"Me too," she breathed.

I wrapped my arms around her, pulling her in tight. And now that I had her, I never intended to let her go.

CHAPTER FOURTEEN

JO

Matt held me tight, and I was grateful for the sensation to help convince myself this was real, and our kiss hadn't just been a figment of my imagination or a vivid dream. But as his arms pulled me in tighter, I knew this wasn't just in my head.

The kiss was real.

We were real.

"Wow," I breathed, still stunned from the unfamiliar emotions raging inside me.

"Wow," he responded.

His grip loosened, and I slid back, lifting my chin so I could look up at him. I needed to see his face, one more confirmation that this was happening. That I was here with Matt. Kissing him. Holding him. Feeling every one of my dreams come true.

When our eyes locked and I saw the same shock and amazement in his stare, I couldn't help but smile.

He smiled back. "We've been missing out on that all these years?"

"Apparently. Yeah."

"Wow. What a couple of idiots we are."

"Yep."

As he smiled down at me, I felt my nerves crackling back to life. When I'd seen the intent in his eyes, felt his hand brush my cheek, I'd been lost in the moment and my body took control. But now as we sat staring at each other, uncertainty rushed in on a wave. It felt so new. So unsure.

Should I kiss him again? Give him a fist bump? Rip off his clothes?

This was Matt. My best friend. And this was territory as unfamiliar as it got. I felt awkward as I struggled for the next move. Nerves and anxiety twisted together in my gut, squeezing the life out of the certainty that had given me the confidence to lean in for that kiss. That incredible, amazing, earth-shattering kiss.

A kiss I wanted again, and again, and again...

"Jo." He took my hand in his and exhaled a deep sigh. "I love you. You were the first girl I loved and you're going to be the last girl I love. I do. I fucking love you, Jo. Always have, always will."

It may have been the boat moving, but it felt like the entire world shifted below me. In a matter of seconds, my whole world changed. His words flipped my life upside down, and I struggled to steady myself... to digest his admission.

He loved me, too.

After decades of keeping the words I'd been desperate to say locked inside me, fighting to never spit them out, I swallowed hard, fighting my fears so I could push the truth out of my mouth.

"I love you, too," I whispered.

His smile lit up so bright it dwarfed the glow of the moon.

As I looked into his eyes overflowing with emotion, I felt the uncertainty drift away with the waves. I remembered the feel of his lips on mine, the way his hands pulled me against him, and the excitement burst back to life and extinguished my anxiety. I wanted him. All of him. And as I stared at the boy I'd always loved... the boy I would always love, I knew which option I wanted.

Rip off his clothes.

I grabbed him by the shirt, pulling his lips back to mine. Pain seared across my mouth when our lips crashed together, but his tongue quickly erased the discomfort. It demanded entrance I was happy to give it.

His hands slid down the sides of my face, holding it tight while I moaned into his mouth. The stars exploding across the sky didn't hold a candle to the passion exploding between us. Years of repression, anticipation, and desire burst into a flame so hot I worried it would start our wooden boat on fire.

My hands drifted to his torso and slid underneath his shirt, traveling along the hard lines of his abs while I worked my way up his body, pushing his shirt off as I went. When I reached the swell of his pecs, I paused to enjoy them. Years of wondering what they felt like were answered as I explored him with my touch.

Matt's lips pulled away, and I whimpered my displeasure. My irritation over the loss of his lips on mine didn't last long when he grabbed the bottom of his shirt and yanked it over his head. I dragged my gaze up his muscular torso, sucking my lip between my teeth as I soaked in every incredible inch of him. The moonlight glistened across his skin and illuminated every impressive feature. Even though my desperate lips ached for his kiss again, I happily sat back and took it all in.

He didn't give me long to enjoy the view. His lips returned to mine and consumed them with his kisses as he pressed me onto my back.

Hot, deep, passionate kisses.

Kisses from the boy I'd loved my whole life.

Relishing the weight of his body on mine, I wrapped my arms around his broad shoulders. While he continued his kisses, his hands drifted down my body, brushing over my breasts as they moved to the bottom of my sweatshirt. When they slipped underneath it and touched my heated skin, a shiver traveled down my spine. With the lightest touch, his fingers ghosted across my stomach as they moved toward my breasts. The anticipation from his slow ascent had my stomach twisting and turning, my body writhing beneath him while I deepened our kiss.

When his hands finally arrived at my breasts heaving with my excited breaths, I gasped as he cupped one. His firm touch sent my heart racing, and I dug my fingers into his back. All the nerves I'd been feeling finally getting to this moment with Matt drifted away as I leaned into his touch, arching my back as his fingers slid beneath my bra and played across my stiffened peaks.

It felt natural to let him explore my body, and not strange like I'd often wondered if it would be... wondered if the fantasies I'd secretly held for him would go up in a puff of smoke if we ever decided to cross the line from friends to lovers. But the only smoke billowing between us tonight came from the smoldering fire that had crackled between us for years igniting into an unquenchable flame. It scorched away any awkwardness as we took our relationship to the next level.

The heat in my body merged and traveled between my legs, that place as desperate for his touch as my other breast. I wanted his hands everywhere. His kisses to never stop. Our bodies to connect in the way I'd never allowed myself to hope could ever be more than a fantasy.

His lips drifted from mine, and I closed my eyes as his kisses moved to my stomach. He dragged his tongue against my skin, alternating it with whisper-soft kisses to my body as he pushed my sweatshirt over my head. The crisp lake air drifted across my exposed skin, and I knew my fantasy was finally coming true.

"I want you, Jo." The sexy timbre of his voice deepened as he spoke. "I've always wanted you."

My pulse climbed as I reached behind my back and unhooked my bra. "Then I'm yours. I'll always be yours." One at a time, I pushed the straps off my shoulders, nerves and excitement twirling together while I pulled off my bra. His eyes smoldered with unquenchable desire as they drifted to my exposed breasts, and I lay there while his gaze traveled over my curves. A warm flush moved across my body everywhere his eyes roved.

"You're incredible," he said as his hands slid up my body, each finding a home on my breasts. I arched my back as he took one in his mouth, his tongue caressing my nipple. The sensation of his warm breath and the cool air sent shivers down my body, and I whimpered at his touch.

As I lay below him spinning with desire, his tongue worked over my breasts while his fingers worked open the buttons on my jeans then slipped them down over my hips. I wiggled as I pushed them off, kicking them off to the side. He traced soft circles along my stomach with his fingers before they dipped beneath the only fabric keeping us apart. When his fingers slid between my legs, I bit my lip to keep from screaming out his name. Pure ecstasy flooded through me as his fingers sunk inside me, moving in rhythm with the tongue still tormenting my breast.

"Oh my God," I breathed as I rocked my hips with him, pressing myself into his palm. The friction combined with the sensation of his fingers inside me and his tongue twirling around my nipple had me ready to explode in moments.

I dug my fingers into his back while I rode the tidal wave of pleasure his touch induced. Clamping my eyes shut, I inhaled a breath, holding it while I reached the crest, floating there in ecstasy for a moment before tumbling back over the other side with a cry.

Boneless and satiated, I opened my eyes to find him staring down at me, a victorious smirk plastered across his face.

"Hi," he said.

A lazy smile lifted my lips. "Hi."

He brushed a piece of hair out of my face, and I pressed my cheek into his palm.

"I can't believe this is happening." He lowered himself down for another kiss. "Is this really happening?"

"This is happening," I whispered against his lips. "And we're not done yet."

Desperate for more, I fumbled to open his pants.. The boat rocked beneath our movement, and he paused, exchanging a smile before we slowed our movements to settle the boat back down. The need to move slow only heightened my anticipation and increased the excitement.

I pushed off his jeans, and with them his boxers, sliding his cock into my hands. A guttural groan escaped him while I worked my hand down his hard length.

"Oh my God, Jo," he breathed as I gripped him tighter.

I watched him kneeling above me, his eyes closed tight while I stroked him and held the proof of his desire in my hand.

When his body tightened and I thought he might come, he slid his hand down over mine and stopped my motion. "As much as I'm enjoying that, I don't want to end this night too soon."

I smiled when I released my grip, proud I'd given him the same pleasure he'd given me.

"Don't. Move." He leaned down, pecking me with kisses to punctuate each word.

I lay back and watched him dig into his jeans, pulling out his wallet, and then a condom from inside.

This was happening. Me and Matt. Together, we'd reached the point of no return. Not that I'd ever want to go back. Everything I'd ever wanted was finally within my grasp. And I wanted it between my legs.

Now.

Matt hooked his thumbs on the band of my underwear, slowly inching them down as he drank in the sight of me naked. I kicked them off and tossed them on top of my pants, carnal desire making me delirious as I watched him lower himself over me, pushing my knees open with his thighs. Our eyes locked while he pressed at my entrance, his eyes begging for permission. The weight of this decision passed between us in a silent conversation, and I answered by wrapping my arms around his hips and pulling him inside me.

A surge of emotion ripped through me as he filled me with the full length of him. Our moans, saturated with pleasure, mingled into one and I dug my fingers into the small of his back.

Pure uninhibited ecstasy traveled between us

while he moved inside me. But as his speed increased, the boat rocked harder, the waves slapping against the sides. Matt slowed his movement to settle the boat, and the slow, deliberate thrusts nearly drove me over the edge.

Forced to contain our passion, we moved together in a slow dance, our bodies connecting in the one way they never had. The fantasies I'd had about this moment, a moment I'd never dared to dream would come, paled in comparison to the reality. My fantasies faded into black and white movies compared to the technicolor of the real thing.

Matt leaned down, pressing his lips to mine while he continued the slow movements that had me ready to explode again. I pulled his body into mine, holding him tight while I felt his rhythm speed up. Whimpering into his mouth, I pushed against him while my body tightened in anticipation. His body froze as he moaned his release, and his name rolled off my tongue on repeat while I shattered into a million pieces.

As we lay wrapped in each other's arms, the boat rocked beneath us, slowing back down to a gentle sway. Matt collapsed at my side and pulled me up against his chest. His lips pressed into my forehead and I closed my eyes and sighed.

"Okay. That was worth the wait." He chuckled.

"Definitely worth the wait." I traced his stomach

muscles with my finger.

"Remind me again why we didn't do this years ago?"

"Because we're stubborn idiots."

I looked up to see his familiar smile. His features were the same... the one's I'd always admired on my best friend Matt. But this time he looked different to me. Better. He looked like someone I wasn't done kissing.

I climbed up his body and peppered his lips with kisses. His arms tightened around my waist as he returned them.

"Now don't go getting me all riled up again. I only had the one condom stuck in my wallet."

Furrowing my brow as I pouted, I broke off our kisses. "Just the one?"

"Well, I didn't exactly expect this to happen when I planned on confessing my feelings to you, now did I?"

"You... you planned on telling me tonight?"

"Yep. Thanks to your sister's encouragement."

"I knew it!" I slapped his chest. "I knew she was up to no good with you tonight!"

Matt caught my hand in his and squeezed it tight. "Well, I would say she was dead on with her superpower, and I for one am grateful she was up to no good tonight. If she hadn't meddled, I never would have had the guts to tell you how I felt. And then we'd have spent another few decades pretending we didn't have feelings for each other. So, I for one, say thank you, Jenna."

Even though I was pissed as hell she'd gone and put her nose where it didn't belong, I'd also never been more grateful in my life. "Thank you, Jenna." I chuckled.

"And don't you dare freak out and bolt on me, Jo. I know you. And I'm not letting you talk yourself out of this. Understood?"

"Is that why you planned on telling me in a boat? So I couldn't run?"

He waggled his eyebrows. "Always thinking. Now no running. Got it?"

With a deep sigh, I nodded. He was right. This would be the time when I would look for the escape hatch and bail before I had a chance to get hurt. Push him away before he could leave me. But if a man existed worthy of forcing myself to ride out my issues, then this was the one.

This was Matt. My best friend and the man I'd loved since I was a little girl. And now I held him in my arms... and I had no intention of letting go.

"So only the one condom, huh?" I bit my lip.

"Yep. No corkscrew. No glasses. One condom. I'm crushing it over here."

"Do you know where there are more condoms?" I peeked up at him.

"Where?"

"Our cabin." Waggling my eyebrows, I gestured toward the shore.

Matt nearly dumped me on the floor of the boat. "Get dressed. I'll paddle."

Laughing, I yanked on my sweatshirt while he pulled up his pants. I snuggled under the blanket as he grabbed the oars and paddled toward shore as fast as if he was in an Olympic rowing tryout.

CHAPTER FIFTEEN

MATT

If it didn't mean moving and waking her up, I'd have pinched myself to make sure I wasn't dreaming. Waking up with Jo wrapped up in my arms was a dream I'd had before. Many times in fact. But in the dream version of this scenario, I couldn't feel the warmth of her skin, hear her shallow breaths, or smell the vanilla hues of her shampoo.

I glanced down toward the end of the bed and saw Petunia's eye boring into me.

That answered that question.

Nope. Not a dream. A terrifying feline interloper didn't exist inside my Jo dreams. While I stared at Petunia, a thought did cross my mind. *At least she's near me without growling, hissing, or swatting at me.* In fact, Petunia was lying on my legs.

Shit. Was this a dream?

I blinked hard and pressed my body tight against Jo's. She shifted, wiggling in my arms before settling back against me.

Not a dream.

"Good morning, Roomster," I whispered into her ear.

Her body stiffened for a moment, and then a slow turn of her head brought us face to face.

"Holy shit," she breathed while she blinked back at me.

I knew that look. I'd probably worn the same one when I woke up with her in my arms. Memories had flooded through my mind while I'd pieced back together every moment that brought us here.

Every incredible, perfect, mind-blowing moment.

"Yep. I'm here. In your bed."

She brushed against my legs and her eyes widened even more. "And you're naked."

"Yep." I pulled back the covers and peeked beneath them. "And so are you."

"Holy shit. We're naked. Together."

"And we did a *lot* of fun stuff naked." I grinned and waggled my eyebrows.

The shock on her face started to dissipate, and I felt her body relax.

"I mean, I remember everything, but it still feels..."

"Surreal."

"Yes! Surreal. That's the word."

"Right there with you, Jo."

She pinched her brows together. "Good surreal, or bad surreal for you?"

"Good surreal. Amazing surreal. It feels like... it feels like a snow day."

"A snow day?" she snorted. "What the hell are you talking about?"

I pulled her tighter against my chest and rested my chin on the top of her head. "Do you remember when we were kids and a big snowstorm was coming the night before school, and we'd go to bed wishing and praying that we'd wake up to find school was canceled?"

"Yeah."

"Well, on the mornings of snow days when I would wake up not to my alarm, or my mom yelling at me to get up, or my sisters screaming at each other over the bathroom, I would realize I'd gotten to sleep in because they had canceled school. And that feeling of excitement... of pure, unadulterated bliss was the happiest I'd ever felt. Just sheer fucking joy. And my whole life, I've compared moments of happiness to how I felt waking up on a snow day. Very few have come close, and none have ever matched it. But waking up with you? Well, it feels like a snow day."

"Oh," she breathed, and then wrapped her arms around me tight. I felt her warm breath drift across my skin with her sigh. "It kinda does feel like a snow day."

I kissed the top of her head and left my lips resting in her hair. Closing my eyes, I squeezed her tight, and I didn't think I'd ever convince my arms to let go.

Not after waiting all this time to hold her.

"Too tight," she squeaked out. "Can't breathe."

I released my grip. "Oops. Sorry. I guess I got a little excited you're actually in my arms."

"You're excited? I've been dreaming about this forever."

"Why didn't you say anything? Damn it, Jo!" I laughed.

"Why didn't *you* say anything? You're as much to blame in our delay to the sack as I am!"

"Ugh. Biggest dumbasses ever."

"Ever."

"But," I said, pulling her around to face me, "we're here now. And I'm not going anywhere. And I *know* you, which also means I know deep down you're wanting to bolt out of here and run away."

"That's not true." She scowled. "I don't want to go anywhere."

Lifting her chin with the tips of my fingers, I drew her in for a soft kiss. "I'm just saying, when you got freaked out about relationships, it has always been me you ran to who'd talk you down from the ledge. But now *I'm* the relationship, and I want you to know you can still run to me and tell me how you're feeling. I'm still me. And you can be honest when you start to freak out, because you *will* start to freak out. And I sure as hell don't want you bolting out of this... bolting from us."

"You want to be the guy I run to so I can talk about the guy I want to run away from, which will also be you?" She arched a brow.

"Yep. I am still your best friend, Matt. Always will be. So, don't you dare go through your freak-out phase without me."

She smiled and pressed another kiss to my lips. "I have a feeling we're not going to go through that phase this time. I ran because I was scared of being hurt. I ran because I didn't trust them. I ran because... well... because they weren't you."

My heart swelled inside my chest, pushing against the walls trying to constrain it. "I love you, Jo."

"I love you, too."

She crawled up my body and pressed against me, our skin heating as our bodies tangled together. Grabbing her face, I pulled her in for a deep kiss. Tongues twisting, breaths quickening, our hands restarted the exploration they'd indulged in last night. I stroked the soft skin on her back, sliding my hand down to cup her ass and pull her on top of me.

A low growl vibrated through the room, and we paused, turning our heads to see Petunia glaring at us.

"Um," I whispered into her ear, "I think we need to kick out the cat."

"Hey, she's in the bed with you! That's a big step!" Jo turned back and smiled. "She's starting to like you!"

"She's also got really sharp claws, and she's extremely close to my nuts. I'm having visions of how this could go and none of them end well."

Jo laughed and kissed my cheek. "Come on, Petunia. Let's get you some food and... oh shit! Is that the time?" She snatched up her phone.

"I haven't looked yet."

"Shit. I'm covering the day shift, and I have to be at JJ's in thirty minutes!"

She started off the bed, but I caught her by the wrist and yanked her back into my arms. "It's a snow day, remember?"

After putting up a half-hearted fight, she settled back into my arms. "Unfortunately, I don't think JJ's will agree considering it's August."

"Just call in sick."

"Don't you have to work today, too?"

I sighed. "Nope. Day off. You can have a day off, too, if you call in sick." Waggling my eyebrows, I brushed a finger against her nipple.

"Not fair!" She swatted it away. "Don't tease me."

"It's not teasing if I intend to follow through. And I *definitely* intend to follow through." I dragged a finger down her abdomen and heard her breath hitch as I neared the place I'd given lots of attention last night.

Her ragged breathing sped up as I inched my way closer, but just before I reached the spot I wanted to touch, taste, and plunge myself into, she stiffened and pushed my hand away.

"You're terrible. Mean and terrible. Now I'm going to be all fired up at work today."

"I can put that fire out." I grinned.

"I'll be off work around five tonight, so we can pick up where we left off then. Deal?"

Grumbling, I tightened my grip. "No deal."

"Matt!" She laughed and swatted my shoulder. "I have to shower!"

"*Grrr*. Fine. But I get you the second you get off work. Deal?"

"Deal."

She started to get up, but I held her tight. "Wait. One more requirement to our deal before I let you go."

"What's that?"

"A date."

"Huh?"

"Tonight, I'm taking you on a date. A real one. A real couple date."

"Matt, we don't need a date. Dates are for getting to know each other before we get to this part... the sex, video games, and Netflix and chill nights. We're already there!"

"Nope." I shook my head and squeezed tighter. "We are a couple now, and couples go on dates. Tonight, it's you and me, romance all the way. If we're going to start this thing, we're going to do it right... not just add sex to what we already have. I say dinner at The Boathouse. We'll sit up on the flybridge and watch a spectacular sunset, have cocktails, and indulge in those lobster rolls I keep hearing about and have yet to try."

Narrowing her eyes, she pressed her lips together. "I *have* wanted to try the lobster rolls."

"Lobster rolls, mojitos, a gorgeous sunset... this guy." I waved a hand over my chest. "Date night. Deal?"

She chewed on her cheek and then nodded. "Deal."

"Yes!" I grabbed her face and pulled her down for a kiss.

"Okay," she mumbled against my mouth. "I have to shower."

"Fine," I breathed against her. "Abandon me. Go on."

"I'll be counting the seconds until I can be back in your arms." She pressed her face against my chest, then stiffened. "Are you wearing my deodorant?"

"What?" I said, stalling.

"Um, your armpits smell like my cocoa butter scented deodorant." She lifted her head and impaled me with a knowing stare.

A sheepish smile lifted my lips as I clenched my teeth and smiled. "Um. Maybe?"

"Matt!" She slapped my shoulder. "Gross!"

"Gross?" I huffed. "We just spent an entire night exchanging bodily fluids, but you're grossed out by sharing deodorant?"

"Don't use my deodorant! There's probably like, armpit hair in it now." She pulled a face.

"I ran out! And I was so freaked out about confessing my love for you last night I didn't want to be seducing you in a pool of sweat, so I may have..." I shrugged, "you know, used yours."

"Get your ass to the Piggly Wiggly today and get your own damn deodorant!" She laughed. "We are going to share a lot of things now that we're together, but deodorant and toothbrushes will never be on that list. Deal?"

Chuckling, I sniffed my armpit. "It does smell pretty good, though."

"Matt!"

"Deal!" I laughed and yanked her back down for a kiss.

She pecked me one last time and then stood. The sight of her naked body sent blood racing back down below.

"You'd better hurry up out of here if you don't want me to pull you back into this bed."

She peeked over her shoulder, and the look in her eyes would have dropped me to my knees if I wasn't already laying down. Desperate to touch her again, I sat up and reached for her, but she danced just out of my grasp.

"Ah, ah, ah!" She shook her finger as she backed toward the door. "Later. Now I shower."

With a kiss blown off her fingertips, she ducked out of the bedroom.

Holy shit.

I was with Jo. My Jo. This thing between us was happening. Finally. And even though I'd just held her in my arms and kissed her, I still struggled to believe it was real.

Yesterday I'd thought I had a whole life of yearning for her ahead of me. A life of chanting *just friends* any time she would walk into a room. A life of pure torture when she settled down with someone else and I'd have to shake his hand and watch him be the one who got to kiss her. But today that man was me. Today there was a new vision for what my life would be. A life with her at my side and in my arms. A life I'd never dared to dream was a possibility.

"Feed Petunia!" she called, and I heard the shower start up.

I looked down the bed and found Petunia retaining her threatening stare.

"Hey, Petunia. So, I'm gonna move now. And I'm gonna need you to not attack me. Especially because, well, I'm naked, Petunia. And your claws don't need to come anywhere near me and my bits. So, let's just do this nice and slow."

One cautious move at a time, I peeled back the covers, keeping as much space as I could between myself and the scowling cat.

"Easy, now." Moving my hands to shield my crown jewels, I stood and took one cautious step after another between the bed and the wall, inching past Petunia. Her intense gaze remained fixed on mine while I crept by, holding my breath as I got within swiping range.

"Easy. Eassssy, Petunia."

After I made it clear of the immediate danger zone, I leapt to the corner of the room where Jo's beach towel was draped over a chair. Quickly wrapping it around my waist, I exhaled my first deep breath.

"Okay. So, I'm coming closer again to get your food. Okay? Can we agree you don't attack me? Deal?"

Her golden eyes remained unblinking.

I padded to the food bowl, then reached to the shelf above and pulled down her food bag. When I glanced over my shoulder, the cat was no longer there. While I swiveled in circles to locate the missing threat, I felt her soft body rub up against my legs.

"Holy shit," I breathed while I looked down to

see Petunia purring against my leg. She chirped and looked up at me, the malice in her eyes replaced with the same softness she'd previously reserved only for Jo.

"So, this is it? I just had to feed you to get you to stop trying to kill me?" I laughed as I poured the food into her dish. She dove in headfirst, purring while she chomped on the little brown morsels of food.

I placed the food bag back on the shelf, and backed away, carefully stepping over her since things were still pretty vulnerable down below, and one swipe of her claws could end the fun I intended to have with Jo tonight.

Tonight. Ugh. Tonight felt like an eternity before I could taste her again. Explore every inch of the body I'd fantasized about since I even knew what things I *could* fantasize about. After twenty-plus years of waiting, even the four times we'd done it last night couldn't satisfy the desire I had to touch her again. When we'd run out of condoms, our unquenched desire still unsatisfied, Jo had said she was on birth control and we'd dove back in headfirst. The feeling of our bodies connecting with nothing separating us had been an ecstasy I'd never imagined possible.

I listened to the shower water hitting the floor and felt jealous it got to touch her naked body when I couldn't.

Or could I?

With a mirthful smirk, I tiptoed out of the bedroom and over to the bathroom. Carefully twisting the handle, I opened the door and slid through, pressing it closed behind me. Jo stood naked just on the other side of that curtain.

A curtain that couldn't keep me away.

I pulled it back, and she gasped, spinning toward me.

"What are you doing?" she demanded as she stood naked before me, her hands buried in the white suds on her head.

"You said you had to shower." I dropped my towel. "You didn't say I couldn't join you."

"Matt..." she warned. "I can't be late for work."

"It's called multi-tasking, Jo. You just keep washing your hair, and I'll put out that fire you're so worried will be burning all day."

I stepped inside the small space, pulling the curtain closed behind me. A cocky grin played on my lips as I edged closer to her.

"What are you doing?" She lifted an accusatory eyebrow but made no efforts to resist me when I slid my hands over her hips and yanked her against me.

"Like I said, I'm putting out the fire."

Her eyes pooled with desire as she watched me lower myself between her legs. I nudged them open and held her gaze while I let my tongue slip into her heated core. Her moans bounced off the shower walls as I teased and tortured her the way I'd learned last night made her body quake and tremble. I'd spent all night memorizing everything that made her moan, wanting nothing more than to bring her pleasure over and over, for the rest of our lives... which is how long I planned on loving her.

The water slid down her body as she leaned back against the wall, her arms dropping heavily to her sides.

I paused and peeked up at her. "You're supposed to be multi-tasking, remember? You keep washing your hair, and I'll handle things on my end."

She did as I said, rubbing the suds into her head while I slid my fingers inside of her. Paired with that thing she loved that I did with my tongue, her legs shook only a few moments later.

I peppered kisses up her wet body until I rose and stood before her, my proud grin meeting her eyes hooded with desire.

"Holy shit," she breathed.

I couldn't withhold my chuckle at the crown of foam towering on top of her head. "I think I distracted you. You may have gone a little overboard on the sudsing. Here. Let me rinse it off."

I reached up and grabbed the shower sprayer, then

spun her around, pressing her up against the shower wall. As I angled the sprayers over her to rinse the shampoo from her hair, I lowered myself and pushed inside of her with a groan.

"See. This is multi-tasking," I whispered in her ear as I moved inside of her while running my hands through her hair, the soap rinsing off and sliding down our bodies.

"Oh my God," she breathed, her soft moans blended with the sounds of the water pummeling the floor around us.

This. This was where I belonged.

In her.

With her.

Always with her.

Her whimpers drove me on while I picked up my pace, my desire for her building with each movement— our connection deepening as I buried myself deep inside her. As I closed in on my own orgasm, I let go of the shower sprayer and let it swing freely as I reached around, cupping her breast with one hand, and reaching around to tease her bundle of nerves with my other. I pulled her back into me, and even though there wasn't an inch of space between us, I still didn't feel close enough to her. I didn't think I'd ever feel close enough to her. After so many years of praying for this, of dreaming of making her my own, I just wanted to hold her against me like this forever and never let go.

She quivered and shook as I brought her back over the edge, only letting up when my name bounced off the walls of the bathroom on repeat. The sound of her ecstasy sent me tumbling over the same edge, and I held her against me, brushing kisses along the back of her neck.

"Holy shit," she breathed.

I panted, holding her for a few long moments before releasing my grip on her. "Yeah. You can say that again."

"Holy shit," she repeated, turning around to face me with a crooked smile.

"See? I told you we could accomplish two things at once." I lifted my chin and gave her a nod of approval. "Your hair looks clean, and if you finish up soon, you won't be late for work." I leaned in, brushing a kiss on her cheek before grinning and backing out of the shower.

Her jaw slackened as she collapsed back against the shower wall. "What? You're leaving?"

"My job here is done. My girl is satisfied, and we'll pick up where we left off after our date tonight."

With a wink, I blew her a kiss and pulled the curtain shut. Proud of my accomplishment, I wrapped myself up in the towel and strode back to the bedroom. This time Petunia greeted me with a chirp, and I grinned back.

"Snow day, Petunia. It's a snow day."

And I had every intention of enjoying every single snow day that lay ahead of us now that Jo was mine.

CHAPTER SIXTEEN

JO

My cheeks hurt from smiling as I glided behind the bar at JJ's. Maybe it was the mind-blowing orgasm Matt had given me in the shower this morning... or the four I'd had last night, but even though I knew those had cranked up the dial on my happiness, it was the fact that Matt had told me he loved me that took it up to an eleven.

No. A hundred.

Actually, there wasn't a level on the happiness dial high enough to handle how incredible I felt knowing that Matt was mine. That he loved me. That I wouldn't have to spend my life pining away for a man I couldn't have. A man I thought would always be just a friend. But after what we did last night, and all the incredible things he'd said, we had blown out of the friend zone and straight into happily ever after.

Happily ever after.

Now there was a concept I didn't think would

ever apply to me. Sure, I was happy enough, nothing to complain about, but I never expected my life could turn into a bona fide fairytale.

"Two margs, Jo," Sheena, our newest waitress, called from the corner of the bar.

With a happy sigh, I twirled around and floated over to the margarita glasses.

"What's gotten into you today?" she asked, peeking up from the iPad she was punching her order into. "You're like a freaking ray of sunshine."

"Nothing," I sighed. "Just a good day."

"I've been working with you for a month. You don't glow. You're glowing. Giggling, glowing, and humming. You've been like this for three hours. Something is up." She arched a dark brow, and her gaze followed me as I swayed over to the ice bin.

"Nothing at all. Just a good mood." I smiled over my shoulder at her.

Her eyes bulged and a sly smile stretched across her face. She glanced over both shoulders then leaned over the bar. "You got laid!"

"What?" I gasped, standing up straight. "I did not!"

With pursed lips and a knowing smile, she nodded. "Yep. You've got the sex glow."

Damn it. I did have the sex glow. Something *I* usually pointed out when I saw it. Hell, it was me who'd figured out Jake and Cassie had gone for it last year because they were glowing like freaking lanterns. Today, though, the one lit up like an LED was me.

"Busted," she reiterated and grinned. "Who was it? Anyone I know?"

"Just... shush. I'm not talking about it."

"Well, damn girl, it must have been hella good to get you glowing like that." She pointed her tablet pen at me and drew a heart in the air.

"Shut up!" I laughed, and heat scorched my cheeks.

"I'll figure it out." She pursed her lips again.

"Just go help your tables. That guy over there is trying to get your attention." I pointed to the man in the booth craning his neck so far back to catch her attention I worried he'd need a chiro adjustment after lunch.

"This conversation isn't over." With one more point of her pen, she spun and raced off to her table.

Struggling to strip away the smile on my face and regain some semblance of composure, I finished making her margaritas and placed them at the end of the bar. The afternoon shift had been slow, so when I heard the door open, I hoped the newcomer would head for the bar instead of the tables so I could make some tips.

"Hey, gorgeous," Matt said, and I spun to see him sliding into a stool.

My face lit up, my smile broadcasting my

excitement to see him. I only tried for a second to contain it, then gave up the struggle. "Hey, hottie. What are you doing here?"

"Missed you." He smiled, and I wanted to jump the bar and cover him with kisses.

Forcing myself to stay put, I crossed my arms. "Is that so?"

"Yep. That's so."

"Well, I guess I kinda missed you, too."

"Kinda?" He arched a brow.

With an eye roll, I dropped the facade. "Okay. A lot."

"Petunia misses you, too, but I told her she couldn't come with."

"You're talking to Petunia now?"

"Oh yeah. We're like this." He lifted his hand, twisting his fingers together. "Best friends."

"Well, I guess ours wasn't the only relationship to change last night, huh?"

His smile stretched wide, deepening his dimples. "I moved you out of the best friend spot to the girlfriend spot, and Petunia leapt from arch-nemesis to best friend."

"I still get to be your best friend, too." Leaning forward onto the bar, I pushed into his space, stopping before I let my lips do what they wanted to do.

Kiss him. Because for the first time in our lives, I

could.

Desire flickered in his eyes and I glanced to his lips as they inched toward mine.

"Thanks for the margs!" Sheena called, snapping me back to my senses.

I was working. Making out over the bar with my new hot boyfriend was definitely not on the list of acceptable behaviors at JJ's.

"You got it," I responded, leaning back just before our lips met.

"Oh!" Sheena called, and I spun to see her grinning, eyebrows waggling as she looked at Matt. "Now I get it. Niiiiiice."

"Go!" I laughed, shooing her away.

"Get what?" Matt asked, settling back into his stool.

"Nothing. But we need ground rules."

"Rules? That doesn't sound like fun."

"No kissing at the bar while I'm working."

"Definitely not fun."

"I'm at work. You can't be coming in here looking all hot and giving me the bedroom eyes."

"You can come to my work and kiss me. Ted won't give a shit. Hell, he'll probably give me a high-five when you leave."

Laughing, I shook my head. "No making me want to make out with you at the bar. Deal?"

"Deal," he grumbled, crossing his arms.

"So, since you're here for non-seductive reasons, do you want lunch? Perch special today."

"Actually," he said, his scowl lifting into a huge smile, "I came to tell you I have news."

"News? What kind? Good or bad?"

"Neither. It's *amazing* news."

"What is it?"

His smile was contagious as he leaned forward on the bar. "So, our neighbors two doors down have apparently been watching my progress on the cabin."

"Yeah?"

"And, while I was out finishing the railing an hour ago, the guy, his name is Jeff, walked down the beach to talk to me. And he said he is looking to hire someone for a remodel, and he offered me the gig!"

"Shut up!" I slapped him on the arm. "Seriously?"

"Yep. Seriously. And it gets better. So, not only do I have a long-term job with him, but he's got like a huge list of friends also needing work and he's going to hook me up."

"You're kidding? That's amazing!"

"*And* it gets one step better."

"How is that even possible?"

"The glass for our driftwood coffee table arrived, so I put it on today, and when we were talking about his home revisions, he noticed it and *loved* it. He asked to contract me to make him some driftwood furniture.

Said he'd pay top dollar."

My mouth refused to close.

"Looks like I really can start a business doing handyman work and making driftwood furniture and stuff. Pretty amazing, huh?"

"It's unbelievable, Matt. I'm so happy for you."

"And none of this would be happening if it weren't for you. Thanks to you letting me move in, it looks like I really will have a whole new career ahead of me. And one that I'll love and won't get bored with."

"I'm glad I could help." Reaching forward, I took his hand in mine. "I'm so happy for you, Matt. Whatever I can do to help you get your new business off the ground, just say the word."

"Matt's Manly Masterpieces is alive!"

"Ugh!" I dropped his hand. "You are not calling your new business 'Matt's Manly Masterpieces.'"

"Well, then you'd better think of a better one fast, because I've got to get business cards printed up so Jeff can give them to his friends."

Pursing my lips, I took a deep breath. "What about 'Handy-Matt'. Like handyman, but you're Matt."

He scrubbed a hand down his face, tipping his head while he mouthed the words. "You know... I like it! It's catchy!"

"Eh?" I nodded. "Not bad, huh?"

"'Handy-Matt'," he said, forming a sign with his

hands. "That's it. That's the one. Again... you're a lifesaver."

He leaned forward to kiss me, but I pressed my hand to his lips, pushing him back in his seat. "No kissing at the bar!"

"Ugh!" he grumbled. "Then sneak outside with me and kiss me out there."

"Matt! I'm working!"

"There's no one at the bar, and I'm not leaving until you do." I saw the determination stiffen his face, and I knew he meant it. Matt had been stubborn as hell since we were kids.

Sheena came around the corner, a playful smirk growing while she eyed us up.

"Hey, Sheena?" I bit my lip.

"Yeah?"

"Can you watch the bar for a minute? I just have to run outside for a second."

Her smile grew as she passed another look between us. "Absolutely. Have fun, kids."

I opened my mouth to argue her spot-on accusation, but instead I snapped my jaw shut and gestured for Matt to follow me. We slipped out the sliding glass side door, and before he'd even had a chance to yank it closed, I grabbed him by the shirt and pulled him into me.

Our lips connected, and he grabbed my face,

pressing me back against the wall. I sighed into his mouth, the agony of the last five minutes being near him and not kissing him drifting away on my happy moans. After a lifetime of resisting the kisses I didn't think I'd ever have, five minutes had been five minutes too many.

"I love you, Jo," he whispered between kisses.

"I love you, too." Pulling him in harder, I folded my body against his chest.

The door to the kitchen opened, and one of the cooks stepped out. I pushed Matt away and spun to see the cook grinning.

"Sorry." I gave him a sheepish smile.

He just gave me a thumbs up and ducked back inside.

Matt laughed and pressed back in for another kiss, but I found the will to stop him. "I have to get back to work."

"Just another minute," he said, slanting his mouth over mine.

Another minute wouldn't quench the desire coursing through my body.

I didn't think even a lifetime of kisses could put out this fire.

"Work. I have to go."

His warm breath ghosted my lips, and I closed my eyes and pressed in for a quick kiss before ducking under his arm. I paused at the glass door and turned back. "I'll see you tonight."

He slumped against the side of the building, pushing out his lip in a pout. "I'll be counting the minutes. Hurry up and get off. Date night."

Date night.

I had a date tonight. With Matt.

The thought made me smile, and when he mouthed 'I love you' I almost raced back into his arms.

"I'll text you when I'm done." I blew him a kiss and slipped back inside.

Ugh! If it weren't the heart of the busy season, I'd be taking a week-long vacation just so I could spend every second in his arms, trying to make up for all the time we'd missed.

Okay, maybe a month-long vacation.

I closed the glass door, pausing to regain the composure his kiss stole from me.

Only a few more hours and I could devour him all over again.

For the next two hours, I tried not to stare at the clock. People came and went from the bar, but my excitement remained steady all day. Only twenty more minutes until I could bust free and fling myself back into Matt's arms.

The phone at the bar rang, and I picked it up. "Hello, JJ's," I said, grabbing a pad of paper to jot down what I assumed would be a to-go order.

"Hey, Jo, it's Hanson."

"What up, Hanson?"

"Hey, my wife got a flat tire in Sturgeon Bay. Would you mind staying a couple hours late so I can run down and save her?"

"Of course," I said. Though I was happy to help, it meant a couple more hours away from Matt. But Hanson always had my back, so I didn't mind a couple more hours of suffering so I could have his.

"You are a lifesaver. Running to her rescue like a knight in shining armor is good for major marriage bonus points."

Laughing, I nodded though he couldn't see. "Damn straight, Hanson. Go save your girl."

"I'll see you in a couple hours."

We hung up, and I put the pen back down and picked up my phone, shooting Matt a text.

Me: *Going to be a couple hours late. Need to cover for Hanson. Should be done by eight at the latest.*

He texted back right away.

Matt: *You're killing me, Smalls. I'm dying over here. I miss you.*

Me: *I miss you, too. Where should I meet you? Home? Out?*

Matt: *I'm going to need all the drinks to numb the agony of waiting for you to get off. I'll go to Stabbur and sit at the bar. Alone. Pouting. Sad. Devastated. Distraught.*

Laughing, I shook my head.

Me: *Quit being an ass. You'll be fine.*

Matt: *Yeah, drinks will help. Maybe. Probably not :(*

Me: *Ass.*

Matt: *LOL. Kidding. Text when you're done. I'll save you a stool. We can have a drink then go to dinner.*

I sent back a kiss emoji and set down my phone. Just two more hours. I could make it.

The door opened, and I heard the irritating sounds of high-pitched girly squeals flooding into the bar.

"Isn't it the *cutest*?" a shrill voice asked, eliciting oohs and aahs.

"It is! Darling!" another voice said.

"See, I told you girls we had to come here. And the margaritas are the best!" the original voice said.

Wait.

I knew that voice.

The hair on the back of my neck rose as a snake of rage slithered down my spine.

Spinning around, I lowered my head while I searched the group of girls for the owner of that voice I never wanted to hear again. When I saw her step through the group of six over-dressed girls, my eyes narrowed into slits.

Red hair fell off her shoulders in soft waves. Red hair I wanted to grab and pull while I dragged her back outside. Pink lips pulled into a grin when she saw me. Pink lips I wanted to pummel with my fist. Her ivory skin was unmarked by so much as a blemish, and I wondered what it would look like swollen and covered in the bruises I'd like to paint it with.

"Oh. My. God!" she screeched when she saw me. "Jo! What are you doing here?"

"Fucking, Nikki," I snarled under my breath, clenching my fists. *What the hell is she doing here?*

"You guys!" she waved in her friends. "This is my friend, Jo! We totally grew up together. I told you it was the smallest world up here. Didn't I tell you?"

"Hi, Jo!" they mirrored, their sugar-sweet tones

almost giving me a toothache.

Ugh. It was like Nikki had cloned herself in some apocalyptic plan to overrun the world with an army of shallow, pretentious, shitty people.

"I just can't believe you're working here!" She climbed into a stool, and her minions followed suit, stretching the length of the bar. Just a minute ago I'd have been thrilled for the bodies, but now I would have killed for every stool to be empty. "I didn't know you left the Blue Ox. I mean, I didn't go back there this weekend because, well, you know." She faked an oopsie face and dissolved into giggles. "Figured Jake wouldn't want to see me."

"He's not the only one," I growled through clenched teeth.

"Oh, Jo! You're so funny." Her cackle made me crave the delightful melody of fingernails on a chalkboard.

"What are you doing here, Nikki?" Stiffening my jaw, I leveled her with a glare.

"Oh, you know. Me and the girl squad needed to get out of Chicago for a little getaway. I told them about Door County, and they just *had* to come. Didn't you girls?"

Like bobble-head dolls tethered together by a pole, their heads lifted up and down in unison. Paired with their matching blonde hair and overdone makeup, I began to wonder if they were clones and I was seeing double... or triple... or whatever the hell they called six-vision. Though Nikki sported the same designer clothes and exaggerated make-up, she at least rocked a different hair color. And once again the flash of red begged me to grab it and yank her to the floor and drag her right out the door.

"So, we blew out of the city, rented a some rooms in Sister Bay, and we're here for the whole week. So good to be home. I missed you guys!"

Nikki had always been selfish, trapped in her own narcissistic world where nothing mattered but her. But this complete and utter lack of understanding of how much we hated her was enough to make me wonder if Matt really had kissed me senseless. I mean, I *was* seeing in septuplet vision. Maybe I'd hallucinated Nikki into being. I shook my head and looked again. Nope. She still sat on one of my bar stools like a delusional whore with her whore posse, thinking I could actually be friends with the likes of her.

Friends after she'd cheated on Jake. Friends after she'd kissed... Matt.

My Matt.

The visual flashed into my mind and I closed my eyes against it. It was bad enough picturing Matt with Nikki when we he and I were just friends, but now, after having spent all night in bed with him, the visual amplified to unbearable levels.

And with it, so did my rage.

It ripped open the wound I'd just managed to close, and it made the pain that much more excruciating. My hands trembled as anger coursed through me.

Anger at her.

Anger at Matt.

No. I struggled to stop the spiral. Matt had earned his forgiveness. My anger toward him was gone and it needed to stay gone.

It had to. I loved him.

But the anger inside me needed to go somewhere, and a redhead sitting at the bar made a perfect target.

I stomped my foot like the bull staring at the red cape. Salivating. Snorting.

Charging.

"Are you fucking kidding me?" I spat.

Nikki sat back, the whites of her eyes flashing for a moment before she rolled them and sighed. "Oh, Jo. You aren't still pissy with me, are you? That was *so* last year."

She turned to her friends. "Jo is best friends with..." she covered her mouth and whispered his name, "Jake. My ex."

"Oh!" The echoed and vacant eyes all turned back to me at once.

So creepy.

"How is Jake? Is he still puttering around Baileys Harbor?" she smiled, and I wondered why I couldn't see fangs in place of her perfect white smile.

My eyes narrowed into slits, unable to tolerate her haughty expression. "Don't you dare ask about Jake."

"Oh, come on. It was an accident. Is he all better? I did feel pretty bad."

She faked a grimace, and I glanced at her hair again. One quick sweep of my hands and I could yank her over this bar and start working on those bruises I kept envisioning.

"*Jake* is better than ever if you must know. He's engaged now."

"Is that so? To who?" she scoffed.

I smiled.

No.

I gloated with my mouth.

Leaning forward on the bar, I tipped my head. "Didn't you hear? I figured you would have. Have you girls ever heard of Cassandra Davenport?" I asked, knowing this group of wannabe fashionistas probably worshiped the ground she walked on. The queen of high society, Cassandra Davenport's former lifestyle probably remained the stuff of envy for a vapid bunch of automatons like this crew.

"Oh my God, yes!" one of the clones answered, and the rest excitedly shook their heads. "We love her! I saw her at a club in Chicago once!"

Leaning forward a little closer into Nikki's space, I let my gloating grin grow like ivy up a trellis. "Well, it turns out you cheating on Jake was the best thing that ever happened to him. You see, right after we ran you out of town, Jake met someone. Cassandra Davenport, or Cassie as we call her. And now they're engaged. Engaged! Isn't that the best news ever?" I stopped gloating only long enough to clap my hands together a few times.

If she wasn't wearing so much makeup, I know I would have seen the color drain from her face. Instead, all I got were blinking eyes and a slack jaw.

"Shut up!" one of the clones shouted. "Cassandra Davenport lives up here? Oh my God! Can we meet her?"

They squealed in unison, but I didn't let the assault to my ears break the stare I had with Nikki. Nope. I was enjoying watching the horror dancing in her eyes.

"Yep. She lives here with him." Her confident facade dissolved completely, and I marched in through the opening. "I'd say he upgraded, wouldn't you, Nikki?"

"Seriously! Can we get her autograph?" One girl asked, but I ignored her.

"Thank you, Nikki. Thank you so much for being a trashy, self-centered whore. You cheating on Jake was the greatest gift you could have given him. Now he can be happy. Like *really* happy. And rich! So filthy, fucking rich he could buy a jet if he wanted one. Wait... they already have one. So, thank you."

My unveiled insult finally shook her from her shock. "I— I'm happy for him." Lifting her chin, I watched her struggle to regain her composure. "Really I am." A fake smile lifted her lips, and she shifted in her stool. "And Matt? Do you two still hang out?"

Hearing his name roll off her tongue dumped kerosene onto my wildfire of rage. Heat coursed through my veins like lava, and I was sure it funneled out my eyes in the form of laser beams. Clenching my fist, I pressed into her space.

"If you ever so much as breath his name again, I will come over this bar and finish what I should have done last year. Now take your Stepford friends and get your ass the hell out of my bar. And don't you ever fucking come back."

Nikki rocked back in her stool, but this time she didn't try to deflect my anger and play it off as a simple misunderstanding. This time she knew I meant it.

Because I did.

"Come on, girls. Let's go." Keeping as far out of my reach as she could, she slid off her stool and hurried out the door.

My hands shook as I struggled to quiet my breathing. While I watched the girls rush down the street, I forced my feet to stay planted and not take off after her like they were begging to do.

"*Damn...*" Sheena whistled, and I turned to see her standing at the corner of the bar. "Remind me not to get on your bad side!"

The lighthearted remark and the smile on her face calmed me down. "Sorry. I hate that chick."

"I kinda came to that conclusion when you called her, what was it? Oh yes. A trashy, self-centered whore. Nice."

Laughter shook my shoulders and helped slough off the tension Nikki's sudden appearance had created. "Yeah. I *really* hate that chick."

"I'm sure she deserves it. But again... I'm staying on your good side." Sheena sucked the air through her teeth and disappeared around the corner.

While I wiped the bar and tried to let the last of my fury fade away, visions of her wrapped in Matt's arms kept popping in my mind like a Whack-a-Mole game. Just when I shoved one image out of my head, another popped back in. And with each vision, a little more of my rage returned.

Rage, or was it fear?

Fear he still wanted her. Fear he'd hurt me. Fear he'd abandon me.

Just like my father.

That familiar voice whispered in my ear, goading

me, telling me to run, begging me to pull the ripcord and float far away, guaranteeing me a soft landing.

I knew that voice well. It had controlled my relationships for a long time, and Matt was always the other voice on my shoulder reminding me to be brave. Reminding me that not every man was a liar and a cheater like my father.

But in the end Matt had no right to say those things.

The image of him pressed against Nikki's lips sent my stomach tumbling, and I braced against it again. Despite always being my shoulder to cry on and voice of reason, he'd been the one who'd betrayed his best friend. He'd kissed Jake's girl. I felt my grip slipping while I tried to hold on tight to the memories of how happy I was in his arms. How safe he made me feel. How safe he'd *always* made me feel.

It's over, Jo. He's forgiven, I reminded myself over and over again. Each time hoping I would believe it.

He loves you *now. Remember that.*

One thing I knew for sure, Matt wasn't my father. When my father had left, it had been Matt who'd been there for me. He'd always been there for me, without fail. And as hard as it was for me to trust, if there was one man on this planet that deserved the honor, it was Matt.

Instead of picturing him with his tongue down

Nikki's throat, I tried to flood my mind with images of his tongue in my mouth instead. And his hands on my body. And the sound of his voice whispering "I love you" into my ear over and over again.

Finally, I started to see past the hurt she'd brought with her, and my excitement to see him tonight grew.

The voice in my head warning me to bail quieted down, and I felt my rage and fear quieting along with it.

I didn't want to pull the ripcord this time. This time, with Matt, I wanted to free fall. To throw away all my fears and trust he would catch me before I hit the ground. This time I wanted to trust that Matt would be my safe landing.

I took a deep breath and exhaled the rest of my anxiety. In two hours I'd see him again, and I knew the moment I was back in his arms, I'd be okay again. Tonight was about us. Me and Matt. And to hell if Nikki's appearance was going to put a damper on our first date... a night I'd spent my whole life dreaming about.

Too stubborn to let her win, I forced the last vision of them out of my head. Glancing at the clock, I went back to counting the minutes until I got to see him again.

CHAPTER SEVENTEEN

MATT

"Another?" DJ, the bartender at Stabbur, asked.

I glanced at my cellphone. Jo should be off any minute.

"Sure, and can I get a Malmo Mule for Jo?"

"You got it." DJ smiled and hurried off.

After a day in the summer heat sweating up a storm while I worked on our cabin, I welcomed the cool breeze blowing off the lake across the street. One of my favorite things about moving to Sister Bay were all the open-air bars and restaurants, and Stabbur Beer Garden was no exception. The outdoor bar across from the Sister Bay beach, and right next to Al Johnson's Swedish Restaurant, provided the perfect place to sit outside and enjoy the fresh air. Living in Wisconsin meant spending large chunks of the year trapped indoors hiding from the cold weather. So, when summer hit, I spent as much time outside as I could. Stabbur was the perfect place to unwind tonight, enjoying the beautiful weather and good cocktails that helped to ease the ache of missing Jo.

And the nerves about our first date.

I'm going on a date with Jo.

It felt surreal. Too good to be true. I mean, I'd spent all morning testing ways to ensure I really was awake, and this wasn't a super vivid dream, but I still wasn't convinced yet. Between hearing Jo say, "I love you, too", and getting a job offer all in one day, I began to wonder if I'd hit my head working on the cabin yesterday and maybe I was stuck in a coma in the hospital in a perpetual dream I may never wake up from.

Not that I'd want to.

If being in a coma meant an imagined and realistic life with Jo at my side, then I'd take a coma any day.

"Here you go," DJ said, dropping off our two drinks.

This coma even came with drinks.

"Put it on your tab?" he asked.

Damn it. I still had to pay for drinks in my coma. "That would be awesome."

Another customer flagged him away, and I put Jo's drink in front of the stool next to mine. The bar was filling up, and I'd promised to save her a seat. If there was one thing I intended to do from this day forward, it was to never let her down. Never give her a single reason to doubt me like I knew she eventually would. I'd give her no ammo to blow apart this relationship and bolt off like she'd done with every other guy in the past.

Fear gripped me when I envisioned her "pulling a Jo" as I used to call it. The minute things got serious, she searched for an out. For any excuse to bail. And for Jo and me, we'd hit serious in less than twelve hours. A record time for my gun-shy girl. Hell, a record time for me. Normally it took her months to inch her way deeper and deeper into a relationship. Months to even refer to a man as a boyfriend. And it was always then when she'd slam on the brakes and bail.

Like clockwork.

While I'd always been there to catch her when she'd whipped open the emergency exit and leapt out, I'd also always been secretly thrilled she was single again. It was torture seeing her with someone else. But now, this time, I was the man driving the relationship train, and my stomach twisted in knots thinking it may be our train she would derail next.

She won't, I thought, trying to calm the anxiety rising with the thought of losing her.

She won't because this time it's *us*. This time it's different.

I would give her no excuse. No reason to question my commitment to her. Not one slip-up to shake her trust in me. And that meant even something as small as keeping my promise to save her a stool.

"Is this seat taken?" a woman asked.

"It is. Sorry," I answered, guarding that stool with my life.

Not one reason.

While I sipped on my old fashioned, I checked my phone again.

Any minute now.

"Hey, dude!" Aaron said, and I turned to see him standing behind me. "I didn't know you were going out tonight!" He hopped into the stool, and I opened my mouth to protest, but then closed it. It would be easier to save a stool if I had a body sitting in it for the next few minutes.

"Hey, man. You back out in Sister Bay tonight?"

"Yeah, the Mullet Hunters are having their reunion show here tonight, so we thought we'd make the trek. Remember how much fun we used to have when they'd play?" He leaned back in his stool and played his air guitar.

"Oh, I remember." I laughed. "I'm hungover just thinking about it."

"Good times! Tony is in the parking lot trying to convince his girlfriend to come out and be our DD so he and I can both get lit."

Snorting, I shook my head. "I wish him luck with

that."

"Yeah. Not likely, but he's trying anyway. You out alone? Ready to par-tay? Get your Mullet Hunter jam on?" Rubbing his hands together, he gave me that mischievous smile he'd been sporting since we were kids.

"Nah. Not tonight."

"Why not? Come on, man! It's the *reunion show!* They never play anymore so everyone who's anyone is coming. It's gonna be awesome. And summer will be over before we know it. Let's do some dancing, drink some beers, find some hot girls... it'll be epic!"

I already had a hot girl. An amazing girl. The perfect girl.

A girl I didn't know if I should tell him about yet. Knowing how easily Jo spooked, I wanted her to be in charge of telling people about us. On her schedule.

"I'm good, man. But you guys should rip it up for sure."

"Oh, come on! What else do you have planned tonight? Nothing. That's what. So you're partying with us. It's a done deal."

Laughing, I shook my head. "Not tonight, Aaron. I've got... plans."

His orange eyebrows rose. "Oh yeah? Like, plans with a girl?"

"Plans I'm not talking about."

"Masturbating doesn't count as plans."

Almost spitting out my drink, I choked down my laugh. "That's not the plan!"

"So, it's a girl." His smile grew. "Who is she? Do I know her?" He looked down at the drink in front of him and his face lit up. "Is she here?

While Aaron searched the growing crowd, I just shook my head. "Who she is isn't important. But yes, it's a girl. And it's really, *really* new and I don't want to jinx it and tell you yet. So, just order a drink and get out of here before she shows up."

"A secret girl." He waggled his eyebrows. "I love a good mystery. Is she hot?"

"Very."

"Do I know her?"

"Not answering."

"I *do* know her!"

"Aaron, just please grab a drink and go. Don't fuck this up for me, man."

He blew out a defeated sigh then stuck his finger in my face. "Fine. But I want details later."

"Fine. Just go!" I gave him a playful shove, and he hopped off the stool.

Bob, the other bartender slinging drinks tonight, hurried past us but called over his shoulder, "Aaron, you need a beer?"

"Yeah, Bob! Thanks!"

Glancing over my shoulder, I worried Jo would arrive and see Aaron here and think I wasn't serious about tonight being a date. This wasn't a night to hang out with friends together. Tonight it was about us. Just us. A couple's night.

"Here you go. I'll start you a tab." Bob slid the beer into Aaron's waiting hands while he blew by.

"There. You've got a beer. Now get out of here."

"Who is it?" he asked one more time.

"Go!" I shoved him again.

He chuckled, but as he started away, he stopped and froze. "No freaking way, Matt."

"What?" I followed my friend's stare with my own.

"Dude. That is fucked up. Seriously? You're dating Nikki?"

"What?" I choked, searching the crowd harder. "What the hell are you talking about?"

Aaron spun to look at me, disappointment and condemnation stiffening his face. "Dude. Just because Jake is engaged now doesn't mean it's okay to go for Nikki. Bros before hos, and she is a bona fide ho. Does Jake know?"

"Does Jake know what? What the hell are you talking about?"

"Um, I'm not stupid, Matt. Your secret date? The one you won't tell me about. Yeah. Cat's out of the bag. And for the record, I think it's totally shitty and not even a little cool. Dude, you *just* got people to forgive you for kissing her in the first place. Have you lost your fucking mind?"

What the hell was he talking about?

"Not cool," he said, shaking his head as he started away.

"Aaron," I called after him. "I don't even know what—"

The crowd parted and I saw her.

Holy shit. Nikki.

She stumbled up the walkway with a flock of blonde floozies trailing behind her. It looked just like high school again. Nikki at the lead and her adoring protégés following behind like a row of lost ducklings.

A knot wound its way around my stomach, and I struggled to keep my mouth shut.

Aaron's harsh words slammed into me. Nikki. He assumed Nikki was my secret date.

And nothing could be farther from the truth.

As I watched her stumbling through the crowd, I realized she was already drunk. Her glassy eyes teased every man she passed, and I struggled to see what any guy saw in her. How I had chosen to spend so many years fixating on a distraction, even when she was with Jake.

And then I saw her flip her hair and giggle at a man who smiled at her, and I finally knew. I *finally* understood why it had to be Nikki all those years.

She was the opposite of Jo.

The polar opposite of the woman I really loved.

Putting all my energy into fixating on Nikki had helped me channel my love for Jo away. Far, far away. Convincing myself I was into a girl like Nikki helped me convince myself I wasn't into a girl like Jo.

How had I been so stupid?

The thought of having feelings for a girl like Nikki, even false and forced feelings, made me want to puke. The fact I'd taken those feelings so far I'd betrayed my best friend twisted my stomach into a knot so tight I worried I would never get it loose.

All the pain I'd put everyone through, myself included, had been my way of convincing myself I wasn't in love with Jo... when I knew damn well, I had been. And always would be.

Nikki's blue eyes skated across the crowd and headed straight for me.

Shit.

I spun around in my stool, pressing my elbows onto the bar and lowering my head, hoping she didn't see me. Praying she didn't see me.

"DJ, can I get my tab?" I whispered as he passed by.

"You got it."

Hurry, I wanted to scream. If Jo came here and saw Nikki, it would ruin our night. Hell, it may even ruin our relationship. One look at Nikki and I knew Jo's rage would resurface, and the fragile new bond we'd created last night could easily break. Her anger would incinerate it. I couldn't – *I wouldn't* – take the risk.

I pulled out my phone, clicked Jo's name and shot her a quick text.

Me: *Change of plans. I'll meet you at The Boathouse.*

DJ dropped off my tab and I handed him my credit card.

"Matt?" Nikki said, and I closed my eyes. Like a child, I pretended if I couldn't see her, she couldn't see me.

It didn't work.

"Oh my God!" she squealed and tossed her arms around my shoulders. "It *is* you!"

No. *Hell* no.

I leapt up off my stool and slid out of her grip. "Not happening, Nikki. Goodbye."

"Oh, come on, Matt! Not you, too." She pouted as I stepped farther away. She started to step toward me but teetered on her too-tall heels and stopped short. "I thought if anyone wouldn't be pissed at me, it would be you. I mean, it was *you* that got me into this mess."

"Nikki, you need to get the hell away from me. I've got nothing to say to you. Goodbye."

I turned away, leaning on the bar and silently begging for DJ to hurry and return with my card.

"Come on, Matt. Don't be ridiculous. You can't even *talk* to me now?" She dragged a finger down my back.

Hell no. I'll get my card later.

I shook off her hand and spun away, hurrying through the thick crowd.

"Matt!" she called after me, but I sped up when I made it through the throng of people. Racing through the parking lot, I hauled ass to my truck and away from Nikki.

I got to my truck and yanked the door open, but her hand appeared and slammed it shut.

Spinning around, I raked my hands through my hair. "Nikki. Get the hell away from me. Seriously. Go."

I reached for my door again, but she slid around me and leaned up against it.

"I don't want to put hands on you, but if you don't fucking move, I'm going to pick you up and move you myself."

"Matt. Seriously. Stop it." She stuck out her lower lip, and I saw her teeter.

"How drunk are you?" I asked, hoping she'd teeter again and stumble out of my way.

Gesturing with her fingers, she giggled. "A little buzzed."

"Well, take your way-more-than-buzzed ass the hell away from me, Nikki. We have nothing to talk about. Now go. Please."

"I'm sorry, Matt."

Nikki sorry? Well that had to be a first.

"I am. I'm sorry I caused you so much trouble. But I really did care about you, Matt. I always have." Reaching out, she tried to wrap an arm around my neck, but I sidestepped her. She lurched toward me and away from my door. I used the moment to leap forward, whipping open my door and sealing myself inside.

"Matt! Come on! This is crazy! Just talk to me!" She pressed her hands against my window.

I fumbled to get the keys in the ignition.

"You're not leaving until you talk to me," she demanded, then marched to the back of my truck.

I looked in my rearview mirror and groaned. Nikki stood behind my bumper, arms crossed and wearing that look of determination I knew well enough to know she wasn't moving.

"Fuck!" I slapped the steering wheel, then sat back and exhaled a breath.

I glanced at my phone. No response from Jo. Hoping she was still at work or had at least gotten my text, I opened the door and jumped out. The sooner I dealt with Nikki the sooner I could get the hell out of here.

"What?" I shouted, slamming the door after I landed on the ground. "What do you want?"

"To talk," she whined.

"Okay, then. Talk. But make it quick."

"Why are you so mad at me?"

"I'm not mad at you, Nikki. I don't care enough about you to be mad at you. I just don't want you anywhere near me. You fucked up my life enough already."

"Hey, you were part of that decision, too!"

Exhaling a groan, I scrubbed a hand down my face. "You're right. I was part of that decision. And it was a *bad* one. And I stopped it before it went even farther. *That* was a good decision. And the best decision right now is to get you as far away from me as possible. I don't want you in my life, Nikki. So please, just let me go."

"I still have feelings for you, Matt." She reached forward, but I stepped out of her reach.

"No, you don't. You don't have feelings for anyone other than yourself. You only want me because you can't have me. And you can't. Not ever again."

"Matt, I have *always* wanted you. You know that. And now we can finally be together. Jake is engaged now so he can't even be pissed."

Her motivations slapped me in the forehead. She heard Jake got engaged, and she wanted to use me to get back at him. Typical Nikki.

Not happening.

"We will *never* be together. Are you listening, Nikki? Never. Now, we're done talking and I am out of here. I'm getting back in my truck, putting it in reverse and driving out of here. If you're still behind it when I do, then that's your problem."

I turned to leave, but she grabbed ahold of my shirt. "Matt, stop!"

Desperate to be as far away from her as possible, I yanked myself out of her grip. The force of my movement sent her tumbling forward, and she screamed as she tripped and headed toward the ground. Even though I hated her, I would never be the kind of man who would let anyone, even Nikki, fall.

I scooped down and caught her in my arms, steadying her as she stumbled back to her feet. She wrapped her arms around my neck as I waited for her to find her balance.

"You're my hero," she whispered, pressing her face into my neck.

"You're okay. Just quit drinking for the night and go home."

Nikki snuggled in even deeper while my stomach

churned. "Matt, take me home."

"Your friends can do that. Now you need to–"

My voice stalled out when I saw her standing in the parking lot.

Jo.

I glanced down at Nikki, still pressed against my chest with her lips brushing my neck.

"Jo, this isn't what it looks like!" I called just before she spun and bolted back toward Stabbur.

I tried to shake Nikki off, but she wobbled again, and I had to hold her up.

"Jo!" I shouted just before she disappeared around the corner.

FUCK!

CHAPTER EIGHTEEN

JO

Matt shouted my name, but I didn't turn back.

I couldn't. Tears brimmed my eyes and to hell if I would let him... and *Nikki*, see me cry.

I knew it. I fucking knew it.

Nikki hadn't been home more than two minutes and already she'd wormed her way back into his arms.

Wasn't in love with her my ass. Of course, he was. *Everyone* was in love with Nikki, though only God knew why.

Sure she had perfect tits, legs up to her neck, and that shiny red hair that never seemed out of place. But how could he not see past that? How could he be so blind to her selfish, ugly insides?

I pushed through the crowd at Stabbur, racing back toward my Jeep parked out front in the road. It seemed like the bodies had quadrupled since I'd arrived only a few minutes ago, looking for Matt. When I'd gotten here, I'd expected to find him holding a stool... not holding Nikki.

Ugh! I ripped out an internal scream as the image of her wrapped in his arms invaded my mind again. Her lips on his neck. His arms around her waist.

Nausea churned in my stomach, and I was grateful I hadn't eaten dinner yet because after that sight, it would have come back up.

So stupid. How in the hell had I allowed myself to forget what he'd done just last year? He'd thrown away his friendship with Jake for one taste of her lips, and now he was doing the same damn thing to me.

But it wasn't friendship he was throwing away this time. It was so much more.

Or at least that's what I had thought it was.

Apparently, I was wrong. *Dead* wrong.

Then I remembered the look in his eye when he'd said he loved me. Remembered the passion buried in his kiss. My steps slowed as I tried to get control of my emotions. Maybe I was wrong. Maybe I'd walked in on a moment that had only looked bad, and this was my natural inclination to overreact resurfacing. The broken heart my father had left behind trying to protect me by forcing me to bolt before things got serious. But this time, they already were serious.

I inhaled a deep breath and blew it out.

He wouldn't do this to me. I'm mistaken. He loves me.

I tried to pound that into my head so I could spin back around and go face him. I'd promised him I wouldn't run, and that's exactly what I was doing. I needed to gather my courage around me like my favorite leather jacket and demand he explain what I'd just seen. Talk to my best friend, the man I loved, and hope that he had some other explanation.

He loves me. He wouldn't do this.

As that certainty started to quell the heartbreak seeing him in her arms had caused, I blew out a breath and did the one thing I'd never done before. I started back to face him instead of running away.

"Jo!" Aaron called, but I ignored him as I tried to push through the bodies standing between me and the conversation I needed to have with Matt. "Jo!" he called again, and I felt him grab my arm.

"Not now, Aaron!" I struggled free and started to hurry away.

He jogged to keep up. "Jo, seriously! Stop. You need to talk to Matt. He's your roommate so maybe you can talk some sense into him."

Aaron's concerned tone spun me around to face him. "I'm going to talk to him right now." I pushed my brows together. "Bu what do you mean talk some sense into him?"

"Good. Go talk to him, or better yet, go kick his ass. Did you know he was dating Nikki again?"

My already swirling thoughts refused to stop. "What?"

My heart ached as it began constructing the walls once again, pinning it in with the pressure that made it hard to breathe.

It's real? The unfaithfulness I just saw with my own two eyes? Wait. If Aaron knows, then how the hell long has this been going on?

"Yeah, fucking Matt is dating Nikki again. And it's just the shittiest thing ever. Seriously. You need to talk some sense into him. Jake will kill him if he finds out, and rightfully so. I'm pissed off myself. I guess you were right when you didn't want to trust him again. Totally didn't see that one coming."

The tears stung as I blinked them back, the haze of betrayal causing my vision to blur.

Don't cry. Don't cry. Don't cry.

"Just talk to him, Jo. Tell him that it doesn't matter how dumbstruck in love with her he is, that shit needs to stop. Now. He'll listen to you."

My mouth opened but words refused to form on my tongue. *Dating* her? If Aaron knew about Nikki, then this wasn't some random hook up I'd walked in on. Was it? But how? Why? My mind raced trying to make sense of the scene I'd just witnessed. And now... now I'd heard the truth straight from Aaron's lips.

Had it been going on when he'd kissed me last

night? Told me he loved me? Took me to bed? Had every second that I'd spent wrapped in his arms been a lie?

"I have to go," I whispered, spinning away.

Lick my wounds.

Cry a river of tears.

Harden my heart and regroup.

My strides sped up until I was racing down the street in Sister Bay. All I wanted now was to go home. I wanted to throw myself on the bed and yank the covers over my head and cry. Something I hadn't done in years.

But as I got in my car, I realized home wasn't my sanctuary anymore. Home was where Matt lived. The bed I wanted to curl up in was the same one where we'd spent all night making love. No. Not love. Not anymore. Nothing about home felt safe now, and I hated him even more for taking that away from me. He'd taken away the safety of my own home when I'd let him move into the other room. A room I intended to toss his lying ass out of faster than he could blink.

I reached my Jeep and jumped inside, firing it up and slamming it into gear. The tires squealed as I skidded out onto the street, darting between cars puttering along as their drivers stared up at the goats on the roof of Al Johnson's Swedish Restaurant.

"Move!" I screamed at them, desperate to get the

hell out of here and away from Matt. And Nikki.

Ugh! The image of her in his arms slammed into my mind again.

When the traffic finally gave way, I tore down the street to my cabin. Gravel ground under my tires as I slammed to a stop in my driveway, and I left the Jeep running while I ran inside to grab a few things I needed so I could crash at my sister's house.

The sight of the finished railing on the porch slowed me to a crawl. Matt had put so much time into our little cabin... *my* little cabin, and now I saw visions of him everywhere I looked. I could picture him sitting on the roof, shirt off, smiling down at me while he showed me his handiwork. I envisioned him securing the last of the wood for the railing, his proud grin deepening his dimples while he stood back to admire it. As I made my way up the steps and into my living room, the sadness drove deeper into my gut when I saw the finished driftwood coffee table in front of the new couch.

Its beauty stole the very breath from my lungs. And it reminded me of him.

As I looked around, my whole cabin reminded me of him. Even Petunia, as she rubbed up against my leg, and I remembered he'd finally won her over, just like he'd won me over.

And then he'd betrayed me.

I'd never known true heartbreak until today. Until just now. I'd never let myself care enough about a man to let one truly hurt me. And then last night I'd ripped open the walls around my heart and let Matt waltz right on through into the uncharted territory. Instead of taking good care of my fragile heart, the one already held together by tape and glue after what my father had done to it, he'd ripped it from my chest and stomped it into pieces.

And that emotional deception hurt the most. He knew how hard it was for me to trust and to put myself out there. He knew saying, "I love you" wasn't something I spit out to every hot guy who looked my way. It was special. It was rare. And it hurt more than I'd ever imagined possible that he'd been able to betray me, even knowing how much damage he would cause.

"Petunia, mommy has to crash at your auntie's for a couple days," I said to her as I grabbed her bag of cat food. She purred while I overfilled the bowl. As she munched on the fresh morsels, I grabbed my tote bag and tossed a couple outfits inside, as well as my pajamas, a couple pairs of underwear and some socks. While Petunia chirped away at her bowl, I hurried into the bathroom and grabbed my toothbrush and makeup bag and shoved them inside my tote as well.

Having all the supplies I needed for a few nights at Jenna's, I walked into the kitchen and grabbed the grocery notepad and a pen. With rage guiding my hand, I wrote Matt a note and tossed it on the island.

"Be good, Petunia. I'll be back in a couple of days. Matt will take care of you until I'm home." I leaned down and gave her a scratch then started out the door. With one last look over my shoulder at the cabin I'd been so happy in only this morning, I raced down the stairs and jumped in my Jeep.

I shot Jenna a text I would be staying with her for a few days, then turned off my phone before she could text back. Matt's apologetic calls and texts were certainly coming, and I didn't want to hear it. His apology. His "I'm sorry I hurt you, but I love her." I couldn't.

I wouldn't.

Jake may have forgiven him when he'd been the victim of their love, but not me. I'd gone against my better judgement and let him back into my life, and I wasn't one to make the same mistake twice.

Fool me twice and we're done.

Period.

I'd gone against my better judgement once and let Matt fool me twice, and I wasn't going for a third.

With one last glance at my cabin, I put my Jeep in reverse and backed out onto the highway. The tears blurred my vision as I glanced in my rearview mirror one last time, but I wiped them away, lifted my chin and vowed not to look back again. Not at my cabin, and certainly not at the memories of me and Matt that kept bubbling up in my mind.

No more.

Me and Matt were done.

Matt

"Would someone *please* find her friends!" I shouted to no one in particular while I dragged Nikki back into Stabbur's bar area. Each time I'd tried to set her down and race after Jo, she'd started wailing, and twice on our way from the parking lot, she'd thrown up. Desperate to unload this unwanted burden and find Jo to explain, I dragged her reluctant body back to the bar.

Jo's tragic expression played in my brain on repeat. Torturing me until I couldn't stop the panic choking its way into my throat.

"I want to go home," Nikki whined, words slurring while she clung to my waist.

"I want you to go home, too," I grumbled while I scanned the crowd for the flock of blonde's she'd come with. Finally I saw them preening themselves by the bar, so I lifted Nikki up and dragged her through the crowd.

When I got there, they all turned to look at us, snickering when they saw Nikki slumped in my arms.

"You guys got her this drunk; you guys can deal with the aftermath."

"Oh my God, Nikki!" One girl laughed as she stared at the teetering redhead beside me. "You're wasted!"

The rest of the girls joined in with their drunken giggles, and I rolled my eyes while I pushed Nikki forward into their huddle. "Here. Take her."

"What the hell are we supposed to do with her?" the tallest girl asked, regarding Nikki like yesterday's trash.

"Take her back to the hotel. Now."

"Nikki is the one who knows this place. I don't even know where our hotel is."

"You've got to be fucking kidding me." I scrubbed a hand down my face and looked around for any sign of Jo. But I knew better, she was long gone. And with good right. When she'd seen Nikki in my arms, it looked bad.

Real bad.

"She's pretty wasted." One girl finally acknowledged Nikki's sloppy state. "We should probably get her back to the hotel. Can you like, call us a cab or grab us an Uber or something? My phone died."

"You're in Door County not Chicago. We don't have cabs, but we do have a few Ubers. DJ," I called to him as he ran by. "Can you get these girls an Uber? They need to go. Like now." I nodded to Nikki as she swayed back and forth.

DJ stopped and arched a brow and jutted a finger at her. "Yikes. I didn't do that to her." He shook his head, pursing his lips while he raked her up and down. "I can try an Uber, but it may be awhile. They'll need at least two for that many people, and it's busy as hell up here tonight. You should probably just run her home. That girl needs to be far, *far* away from anywhere serving booze."

"Thanks, man. I'll figure something out."

I didn't want to deal with this. Jo took priority over everyone, especially this selfish pain in the ass. But when I saw Nikki start toppling over, and her entourage did nothing to stop her fall, I caught her in my arms again and groaned.

"Nikki, where is your hotel? Where are you staying?" I asked her.

"At your place," she cooed with a crooked smile.

"Seriously, Nikki. Where are you staying?"

"Your bed." Biting her lip, she winked at me with one glassy eye.

"For fuck's sake," I growled. "And you girls really don't know the name of your hotel?"

The ones still paying attention shook their blonde heads. Nikki dragged a finger across my chest, and I had to stop myself from dropping her on her ass and leaving her to deal with her own mess. But I forced myself to continue propping her up. I may hate her guts, but I wasn't going to leave her out here so drunk she couldn't even find her way home. I needed to get these girls home... if I could even figure out where they were staying.

Aaron leaned against the bar just down the way, and I saw his disdainful glare as he glanced in my direction.

"Aaron! Get over here!" I waved, but he just shook his head and looked away, taking a sip of his beer.

I knew that look. It was the same one Aaron and the entire town of Baileys Harbor had given me for months after I'd kissed Nikki last year.

But this time I didn't deserve it.

"Aaron! Seriously! Get your ass over here!"

With a heavy sigh, he grabbed his beer and sauntered over. "What?"

"Dude. This is *not* what it looks like. But Nikki is wasted, and we need to get these girls all back to their hotel. Nikki can't even walk."

He scoffed. "So not my problem. You can figure out how to get your little girlfriend and her friends home."

"She is *not* my girlfriend. *Jo* is my girlfriend. Or was. Since she saw this shitshow in my arms, she's probably halfway to Canada by now. I need your help to get Nikki back to her hotel safe so I can go find Jo and explain. Okay? Please, man. I'm in a world of hurt here."

"Wait?" He lifted a finger. "Jo is your secret girlfriend?"

"Yes. I'm not dating Nikki, I'm dating Jo. Nikki just showed up here wasted and threw herself at me. Apparently, she found out Jake is engaged, and this is all typical Nikki trying to get back at him. I'm not with her. I swear to God."

His eyes lit up, and he stuck a finger in my face. "Ha! I knew there was something up with you at the Sister Bay Bowl the other night! That was it, wasn't it? You and Jo? Really?"

"Busted. But right now she's hella pissed at me because she thinks I'm cheating on her with Nikki."

With widening eyes, he sucked the air through his teeth. "Shit."

"What?"

"I thought you were dating Nikki, too. The whole secrecy around the girlfriend, and then she showed up."

"Yeah. I get it. But I'm not, and I really need to get her the hell out of here."

He sucked more air through his teeth.

"What?" I asked while Nikki hiccupped in my arms.

"I may have seen Jo running out of here and told her to talk some sense into you because you were dating Nikki."

Son of a bitch.

"You didn't," I grumbled.

He nodded. "I did."

"Well, shit! Now she's *really* going to think I'm a stupid, cheating bastard!"

"Sorry about that, man. I just thought... well, you know what I thought. And I was pissed as hell you were doing that to Jake again. I didn't know about Jo." He paused, shaking his head. "You and Jo? Really? That's so awesome, man!"

"Well it *was* awesome until about fifteen minutes ago. Now, can you help me? I have to get to Jo."

"You got it. Tony's still sober. He can help get them back if we need to drive. Where are they staying?"

"I have no idea. Hey, you," I said to the tall one who seemed most coherent. "Where is your hotel?"

"I dunno." She shrugged.

"Is it close to here? In Sister Bay?" I asked, trying to keep my desperation to get back to Jo from coming out as barks.

"I think so. It's like on a hill or something."

"Are there any landmarks nearby you can think of?"

"Um?" She twirled her hair. "I think it's right near that bar we were at with a garage or something."

"The Garage Bar! Good! That's right up the hill from here. Were you across the street?"

"Yeah. I think so."

"Village View Inn," Aaron and I said in unison.

"Okay. We're going to show you how to get back."

Excited to get Nikki out of my arms and on her way, I started to let my thoughts travel to Jo. How I would explain this to her and stop the runaway train of relationship-ruining thoughts I knew were tumbling through her mind.

"Can you girls walk?" I asked.

They shrugged and nodded, but a few looked nearly ready to topple over like Nikki. She still lay suspended in my arms, mumbling nonsense as she twirled her fingers through my hair.

As much as I wanted to point them in the right direction and run after Jo, I knew they would never make it back to their hotel without help. With a grumble, I said, "Here's the deal. We're gonna walk you girls back to your hotel to make sure you get there safely. But we leave now." I turned my attention to Aaron. "Get Tony. We're gonna need all three of us to make sure they don't stumble into the road and get smoked by a car or wander off the wrong way and fall into the lake."

Aaron pulled out his phone and typed away while I took one last glance around the bar looking for Jo. But now knowing what Aaron had said to her on top of what she'd witnessed, there wasn't a chance in hell she'd stuck around. It would have sent most women running, and for someone with trust issues like Jo, I knew she was long gone.

"Okay, he's on his way from the parking lot," Aaron said as he put his phone away. "DJ! We'll be right back!"

"I'll keep your tab open!" DJ called as he sped past.

"All right, ladies," I said while I bounced Nikki up for a better grip. "You all need to follow us back to your hotel."

Tony appeared and looked stunned by the gaggle of girls teetering around us.

"My girlfriend is not gonna be pleased with me," he said as he slung his arm around the waist of one.

"Yeah. I know what you mean," I grumbled. "But we can't just leave them, so let's get this over with."

"Come on, ladies. Move it along, move it along." Aaron got behind them and herded them behind me. Like a herd of reluctant cattle, they argued every step of the way, but Aaron kept them moving along. Nikki mumbled some nonsense while we made our way through the crowd, but all I could think about was what Jo must be feeling right now.

All I'd wanted was to make sure I never gave her a reason to question my love for her, and yet in less than twelve hours I'd managed to shake us to the core. To hurt her. To make her doubt me. Everything I'd never wanted to do.

"I miss you, Matt," Nikki muttered, but I just rolled

my eyes and kept on walking with her.

"No puking on me, got it?" Tony said to his girl as we started walking along the busy Sister Bay streets with a pack of drunken bobbleheads sandwiched between us.

Nikki's glassy eyes blinked up at me before closing, her body going limper by the second.

Grumbling at the worsening situation, I lifted her up into my arms and held her tight against me while her head wobbled and settled onto my shoulder. At least now that she was passed out, she'd stop hitting on me, so there was that little morsel of joy in this shit situation. Even though it was a pain to carry her her, I hoped she'd stay passed out for the quick walk up the Sister Bay hill. The sooner I got them dropped off, the sooner I could haul ass back to the cabin to talk to Jo.

If she ever talks to me again.

I knew Jo better than anyone on this planet. She didn't need much of an excuse to launch out the emergency exit of a relationship, and what she'd seen with Nikki would give her the tiny nudge she needed to bail. The scene at Stabbur played like a big flashing sign screaming, "Danger Ahead. Exit Immediately." Aaron's slip of the tongue had only cranked up the fluorescent lights on that sign. But I had to find a way to explain what had really happened.

And make her believe it. Because Jo would fight

me every damn step of the way.

"I'm going to be sick," Nikki said, opening her eyes for a moment.

"Do *not* puke on me. We're almost there. Just hold it together a little longer."

She closed her eyes, and deep breaths lifted her shoulders.

Typical Nikki. She loved getting wasted, and this wasn't the first time I'd seen her this hammered, but I hoped it would be the last. I hoped this would be the last time I saw her *period.*

We marched the ladies up the hill past The Garage and The Alley Bar across the street. I saw enough familiar faces staring at me with wide eyes to know the rumor mill would already be churning.

I saw Matt with Nikki! Matt and Nikki are together! Matt's banging Nikki! What an asshole!

I could almost hear the gossip starting as I passed by all the people I knew carrying the woman I'd betrayed my best friend with in my arms. It was like walking the streets with a scarlet "A" attached to my chest. Although this scarlet "A" was the red head in my arms. It brought back all the memories of the scornful stares I'd endured last year, and I knew Jake's phone would be blowing up in a matter of minutes. I made a note to get ahold of him as soon as I could with the truth instead of hearsay. Knowing the way the rumor mill churned up here, people would be testifying they saw me having sex with her in the streets.

But first, I had to handle Jo. This time Jake would have to wait.

I groaned, pushing my way the last few yards to the driveway at The Village View Inn.

"We're here," I said. "Which room is it?"

"My hero," she whispered in my ear as I lifted her down until her feet hit the pavement.

I kept a hand on her shoulder until she stopped wobbling. "You gotta quit doing this shit, Nikki. You're almost thirty. It isn't cute anymore."

"Whatever, Matt. I'm on vacation. Rosé all day! Just having some fun." Her crooked smile started, and she reached out and booped my nose. "You should try it. Stay for a while."

She wrapped her arms around my neck and pulled herself toward my face. The rank mixture of vomit and alcohol wafted up into my nostrils and I cringed against it, turning my head away.

"I'm going to get you settled, and then I never want to see you again, Nikki. Go back to Chicago and stay there."

"Whatever," she huffed, and the smell of that breath almost dropped me to my knees.

I carried her up the steps to the room the other girls were filing into. Tony and Aaron were helping them get situated, and when one started taking off her dress, the two of them exchanged a shocked glance and then looked to me.

Tony lifted his hands and backed toward the door. "I need to get out of here. If my girlfriend knew I was in a hotel room filled with blondes and one of them was half naked, I'd be sleeping on the couch for all of eternity."

"Dude," Aaron said. "Normally this would be my dream come true, but it's feeling a little pervy since I don't think any of them even know their names right now. I'm right behind you."

"Wait up." I carried Nikki over to the bed and tried to lay her down. She clung to my neck, trying to drag my mouth to hers.

"Don't go," she whispered as I reached back and tried to unlock her death-grip from my neck.

"Nikki, let go."

"Stay." She leaned up again.

Her friends giggled and laughed, as I struggled to get free.

"Kiss her!" they egged us on.

"Not happening," I argued, still struggling to get her fingers to unlock. "Nikki, I mean it. Let. Me. Go."

With a defeated sigh, she finally released her grip. "Fine. Whatever, Matt. Go."

"I plan on it." I pushed myself up and rubbed the

claw marks on my neck. "Goodbye, Nikki. I mean it when I say I hope this is the last time I ever see you."

She stuck up her middle finger, then rolled onto her side. The gaggle of girls mirrored the gesture, and I saw one snap a photo of the obscene gesture-fest as I left.

"You alive?" Aaron asked, leaning up against the railing outside the room.

"For now. I still have to find Jo, and *that* encounter I might not survive." I sucked the air through my teeth, and they mirrored the look. "Thanks for the help guys. Wish me luck with Jo."

"I'm really sorry I doubted you, and that I may have made things a wee bit worse with Jo." He motioned with his fingers while he grimaced.

"Not your fault, buddy. It was an honest mistake."

"Let me know how it turns out, and if you want me to talk to her and explain things, I'm totally game."

"Thanks, man." I bumped his fist with mine. "I think I need to deal with this solo, but if shit goes south, you'd better believe I'm making you come and explain your part in it."

"Deal."

With one last fist bump, I said goodbye to them and started jogging back down the Sister Bay hill to my truck. Finally, I could get to Jo. Explain how everything she saw, and heard, was one huge, horrifying misunderstanding.

After I reached Stabbur, I pulled out of the parking lot and drove back to our cabin. My heart sank when I got there and her blue Jeep wasn't in the parking lot. After putting my truck in park, I dialed her number, not surprised when it went straight to voicemail.

This was Jo. And Jo's flight response had definitely kicked in.

The only positive thing about her phone being off was that hopefully I'd find her before she saw all the texts tattling about how I'd been spotted all over Sister Bay with Nikki in my arms. No one knew we were dating, so they'd have no idea the impact those texts would have, but as Jake's bestie, she'd certainly be at the top of the text list to gossip about my exploits. Because *that* would really help my case.

Son of a bitch.

I slapped the steering wheel and slumped back in my seat. Maybe, just maybe, she would still come home tonight. And when she did, I would be waiting. Waiting to beg her forgiveness and make her listen.

With the weight of my disappointment crushing me into the ground, I walked up the stairs to our cabin and went inside. Petunia trotted up, greeting me with a meow.

"Hey, Petunia. I don't suppose Jo told you where she was going, did she?"

I stopped and gave her a scratch and then peeked inside Jo's room. The cat bowl overflowed with food. Not a good sign for her returning tonight.

"Where'd she go, Petunia? Jenna's?" I asked as I walked back into the living room. I saw the note on the counter, and my heart hammered against my ribcage as I hurried over to read it.

Dickhead,

You have 48 hours to get the fuck out. I'm leaving town for a few days, so take care of my cat while you're still there. And if I ever see your lying, cheating, asshole face again, I swear to God I'll tear it off. My phone's off so don't bother trying to call me, text me, or find me. Goodbye for good.

Jo

Well, that answered that. Leaving town? I thought maybe she'd go to Jenna's, but apparently that was still too close to me.

The man who she thought broke her heart.

I pulled the note to my chest and stumbled back to her bedroom. With a defeated sigh, I flopped down onto her bed.

The bed we'd just been in this morning.

The one where we'd spent all night tangled in each other's arms.

The scent of her shampoo still clung to the pillow,

and I inhaled a deep breath of it. Agony ripped through me while I pulled her blankets up over my chest. Jo needed space tonight, and if I tried to force the issue and find her, I knew she'd make good on that promise to tear my face off.

But just in case she checked her messages, I sent her one anyway.

Me: *I am not with Nikki. I swear to God, Jo. It was a total misunderstanding, and you'll know that once you learn the truth. I love you. Only you. Always have and always will.*

Setting my phone on the nightstand, I folded my arms and laid my head back on them. Petunia hopped up on the bed, and after giving me wary stare, she curled up along my side.

"We'll get her back, Petunia. We have to."

Her soft purrs soothed me while I stroked what remained of her patchy coat.

Jo had to come home eventually, and when she did, I'd be waiting.

THE OTHER ROOM

CHAPTER NINETEEN

JO

"Wake up, sleepyhead," Jenna whispered into my ear. For a moment I drifted back in time to high school, and my older sister was waking me up to make sure I didn't miss the bus.

Then I remembered Jenna's favorite wake-up call involved dumping cold water on my head.

I shot up in bed, pressing my back to the wall while I struggled to grasp the current calendar year.

"Whoa! Easy there, tiger!" She laughed.

I looked around, and seeing I wasn't in my childhood bedroom, but instead in Jenna's lavish guestroom, I exhaled a deep sigh.

"Sorry, flashbacks to you waking me up high school."

Her smile grew, and she pulled a glass of water out from behind her back. "You mean when I used to dump water on your head?"

"Don't you dare!" I shouted, lifting my hands to

shield my face.

Jenna's laugh filled the room, and she set it on the bedside table. "Just kidding. Those are expensive sheets, so I wouldn't dare. I thought you might be thirsty."

"Thank God." I blew out the breath trapped in my lungs. "I'm literally traumatized by that. You were such an asshole!"

She dipped into a curtsy, then giggled and flopped on the bed beside me. "Yeah, I was an ass growing up. But aren't you glad you have me now?"

She pulled me in for an obnoxiously tight hug, and I struggled to get free. "Quit hugging me, you weirdo."

"I can hug my baby sis anytime I want." She squeezed harder. "How are you feeling today?"

And just like that, the reason for my tortured night in her guest room came crashing back into me like a semi-truck.

The vision of Nikki with her arms around Matt's neck. His arms around her waist. Her lips pressed to his neck. It felt like time had rolled backward twelve hours, and I shuddered.

"So, you gonna tell me what the hell happened yet?"

Heaving a sigh, I closed my eyes, hoping the vision of Matt and Nikki together would fade to black.

No luck. Even with my eyes closed they stayed stamped behind my eyelids.

Last night I'd lied when I wrote the note to Matt about where I was headed, hoping to prevent him from showing up here. Instead of going out of town like I'd said in my note, I'd dropped in on Jenna. When she'd opened the door, I stood there blubbering, unable to form the words to tell her what had happened.

Having seen me cry on less than a handful of occasions, she'd understood the seriousness of the situation and shuttled me straight up to the guest bedroom, grabbing a bottle of wine off the counter along the way. For two hours I sobbed between sips of wine from the bottle, and for two hours she sat quietly at my side waiting for me to be ready to talk.

But I hadn't been ready. I didn't think I'd ever be ready to talk about what had happened; to find the words to explain how it felt to have my heart torn in two. Instead, I'd fallen asleep on my tear-soaked pillow with Jenna curled up at my side.

"Come on, Jo. You've got to tell me who's ass I need to kick. I've been working out with a punching bag and taking kick-boxing classes. Just give me a name and I'll put my practice to good use."

Her good-natured comradery made me chuckle, and I let my head flop on her shoulder.

"A name," she said again while she ran her fingers through my hair.

With a deep breath, I let it slip out. "Matt."

She pressed her cheek into my head and pulled me a little closer. "I figured that may be the name going to the top of my hit list. But why? I don't understand. Two nights ago he told me he loved you and he planned on telling you that night. What happened?"

"Fucking Nikki," I growled.

"Whoa." She sat up and turned me toward her. "What do you mean 'fucking Nikki'?"

"Well, thanks to you," I paused and gave her the evil eye, "Matt did indeed confess his love to me that night. And then I confessed mine. And for about twelve freaking hours life was perfect. We were well on our way to happily ever after."

"So, I was right! You *do* love each other." A triumphant grin stretched across her face but fell quickly when my glare narrowed. "Sorry, go on."

"What happened, oh meddling sister, was that after Matt and I had one magical night together, I went to meet him out for a date last night and found him in the parking lot with Nikki wrapped in his arms."

"Son of a bitch," she spat.

"Exactly. Son of a bitch."

She lifted her hand, closing her eyes for a second. "Wait. Wait, wait, wait. So, he told you he loved you two nights ago, asked you to meet him on a date the very next day, but then cheated on you with Nikki in the parking lot of the place you were supposed to meet him for a date?"

"Yep." I nodded, then picked up the water and took a sip.

Her nose crinkled. "That doesn't make sense."

"Well, it happened."

"Maybe you didn't see things right."

I scoffed. "Oh, I saw things right. Nikki in his arms, his arms around her waist, her lips against his neck. Trust me. The image is burned into my mind for all of eternity."

"It doesn't make sense." I saw the wheels turning in her mind. "Why would he tell you to meet him where he was going to cheat on you?"

"Actually, he sent me a text to meet him at The Boathouse, so he *was* trying to keep me away from there."

Her lips puckered while she kept searching for a rational explanation. "That is pretty incriminating."

"Oh, you want incriminating? When I took off running after I saw them, I bumped into Aaron who, get this, begged me to talk some sense into Matt for dating Nikki again."

Her eyes bulged and her mouth fell open. "Okay, yeah. Son of a bitch. Which one do you want me to beat up first? Matt or Nikki?" She glanced down at her hands and clenched them into fists. "Scratch that. I've got two hands. I can kick both their asses at once."

Even though forcing a laugh made my stomach flip over, I couldn't help but let a few chuckles slip out while Jenna shadow boxed in front of me.

"Both work great." I smiled, but as quickly as it came, it slipped away, and I felt the tears stinging behind my eyes.

"Oh, shit. Don't cry." Jenna stopped her impromptu boxing match and took my hand in hers. "I'm so sorry, Jo. This is all my fault."

"It *is* all your fault!" I sniffled. "Why couldn't you just keep your big yapper shut?"

"Because I knew you both love each other, that's why. And it's why this still doesn't make sense. I *know* he loves you. It's my superpower, remember?"

"Well, your superpower is busted as hell."

"But it's not," she said, then pursed her lips together for a beat. "I know he loves you. I do. There must be some rational explanation. There has to be."

"Jenna, as much as I wish there were, there isn't. I mean, come on. I saw them together with my own two eyes, and Aaron just confirmed it. And let's be honest, Matt isn't exactly the stand-up guy I always thought he was. He crossed the damn line with her last year *while* she was engaged to his *best friend.* I mean, who does that?"

"I'll admit it doesn't look good."

"I know what I saw. And even though I believed

him when he said he loved me that still doesn't mean he wouldn't fall back into her arms with one crook of her finger. She's like a freaking siren."

"A siren whose ass I'm gonna kick."

"Only after I get done with her."

We exchanged a sisterly smile. The kind we used to share when we were working together to trick mom with one of our sinister schemes.

"I'm really sorry, hun. I wanted this to work out for you so badly. I didn't want you to end up like me."

"What are you talking about?"

Before she could answer, her big bulldog, Arnold, trotted into the bedroom.

"Hey, buddy," I said to him when he reared up on his back legs, struggling to drag his brindle and white squatty body up onto the bed.

Jenna reached down and caught him under his rear and pushed him up the rest of the way. Big slobbery kisses coated my face, and I shut my eyes while I laughed and shoved him off.

"Quit it, Arnold!" He gave me one last kiss, then flopped onto Jenna's crossed legs.

"Hey, sweet baby boy." She closed her eyes and kissed him on his black nose. "Aunty Jo is here, and she's sad so I think she needs more kisses to cheer her up."

"No more kisses, Arnold. But thanks for the

morning bath." I wiped the last of the slobber from my face, then rubbed his wrinkled head and he let it settle into Jenna's lap.

"What did you mean 'turn out like you'?" I gestured around the extravagant spare bedroom in her beautiful house. "I'd say you've got a pretty kick-ass life."

"Yeah. I've got a great career, a gorgeous house, a shoe closet to die for, and this guy." She rubbed Arnold's head. "But notice what's missing from this life of mine?"

I shook my head.

"Someone to share it with. I spend every single day with couples who are madly in love and planning their lives together, and then I come home alone. I never wanted my baby sis to fall victim to the same insecurities I've had ever since Dad left. I wanted you to fall in love and trust someone the way I've never been able to."

"Well, I did trust someone. For all of twelve hours I trusted Matt and look where that landed me." I snorted, and Arnold tipped his head, then laid it back down.

"Yeah, I hear you. I did that once, too."

"You did? Who?"

Jenna rolled her eyes. "Remember? Carter? That dude in college I met on spring break in Hawaii?"

My eyes lit up. "Oh yeah! I forgot about him!"

"Yep. At least I got more than twelve hours of

happiness. I got five days of heaven before I caught him in bed with my roommate, so at least there was that."

"God! Men are such assholes!"

"Yep. He was my one attempt at shaking off the fear I had of trusting men. After that, the trust train chugged out of the station."

"So, at least you understand what I'm going through."

"Oh yeah, I get it. But," she said, lifting her fingers, "that doesn't mean I want you to stop trying."

"Oh, I'm soooo done trying. My trust train is barreling down the tracks as well. Maybe it will run into yours somewhere along the way."

Jenna laughed, but then shook her head. "I'm serious, Jo. Don't do what I did. Don't give up. So, Matt turned out to be a piece of shit... which I'm still having a hard time believing my superpower failed, but let's just say it did. So, he's an asshole, but that doesn't mean you won't meet a guy who isn't."

"And what about you? Will you be opening yourself up again after what happened to you?"

"Oh, hell no!" She laughed, then cleared her throat. "But we're not talking about me, we're talking about you. It's too late for me."

"You're only two years older than me. I'd say you still have plenty of time to find yourself a perfect guy since you think one exists for me. If one exists for me, then one has to be out there for you."

"I already have the perfect guy." She lifted Arnold's head and squished his chubby face.

"Well, I have Petunia. So there."

"That ugly-ass cat doesn't count."

"She's beautiful, and if Arnold counts, then Petunia counts."

"You're a pain in the ass."

"I learned from the best."

Her arched eyebrows mirrored mine, but then we both laughed.

"I am sorry, Jo. I hate to say I know exactly how you feel, but I do. Ugh, I was so freaking in love with Carter. Even though I only knew him for like a hot second, I was totally in love. From the second I saw him running out of the ocean with that surfboard in his hand, I was *gone*." She palmed her face. "Then add in some spring break cocktails, romantic nights on the beach, and that six-pack I could have washed my clothes on. Gone, gone, *gone*."

"Whatever happened to him?"

"No idea. I went back to my hotel room to meet him for our date and found him with his shirt off and Janine in his arms on the bed. I didn't even say anything. Just turned and ran out and never saw him again."

"He didn't call or anything?"

"He didn't have my number. Our cell phones got no reception in Hawaii, so we'd just been using our hotel room numbers to connect. And I was so pissed at Janine I didn't go back to our room until I had to get my bags the next day. I spent the whole night crying alone on the beach. The next morning I flew home. He went to school somewhere else, so after I left, that was it. Just gone for good."

"Oh, Jenna! That's so sad!" I reached out and took her hand. "I'm going to find him and do a little damage to his face while you kick the crap out of Matt and Nikki."

"The severely damaged Parker sisters are kicking ass and taking names." She smiled, and we both blew out a sigh.

"Dad really messed us up."

Nodding, she pursed her lips. "Yeah. He did."

"And now we're doubly messed up because we both tried the whole love thing once and it was an epic failure."

"Disasters."

"So, it's just us and our pets. Oh God." I shook my head. "We're going to be those weird, lonely sisters in the retirement home together, aren't we? The ones who never married and only have each other."

"We'll be the baddest bitches in there, though."

"Damn straight."

We exchanged a smile. "What are you going to do? I mean, you live with the guy."

"Not for long. I left him a note he has forty-eight hours to get out. Until then, I'm hiding out here until I'm sure he's gone."

"Has he called or texted?"

"Not sure. I shut off my phone last night."

"How are you not checking it? OMG! Turn that thing on and let's see what he has to say for himself."

I didn't want to look. I knew he'd have messaged by now and I dreaded reading whatever words he'd strung together to apologize. Or make excuses. Whatever it was, I didn't want to know. It would hurt too much.

"I think I'm going to throw my phone in the lake and change my number."

"Give me the phone. I'll look."

Even though I didn't want to see it, part of me was dying to know if he'd reached out. Or maybe he was still curled up in Nikki's arms and he hadn't even thought about me since.

That image almost made me toss up the half of a bottle of wine I'd downed last night.

"Fine. But don't tell me what it says."

"Deal."

I grabbed my purse from the nightstand and fished out my phone. After turning it on, I unlocked it and saw the message from Matt waiting.

My heart hammered at the sight of his name, and I passed it to Jenna with a shaky hand.

While she read the message, her lips pressed into a thin line, and worry lines creased her forehead.

"What? Is it bad?"

"It says—"

"Stop! Never mind. I don't want to know."

Ignoring me, she went on. "It says, 'I am not with Nikki. I swear to God, Jo. It was a total misunderstanding and you'll know that once you learn the truth. I love you. Only you. Always have and always will.'"

She looked up, and I swallowed the golf ball-sized lump forming in my throat.

"Are you *sure* you didn't misunderstand what you saw?"

Her arms around his neck. His arms around her waist. Her lips against his neck.

The same visual crashed back into my mind, and I shook my head. "No. I definitely saw what I saw. Aaron even confirmed it when I started to question it."

"Well he sounds pretty sincere."

A year ago I would have believed anything Matt told me. A year ago he was a stand-up guy. The person I trusted most in this world. And then he'd gone and done what he did and blew my trust in him out of the water. Now I didn't even recognize him anymore.

The phone rang, and she screamed and turned it toward me. Matt's name flashed across the screen, and I flew backward and slammed against the wall. "Turn it off! Turn it off!"

Fumbling with the buttons, Jenna hit ignore and squealed until it finally powered down.

"Oh my God! He called!" She tossed the phone back at me. "He must have been trying you all morning! That phone was on for like a minute!"

My heart raced so fast I thought it might jump out of my chest. I looked down at the dark screen and wondered if he was leaving a message.

I love you. Only you. Always have, always will.

The words Jenna had read bounced around in my head. But then they collided with the image of Nikki in his arms, along with Aaron's disgust with his friend, and I swallowed down my doubt.

"Doesn't matter. I'm not talking to him again. Matt's not who I thought he was, and the sooner I get him out of my life the better."

"Well, whatever you need, you know I'm here for you. You can stay as long as you'd like, and whenever you're ready for me to start kicking some ass, just say the word."

Exhaling a stilling breath, I nodded. "Deal."

"But we need to make one more deal."

"What's that?"

"You don't let this stop you from trying to find love. Don't let Dad, and Matt, win. You're a fighter, Jo. When this whole thing blows over, I want you to promise you'll put yourself back out there and try to trust again. Try to find someone who sets your world on fire."

I'd already found the man who lit my world on fire. Hell, he'd been scorching my world for over twenty years. Right now, the only thing I wanted to focus on was finding a fire extinguisher to finally douse his everlasting flame.

"Do we have a deal?" She arched a brow.

I didn't want to be too scared to trust again, but I didn't think I'd ever get past the hurt that had lived inside my soul since the day I found out my father wasn't ever coming back. That he didn't love me enough to stay. A father was supposed to be the person you could rely on no matter what... through thick and thin. And when he'd let me down, Matt had been my unshakeable foundation. But now, even he had cracked and crumbled beneath me, and I could feel my entire world shaking as it all fell apart.

"Jo, you have to promise to try. Don't end up like me."

"I can't promise I'll succeed, but I'll promise to try," I said, then stuck my finger in her face. "But only if you promise you will, too. Deal?"

Her dark eyes narrowed, and she bit her lower lip. "You suck. But deal."

I extended my hand, and with an exaggerated shake, we made our pact.

Deep down I knew I'd never find another man who made me burn like Matt, but I also wasn't one to go down without a fight. Men had taken so much from me, and Jenna was right that I couldn't let fear control my life anymore. Though I didn't know if I'd ever find someone I could trust again, I knew I at least had to try.

"I love you, Jo. You're going to get through this." Jenna pulled my hand into her lap. Arnold woke with a start when our hands brushed his head. His big brown eyes looked between us before he flopped his head back down and the sounds of his snores filled the room again.

"At least we've got Arnold and Petunia to keep us company in the meantime." Jenna smiled as she patted her dog.

"And each other."

And we did. As heartbroken as I was today, I knew I'd get through this with Jenna at my side. Now I just needed to get Matt the hell out of my cabin so I could move on with my life. A life without him.

CHAPTER TWENTY

MATT

"Call Jo," I said into the phone for the hundredth time today. It dialed her number, going straight to voicemail again. It rang only once, and when I'd heard that sweet sound I'd almost dropped it, so excited she was ready to take my call.

But two rings later it flipped back to voicemail.

Damn it.

I steered my truck down Jake's gravel driveway and pulled up in front of the house. Hank came bounding around the back of the house with Cassie's Brussels Griffon, Poppy, in tow.

"Hey, Hank!" I said as I hopped out. "Hey, Poppy!"

She hopped up and down on her back legs until I scooped her up in my arms.

"Well, what do we have here?" Cassie said as she opened the front door.

"Hey, Cassie! Welcome back!" I said between kisses from Poppy.

"Thanks! We got home last night. We had an incredible time."

"I'm so glad you two got some time away. Is Jake home?"

"Yep. Out on the dock fishing."

"Good. I need to talk to him. And you."

"Yeah?" She leaned against the doorframe and pushed a piece of blonde hair back into her casual ponytail. "About what?"

"Jo. Nikki. My hellish life."

Her eyebrows shot to her hairline. "Oh, boy. I'll get the coffee."

"Thanks, Cassie." I set Poppy down and reached into the back of my truck and snagged my fishing pole.

If there was anything that could help me dig myself out of this hole, it was a little fishing therapy with Jake. I walked around the house and back to the dock he had on Kangaroo Lake. Jake stood on the edge of the dock casting into the still water.

"Welcome home, buddy!" I called as I came down the dock.

"Hey, man! What's up?"

"Everything." I heaved a sigh. "I need help."

Jake arched a brow then reeled in his line before setting his pole down on the dock. "What did you do?"

"It's what I *didn't* do that has me in trouble. And I wanted to come tell you about it in person, since last time I was in this situation I didn't come to you right away and all hell broke loose."

"Is this about Nikki?" he said, his accusatory eyebrow lifting with a playful smirk.

My mouth fell open for a heartbeat but then I remembered where I lived. "Christ. You've already heard. Freaking people and their damn rumors. It's not what it looked like, okay?"

"I know," he said convincingly.

"You do?"

"Yeah. I mean, my phone blew up with pictures of you and Nikki, and texts saying you two were together, but I didn't buy it. I knew it was a misunderstanding. I trust you man. I know you wouldn't do it twice."

"Thank you!" I tossed my hands up in the air. "Now why can't Jo have come to the same damn realization as you? Of *course* I wouldn't do that again. It was all just smoke and mirrors manipulated by a self-centered bitch."

"Jo?" he asked, then crossed his arms as Hank settled at his feet.

"Here, coffee." Cassie came up behind me and stuck a mug in my hand.

"Thanks, Cass."

Jake stood waiting while I shook my head. "You

two can't go out of town anymore. A *lot* has happened since you've been gone, but I'll give you the short version. So, you know I moved in with Jo, who hated me."

"Yep," Jake said.

"Well, I got her to forgive me, and we got to be friends again. Which was great. But I've been hiding something from everyone, myself included. I'm head over heels in love with Jo."

"No way!" Cassie slapped my shoulder.

"Yes way." I nodded. "Like soooo in love. Like for forever."

"And how does Jo feel?" Jake asked, then gestured for me to pick up my pole.

I set down my coffee mug, then unhooked my lure from the eye and stepped to the edge of the dock. Jake picked his pole back up again, and together we cast into the water.

"Well, I fessed up a few nights ago, and it turns out she loves me, too."

"No *way!*" Cassie squealed and clapped her hands. "This is amazing!"

"Yeah, it was amazing... for about two seconds."

"Uh oh," Jake said. "Is this where Nikki comes in?"

"Yeah. This is *exactly* where Nikki comes in, and I wanted to come here and tell you in person before it got back to you in a bad way, which is what happened with Jo. But apparently you already know."

"Oh, boy." Cassie said. "What happened?"

"Nothing! I swear! But Nikki showed up in town, as you know. I was meeting Jo out for our first official date, and while I was waiting for her at Stabbur, Nikki appeared. And she was wasted. Darling Nikki was so drunk she almost puked on my shoes. I swear to God I tried to get away and avoid her. I would *not* get tangled up with her again. You've got to believe me on that. Okay?"

"Okay." He kept cranking his reel.

"But when I was getting in my truck, she showed up and blocked the door. And she was totally hammered. I tried to convince her to get away, but she stood behind my truck and blocked me from backing out. When I went to move her, her drunk ass fell, so I caught her. And that's when Jo appeared. Right when I had Nikki in my arms."

"Mother..." Cassie whispered. "That's not good."

"No. Not good at all. But I swear on a stack of bibles I was just trying to be a decent human being and make sure she didn't die on her way to the hotel. I never make the same mistake twice."

"Matt, I believe you. You screwed up once, and I know you wouldn't do it again. And that sounds exactly like something Nikki would do. She has a way of bringing drama with her everywhere she goes."

I scoffed. "Yeah, she does. So, here's the dilemma. I can't find Jo. When she saw us together, she bolted. But I couldn't go after her because Nikki and her pals were so wasted I couldn't leave them wandering around in that state, so Aaron, Tony, and I had to carry them up to their hotel."

"Ah, that would explain the pictures of you outside The Bowl with Nikki in your arms." Jake twisted his face into a grimace. "Man, people really know how to spin shit up here."

"Yeah. They should all be screenwriters or novelists with how imaginative they can be with things. I knew they would be spitting out rumors like a dirty game of telephone."

"Pretty much," Jake said on a chuckle. "I'd heard a handful of strange ones when I woke up this morning and saw the texts."

"Great. That probably means Jo has too." I slapped my head. "I didn't even get a chance to talk to her. By the time I got back to our cabin, she was gone."

"She must be so heartbroken," Cassie said, and I turned to see her hugging Poppy to her chest.

"Yeah. I'm sick about it. Not only did she see Nikki in my arms, but Aaron's dumbass assumed the same thing and as she was running away from me, he told her to have a talk with me about not dating Nikki."

"Shit," Jake mumbled. "Jo's gotta be wild. I'm

surprised you're still alive, to be honest."

"She won't take my calls and she said she's going out of town for a few days. Can you two try calling her? Maybe she'll pick up for you?"

"Of course," Cassie said, then pulled her phone out of her jean shorts pocket. I held my breath while she dialed, but after pressing the phone to her ear, she shook her head. "Straight to voicemail."

"Damn," I grumbled. "I love her so much you guys. I've always loved her, and it turns out she's the freaking reason I got myself mixed up with Nikki. Years of trying to convince myself I wasn't in love with Jo led to the whole shitshow last year. And the worst part? Turns out Jo's been in love with me all these years, too. All these years we could have been together, but we were both too stubborn and scared to admit it."

"Matt, this is awful." Cassie stepped forward and rubbed my shoulder while I cranked on my reel. "We'll fix it."

"We have to. I can't lose her, guys. I can't."

"It's Jo," Jake said, then cast his line again. "She runs hot, and she runs... like away."

"Yeah, don't I know it. My whole goal was to never give her a reason to doubt me ever, and it lasted all of twelve hours."

Jake shook his head. "Well, she may be able to avoid your calls, but she can't avoid you forever. You just need to push your way back in and force her to listen. You, my friend, have the truth on your side."

"She's stubborn as hell," Cassie added, "but she's also not crazy. She'll listen. Just stalk her at the cabin and JJ's until you can make her listen. You two love each other, and there's no way we're letting Nikki blow up another relationship."

"You think I should just wait around at JJ's and catch her at work?"

"Yep." Cassie nodded. "Go there every night and look for her. I had to force this guy to listen to me last year, and I'm so glad I was persistent."

The two of them exchanged a smile, and I hoped that someday Jo and I would share the same love they had.

If only I could find her.

"Thanks for listening, guys. I just needed to let you know to ignore any rumors you hear about me and Nikki and get your advice on Jo. I can't believe this happened at the worst possible time."

"Have faith in Jo and your love," Jake said. "She'll forgive you. She has to. You and Jo are meant to be. I'm surprised it took you two this long to figure it out."

"You knew?" I spun to look at him.

"No, I didn't *know,* but I suspected. More like, wondered why you two didn't get together. You're perfect for each other."

"You are perfect for each other," Cassie added.

"Well, let's hope I can convince her of the same thing."

I pulled in the last of my line and hooked my bait back onto the eye to keep it from swinging.

"Let us know if there's anything we can do to help." Jake gave me a smile. "We've got your back."

"You guys are the best. And seriously. No going out of town anymore. I was totally lost without you both."

Cassie laughed and tossed an arm around my shoulder. "Don't worry, Matt. It's going to be fine. Just get out there and go find your girl. Then tell her to call me when you're all patched up because I want to hear all the details about how you finally confessed your love for her." She waggled her eyebrows, and I burst into laughter.

"I'm sure she'll tell you all about it. Just give me some time to fix it."

"You will." Cassie kissed my cheek. "Good luck, Matt."

"Jake, I'll call you later."

"Keep me posted, buddy. Good luck."

I handed Cassie back my coffee mug and gave Poppy a scratch on the head before marching back up to my truck. When I climbed inside, I dialed Jo again.

Voicemail. Damn it.

With a new sense of hope, I pulled out and drove

back to Sister Bay. Her Jeep wasn't at the cabin when I got there, but Cassie and Jake were right. She may have told me to get out, but I wasn't going anywhere until I got a chance to talk to her and set things straight. And if that meant sitting all day in this cabin and ambushing her at JJ's, then that's exactly what I would do.

CHAPTER TWENTY-ONE

JO

I felt like a zombie while I went through the motions at JJ's. Just yesterday at work I'd been floating behind this bar like I had clouds beneath my shoes. Tonight it felt more like someone strapped cinderblocks to my feet. Every step took more effort than the last, but fighting the tears took the most effort of all.

Being a girl who rarely cried, fighting the desire to flop down on the floor and sob a sea of tears felt foreign to me.

Tears were for weak people. People who weren't strong enough to push through whatever shit life threw at them. I never cried because it fixed nothing. Crying didn't change a shitty situation, and it sure as hell didn't make anything better. Yet here I was struggling to contain the tears begging to burst free.

It turns out having a broken heart could crack open the dam of tears even for people like me.

Don't cry.

"You sure you're okay?" Hanson asked as I stared blankly at the row of tequila bottles on the shelf, blinking hard to contain the flood of tears.

"Yeah. Fine," I lied.

No, I wasn't okay. I was as far from okay as I'd ever been. Yesterday Matt and I were heading for happily ever after. Today I was trying to process that not only had that future been snatched from me, but the future where he was my best friend was gone, too. Matt held no place in my new future.

"If you want to talk about something, just let me know," Hanson said, and I nodded.

"Thanks. I'm okay."

The drink printer beeped, and I heaved a heavy sigh then walked over to see what drinks were waiting to be made.

Two margaritas and a rum and coke. Easy enough.

While I stumbled through the motions, memories of Matt in my arms kept invading my mind. But they were quickly replaced with visions of him in Nikki's arms and then... that photo on Instagram flashed back into my mind.

This morning Jenna had gone stalking Nikki's Instagram account today for any proof to exonerate Matt and prove her superpower was still intact. Instead, we'd found proof of the exact opposite.

When I'd seen it on Jenna's phone this afternoon,

I'd almost thrown up, and just thinking about it brought the same gag reflex that had kept me from eating a single bite of food today. Not only had I caught Matt in Nikki's arms last night, but instead of coming after me, it turned out he'd gone back to her hotel with her. One of her friends had posted a photo of her in bed with him, pounding the final nail on the coffin of his guilt. And the final nail of the wall I had quickly resurrected around my heart.

And when I'd finally turned my phone back on this morning? Little pinging notifications of pain had announced every single indiscretion. It seemed everyone on the planet had to text me to say how right I'd been to stay mad at Matt, because as it turned out, he was exactly who I'd thought he was.

Little did they know, I hadn't stayed mad at him at all, and instead had gone and revealed my love for him.

So stupid.

All morning long I got my mistake thrown in my face. My texts had blown up with other people sending pictures of Matt cradling Nikki in his arms up by the Garage and The Bowl. I'd had to shut off my phone the rest of the day to stop from being bombarded with proof that took away any doubt trying to creep into my mind that maybe I'd been mistaken. I hadn't. It was true. Matt had been with Nikki. He'd lied to me. Betrayed me. Broke my damn heart.

"Jo? I think it's full." Hanson pressed a hand on my shoulder.

"What?" I looked down to see the glass overflowing with Coke, my finger still pressing the button on the gun. "Oh shit."

"If you need to take a night off and go home, I'll totally cover for you. You saved my ass yesterday. I owe you."

I dumped the drink out down the drain and turned back to face him. He pressed his glasses up on his nose and gave me a sympathetic smile.

"Hanson, I really appreciate it, but I don't want to go home."

Home was where Matt likely was.

Home was filled with memories of him.

Home was the last place I wanted to be.

"Just let me know if you change your mind."

"You're the best. Thank you. But it's getting busy and I'm not going to leave you in the lurch."

Get it together, Jo.

I'd survived worse, my own father leaving, and even though it didn't feel like it, I knew I'd get through this, too.

I refilled the rum and coke and carried it over to the waitress station. One by one the stools filled up, and I welcomed the distraction. Hanson and I flew into gear like a well-oiled machine, and soon my memories of Matt were overrun by drink orders, food orders, and the bar of people three-deep all vying for my attention.

"Behind!" Hanson shouted while he blew past me.

I scooted out of his way, careful not to spill the three margaritas clutched in my hands. While I scanned the crowd trying to remember which customer they belonged to, my gaze skidded to a stop when it moved to the huge window overlooking the street and caught sight of a truck driving by JJ's slowly.

Matt's truck.

No. Hell no!

So much for my ruse about leaving town.

Hoping he'd not seen me behind the wall of bodies all vying for my attention, I slouched down a little for good measure. My heart hammered in my chest as I watched the doors waiting for him to walk in, but after ten minutes of nothing, I finally exhaled a breath of relief.

Grateful he'd either not seen me when he crept by or decided showing up here would be a terrible idea, I switched my focus back to digging myself out of the hole that had swallowed Hanson and I up. Getting through the dinner rush was a pain in its own right, but getting through the dinner rush trying to hold together the pieces of my shattered heart proved a different beast entirely.

A gnarly, carnivorous, unrelenting beast that tried

to devour me every second of the night.

A couple hours later, the crowd had cleared, and Hanson and I stood side by side downing our first glasses of water all night.

When I finished my glass and turned around, my breath trapped in my throat when I saw Matt leaning against the door. Instantly those damn tears made a move back into position. But before they could spring free, my rage won the race of emotions, and I narrowed my eyes.

"Jo," he said as he started toward me. "It's not what it seems. Please, just talk to me."

Not what it seems? Is he kidding right now?

It was *exactly* what it seemed.

Matt was still the lying, cheating asshole I'd thought he was all year long.

"Bartender!" one of the few remaining customers called, shaking me from our stare down. "Can we get a couple margaritas?".

"Yep!" I answered, shaking my head to get my shit back together.

I scolded Matt with my stare, and with a heavy sigh, he backed away from the bar and slipped back out the door.

For the next two hours, even though only three customers remained, I tried to keep busy, washing every surface of the bar in an attempt to bide my time before having to go. I knew Matt would be waiting for me, and the last thing I wanted to do was hear more of his lies.

"I think he's still out there if you want to go talk to him," Hanson whispered as he peered out the front window. "I mean, you can keep polishing the same glasses over and over if you really want to, but really, your shift ended like two hours ago. Why don't you head out and put the poor guy out of his misery?"

Shaking my head hard, I straightened back up from the glassware and my towel. "I don't need to talk to him. Just ignore him."

"Want me to tell him to leave? Maybe rough him up?" Hanson asked, and a slight smile lifted my lips.

"You'd do that for me?"

He scoffed. "Hell, yeah! I haven't tossed a guy out of a bar in a while, but you'd better believe I'll send that one sailing if he's bothering you. Granted, he's not in the bar, but I'll still get rid of him if you want."

For a moment I contemplated it, but then realized as much as I appreciated the comradery, I didn't need Hanson fighting my battle. Lifting my chin, I dug deep to find the strength to face Matt.

"I'll handle it," I said, and Hanson gave me a nod of solidarity.

I punched out and told Hansen I'd grab my tips tomorrow. Wanting to get this over with, but also wanting to avoid it at all costs, I took a deep breath and walked out the front door. It only took a second for me to see Matt sitting on the bench just off to the side. I opened my mouth to say something to him, but when I tried to speak, I couldn't get a word out over the lump forming in my throat. Instead, I spun on my heel and started hurrying toward home.As my aching feet hit the street, I could practically feel his breath down the back of my neck.

"Jo. Please. Just talk to me," he begged, but I ignored his pleas.

Quickening my steps, I struggled to breathe while the heartache tightened in my chest and crawled up my throat.

"Jo!" Matt called again.

Just the sound of his voice sent a shiver down my spine. An enraging blend of lust, hurt, and anger all twisted together and traveled through my body.

Lust had no place in my emotions right now, but I couldn't get the soft tones of that same voice whispering "I love you" into my ear out of my head.

He's a cheater.

A liar and a cheater.

Trying to shake off the emotions punching through me, I stopped and inhaled a ragged breath.

Matt's footsteps drumming on the pavement grew louder as he walked up behind me. "Thank you for stopping. I just want to explain what happened."

"Explain what happened?" The absurdity caused me to choke out a laugh.

"Yes. When I saw Nikki—"

Just hearing her name on his lips sent a whoosh of rage rushing through me. I spun around and impaled him with a glare just before letting that same rage rip out of my arm and explode against his face with a slap.

He stumbled back clutching his cheek.

"Get the fuck away from me. And don't ever come near me again. We're done. *So* done. Now leave me alone."

"Jo," he started as he regained his balance. "I know it looked so bad. I mean *so* bad... but nothing happened with her, I swear!"

The empty words fell flat between us. "You're such a liar."

"Jo, I would never do that to you! Nikki followed me to my truck, and her drunk ass fell, so I caught her. That was it."

"Oh? That was it, huh?" I snorted.

I reached into my purse and pulled out my phone, then turned it on. With a few clicks on the screen, I went to Nikki's Instagram page and found the photo of her lying in bed with him hovering above her. I whipped the phone around and shoved it in his face. "And did she fall into your arms in her hotel room, too?"

His mouth fell open as he took the phone from my hand. "Holy shit."

"Yeah. Holy shit is what I said, too. Do you need more proof? I've got it. We can go through text after text with pictures of you and Nikki. Don't even get me started on the text messages from *concerned* citizens worrying you're screwing over Jake again. It's over, Matt. Now get the hell out of this bar and out of my life."

"Jo, she was hammered. I just helped her and her friends back to their room. That's *all*. Tony and Aaron were with me for Christ's sake! Drunk chicks falling down could be dangerous! I couldn't leave them—"

"Enough!" I screamed, and the volume of my voice startled even me. "I've heard enough! You hurt me more than I ever knew was possible. And it's done, Matt. You've done enough. Now please... go!"

The tears burned behind my eyes, and I blinked fast to keep them at bay. One tear slid past my defenses and dripped down my cheek.

"Jo, I swear to you that this is not what it looks like."

I ripped the phone from his hand and pointed to his truck parked just down the street. "Go."

"I'm not leaving, Jo. Not until you listen."

Burning hot tears stung my eyes, and my rapid blinking lost its battle against them. "If you won't go, then I will."

I took off toward the cabin, but he raced in front of me, blocking my path.

"You are not running away this time, Jo!"

"Get out of my way! And don't fucking follow me!"

The tears exploded as I veered from my path and turned toward the docks. Hurt, anger, and humiliation ripped apart my insides as the sobs shook my body. I bolted onto the docks, praying Matt wouldn't follow me. Praying this would be the last time I saw him.

Praying I would remember how to breathe again.

Matt

Nikki's friends had posted a picture of us? Of course, they had. If her goal was to make Jake jealous, she'd have leapt at the possibility. And if it didn't look bad enough before, it was catastrophic now. Me actually struggling to get Nikki's arms from around my neck so I could get out of there looked a hell of a lot like a hot make-out session between me and the devil herself. Between the picture she posted and the ones I was sure Jo got from people who saw me carrying her around, it looked as damning as if she'd caught us in bed together. I pressed my hands to my head while I watched Jo sprint down the docks.

I glanced inside the window into JJ's, and Hanson's condemning eyes bore through me. A soft shake of his head warned me not to go after her, but I couldn't let her keep believing lies. I couldn't leave her in pain when there was still a chance to fix this.

A small chance.

A miniscule chance.

But a chance.

I took off after her, screaming her name while I tore down the sidewalk and onto the docks. Jo glanced over her shoulder and picked up her pace, racing between the boats bobbing in the water.

"Jo, stop!" I called, my calves burning as I tore after her. When I turned the corner, she stood at the edge of the dock staring out at the water with nowhere left to go. Slowing to a crawl, I approached her carefully, my heart shattering when I saw her shoulders shaking with her sobs.

Sobs I'd caused.

"Jo, please don't run."

"Get away from me," she whispered, her voice cracking as she struggled with the words.

"I didn't do anything with Nikki. I swear to God, Jo. It looks so bad, and I know that, but I need you to believe me."

She shook her head. "You're a liar, Matt. I never should have let you back in my life."

"I'm not a liar." I stepped toward her, careful not to move too fast. "Nikki was—"

"Don't say her name," she spat.

"I'm sorry. The devil was wasted and what you really saw was her falling in my arms while I tried to get away. And what Aaron said to you was wrong, and he'll tell you that. He'd seen me saving a stool... a stool for you. But I didn't want to tell him about us until you were ready, so I just said I had a secret girlfriend. And then he saw Nikki and put two and two together... which was a completely incorrect attempt at solving the puzzle."

"Go away," she whispered again. A soft breeze lifted her hair, and I caught the light scent of her shampoo.

Torture. It was pure torture being this close to her and not touching her.

Torture seeing her body quake with the tears I'd caused.

Torture knowing I had hurt the woman I loved more than anything in this world.

"Not until you listen to me."

She spun around. Red, swollen eyes met mine, and she stiffened her quivering lip. "Fine. If listening to you means I can finally get you out of my life forever, then talk. Quick. Because once you're done, so are we."

I moved toward her but stopped when she recoiled. The few feet left between us may as well have been the Grand Canyon.

"It all looks so bad. But *nothing* happened. I can't stand Nikki. And I would never hurt you. I love you, Jo. I fucking love you."

"So, you loved me so much you took the girl you hate to bed?" She arched a brow and impaled me with a glare.

"Nikki and her friends were wasted. I tried to run after you, but Nikki almost fell down again. As much as I wanted to come after you, I'm not the kind of guy who can leave a drunk girl, even one I hate, lying in a heap in the parking lot. That's not me, Jo. And if it was, you wouldn't ever have been friends with me in the first place."

Her face softened for a beat but stiffened back up just as quick.

"So yeah, I ended up with Nikki in my arms. And when I tried to dump her off on her friends, they didn't even know where they were staying. I got Aaron and Tony to help me carry them all home. Because again, I'm not the kind of guy who can leave wasted girls wandering around town where they could get hurt. Though I'm so sorry that because of my morals it hurt you and looked so much worse than it was."

"It looks really bad, Matt. And the bed? I suppose

Nikki needed mouth-to-mouth resuscitation or something?"

"No. My lips never touched hers. But she couldn't walk, so I carried her up to her room and threw her in her bed. Then she refused to let go of my neck, so there were a few moments where it looked like things were happening that weren't happening. Apparently, her crappy friends snapped a photo and posted it because she's pissed Jake is engaged and I'm sure this is her 'fuck you' to him. Because she's Nikki. She's selfish and cruel. But that's all it was. A photo of me struggling to get out of her death grip. Call Aaron. He'll tell you."

"I don't need to call Aaron. I'm sure you two already worked out your stories."

"Yes, you do. Or Jake or Cassie. They'll all explain that this was just a huge misunderstanding."

Her gaze darted out to the lake, and I saw the struggle happening in her mind.

"You weren't wrong to trust me again. And I know deep down you know I'm telling the truth. Misunderstanding the situation just gave you a valid reason to run. You *know* I would never do this to you."

"Do I?" She spun back around. "Do I know? Because I also know you were so ensnared by Nikki last year that you kissed her while she was engaged to your *best friend*. What's to say you're still not trapped in her claws?"

"Because I'm in love with *you*, Jo. Totally, completely, madly, and irrevocably in love with you. And now that I know that, the thought of touching Nikki again makes my skin crawl. You're the only one for me. I swear it. Please, don't throw us away. Please, Jo."

My heart hammered against my chest while I stared into her eyes. Watching for some shift in her convictions. Looking for some flicker of the love I'd seen in her eyes just yesterday.

"I can't, Matt. Even if you're telling the truth, I just can't." Her chin quivered, and I reached out to touch her, but she pulled away.

"Yes, you can."

"No, I can't!" she shouted, but I felt her resolve sliding. "I can't do this. You'll just end up breaking my heart, and I just can't, Matt. This whole thing was just a huge wake-up call that this, we, are a terrible idea."

"Jo, we are not a terrible idea. We are the best idea anyone has ever had. I love you, and I know you love me. Please don't throw that away because you're scared."

I reached out again, and she stepped back. But this time I didn't stop, and I pulled her into my arms.

"Don't!" She struggled for a moment, but I held her tight.

"I'm not leaving you, Jo. Ever."

"Go!" She fought harder, but I held on, pressing her body against mine.

"I'm not leaving you, Jo," I whispered against her hair. "I'm never leaving you."

Over and over I repeated the phrase, and with each admission, her struggle softened.

"Go," she tried again, but I knew about the root of her hurt. The fuel for the rage and anger burning inside of her.

Deep down she believed me. I knew Jo... better than anyone. And I'd seen that look in her eyes before. It was the look she had when things were getting serious and her walls went flying up. The look she got just before she launched back to the safety of her life alone. A life where no one had the power to hurt her again. Abandon her.

For all her anger and rage right now, I realized she knew I'd never fall for Nikki again and betray her. But her fear of me leaving her had sent her launching for the emergency exit, desperate to protect herself from being abandoned once again. Desperate to avoid a future I knew wouldn't come. In her warped version of the future, I left her when she needed me most.

Just like her dad.

But I would never leave Jo. Not ever.

And I wasn't going to let her fear push me away like it'd done with every other man. Where they'd given up,

I would hold strong. I would fight to my dying breath to show her I was the one she could depend on.

Always.

"I'm not leaving you," I whispered again. "Ever. I love you, Jo. And I need you to accept that."

Slowly, her body folded against mine, her fight against her fears petering out. I pulled her tighter, pressing my lips to the top of her head as she slid her arms around my waist.

"We're going to have a long life together, and I need to know that you won't bail on me because you're scared. I can't live without you, Jo. You need to find a way to trust me. Trust in my love for you and that I'm never *ever* leaving you. In the twenty-eight years we've been friends, name one time I've let you down. One time I wasn't there for you when you needed me."

I felt her head shake against my chest.

"The answer to that question is never. Not once have I ever abandoned you, and I fully intend to keep up that track record until we're old and wrinkled and gray. I will be here for you always. Always and forever. And that's how long I'm going to love you."

"I'm so scared," she whispered, and I felt my own tears threatening to spill out.

How could someone ever hurt a girl as wonderful as my Jo. Who could ever leave her?

"When you're scared, you lean on me, okay? I'll be

brave for the both of us. But I need you to trust me. No matter what. Because I will never ever hurt you. And I will never let you go. Understood?"

She sniffled and nodded, and I squeezed her tighter, then released my grip and leaned back.

Fearful eyes brimmed with tears met mine, and I slid my hand beneath her chin, stroking away a tear with my thumb.

"I love you, Jo. More than anything."

"I love you, too," she whispered.

The power of those four words seeped into my soul, and I closed my eyes and pressed my lips to hers. I tried to kiss away all her insecurities, all her pain, and all her doubts. With each brush of my lips against hers, I tried to mend the cracks in her heart and fill them with my love.

"I love you so much," I whispered against her mouth. "I'll love you until the day I die."

"Don't hurt me, Matt." Her breath ghosted my lips as she whispered the words.

"Never," I whispered back, then deepened our kiss.

When I felt the last of her fears drift away on the summer breeze, I softened my grip around her and brushed her lips with one last kiss.

"I promise I'll never hurt you if you promise you won't be searching for any excuse to leave me." Arching a brow, I smiled. "I mean, I have every intention of giving you no ammo in that department, but I'm a dude. And sometimes we make stupid decisions. And sometimes things look a hell of a lot worse than they are. Sometimes I'm going to do the wrong thing or say the wrong thing. But not because I don't love you or I'm going to leave you. Because I'm a guy and we do stupid shit sometimes. And I'm not perfect. But even then, I need you to trust in my love for you. Deal?"

She bit her lip, and a smile started on her lips. "Deal."

I kissed her once again, and this time she met my lips with the same desire I'd felt before her confidence had been shaken.

"I love you, Matt. I'm sorry I jumped to conclusions."

"You don't need to apologize. Anyone would have jumped to that conclusion. But now you know... no matter what, you never need to worry about my loyalty to you."

"I'm holding you up to that." She smiled and I felt it down to my toes. "If you screw me over, I'm siccing Petunia on you."

"A fate worse than death." Laughing, I kissed her again.

"As much as I want to keep doing this," she said between our kisses, "I should really get back to work and help Hanson clean up."

"You go back to work, and I'll go home and hang

out with our cat until you get done. Then I want that date night you agreed to."

"Our cat?" She arched a brow as she slipped out of my arms, stepping to my side and taking my hand.

"Yep, our cat." I walked along with her. "Petunia and I bonded even more last night while I was lying in your bed waiting for you to come home."

"Is that so?"

"Yep. We both missed you. She's going to be pretty excited you're not still kicking me out."

"Oh, will she?"

"Hell, yeah. Petunia will probably throw a party."

"Well, I suppose I don't want to let her down, so I guess you'll be staying."

"Forever." I squeezed her hand. "I'll be staying forever. Although, I'm wondering if we can make some new arrangements."

"Like what?" she arched a brow.

"Like, I was thinking about what we could do with the other room now that I'll be staying in yours."

"You're moving into my room now?" She laughed.

"I'm not spending another night away from you, baby. It's you and me. Always. So yeah, I'm moving into your room."

"I suppose we could figure out something to do with the other room. Maybe a workshop for your new business?"

My smile grew, and I slung my arm around her shoulders. "Exactly what I was thinking. This is why I love you."

"I love you, too."

I pulled her to a stop and yanked her into my arms. "I'll see you at home, Roomster," I said, and she laughed before I pulled her in for the kind of kiss I intended to give her over and over again... for the rest of our lives.

Stay tuned for the next Door Peninsula Passions book, THE OTHER PLAN, coming in early 2022! Visit my website to find out more or sign up for my Enews to get notified when it releases.

DOOR PENINSULA PASSIONS

THE OTHER PLAN
Door Peninsula Passions Book Three
Releasing Early 2022

The only thing this wedding planner didn't plan on was him.

As the top wedding planner in Door County, Jenna is prepared for anything. But when she gets hired to coordinate a week-long wedding celebration for an affluential family, there was one thing she hadn't planned for... the man who broke her heart in college showing up as the best man.

Carter hadn't seen Jenna since she bolted from Hawaii where they'd met on spring break ten years ago. The romance only lasted a few days, but she'd left a permanent mark on his heart. Now he needs to figure out how to win her back, but Jenna has other plans... plans that don't involve her ending up back in his arms.

As Carter tries to win her heart again, Jenna struggles to shield it from his grasp. One heartbreak had been enough for her, and she doesn't intend to fall for Carter's charms again.

At least that's the plan. And in Jenna's world, plans always go her way... or at least they did until Carter waltzed back into her life.

Sign up for my news to get notified when it's available!

www.katherinehastings.com

Did you miss the first book in this series, *The Other Half?* If you did, grab it now to read Jake and Cassie's story!

THE OTHER HALF
Door Peninsula Passions Book One

When a spoiled socialite is forced to live like the other half, will she find her other half?

When spoiled socialite Cassandra Davenport takes things one step too far, her grandfather gives her an ultimatum—prove she can live without her famous name and riches or give up her place in the family legacy. With nothing but a hundred dollars, her tiny dog, and a car that should've died in the eighties, she heads to the family cabin to prove she's more than just a pretty face with a trust fund.

Local fisherman Jake Alton doesn't know much about the woman who showed up at the rundown shack next door, other than the fact she's putting a damper on his solitary and secluded lifestyle. Even though he tries to avoid this intruder to his sanctuary, the beautiful woman proves impossible to ignore.

As Cassandra struggles to adapt to her new rustic lifestyle, Jake struggles to keep his wounded heart out of her hands. But even though they try to resist each other, these two opposites do more than attract... they collide.

OTHER BOOKS TO READ

Take a look at my other books available, including historical romance, contemporary romance, paranormal romance, and women's fiction. Find them all at

www.katherinehastings.com

THANK YOU FOR READING

I hope you enjoyed *The Other Room*! The greatest gift you can give a writer is your review. If you enjoyed this book, I would be forever grateful if you'd take the time to leave a review on Amazon or Goodreads. Find out more about my other books and upcoming releases at www.katherinehastings.com

You can also get new book releases, sales, and free book specials delivered right to your inbox by signing up for my Enews!

Get social with me and join me on:

Facebook
Instagram
Twitter

Follow me on:
Bookbub
Goodreads

Made in the USA
Monee, IL
30 January 2022